DATE DUE

JUN 28	
NOV 1 3 1999	
JUN 1 5 2000	

Also by C. J. Hribal

MATTY'S HEART

AMERICAN BEAUTY

C. J. Hribal

Simon and Schuster
New York

Copyright © 1987 by C. J. Hribal. All rights reserved, including the right of reproduction in whole or in part in any form. Published by Simon and Schuster, a division of Simon & Schuster, Inc., Simon & Schuster Building, Rockefeller Center, 1230 Avenue of the Americas, New York, NY 10020. SIMON AND SCHUSTER and colophon are registered trademarks of Simon & Schuster, Inc. Designed by Irving Perkins Associates. Manufactured in the United States of America.

1   2   3   4   5   6   7   8   9   10

Library of Congress Cataloging-in-Publication Data
Hribal, C. J.
American beauty.
I. Title.
PS3558.R52A8   1987   813'.54   87–12997
ISBN 0-671-62523-3

The author is grateful for permission to reprint material from:
"The Girl from Ipanema (Garota de Ipanema)." Music by Antonio Carlos Jobim. English words by Norman Gimbel. Original words by Vinicius De Moraes. © Copyright 1963 by Antonio Carlos Jobim and Vinicius De Moraes, Brazil. Sole Selling Agent DUCHESS MUSIC CORPORATION (MCA), New York, NY for all English-speaking countries. USED BY PERMISSION. ALL RIGHTS RESERVED.
"The Dutchman." Words and music by Michael Peter Smith. © Copyright 1971, 1978 by DUCHESS MUSIC CORPORATION, New York, NY 10022. USED BY PERMISSION. ALL RIGHTS RESERVED.
"Wild Children" by Van Morrison. © 1973 & 1974 CALEDONIA SOUL MUSIC and WARNER–TAMERLANE PUBLISHING CORP. All rights reserved. Used by permission.
The Street of Crocodiles by Bruno Schultz. Reprinted by arrangement with Walker and Company.

c.1

ACKNOWLEDGMENTS

Many thanks to Bob Asahina, Charles Baxter, Walter Howerton, Jonathon and Wendy Lazear, Terry Maguire, Patricia B. Soliman, Tom Townsley and Bill Truesdale. And especially to Ron Block, friend extraordinaire.

The author also wishes to thank The National Endowment for the Arts for its generous support, and to acknowledge receipt of a Bush Foundation Fellowship.

To
KRYSTYNA

and
To our parents:
CLAUDE

and
MARY

and
MIECZYSLAW

and
ZDZISLAWA

It was a moment when time, demented and wild, breaks away from the treadmill of events and like an escaping vagabond, runs shouting across the fields.
—Bruno Schulz, *The Street of Crocodiles*

We were the wild children. . . .
—Van Morrison

And now, after much time, Greece is where I am. I'm twenty-eight. It is strangely difficult to say how I got here. As if the moving happened inside Tweed's lens, everything compressed, everything hurrying by, and when you can focus clear again you're arrested by the simplest facts. I am in Greece with a year-old son. I am woozy from booze and the heat has sapped everything out of me. Leached it away so it seems I'm carrion swelling heavily in the heat. Even the breeze seems to bake wet the linings of my eyes, making them hot and swollen and heavy. High up in my nose I can feel the heat, feel it in the droop of my swollen breasts and in the weight of a nonexistent blanket across my thighs. Everywhere lazy heat. Time ticks away, but at least I'm in one place and notice it. White and blue heat. Liquid. This afternoon is the first serious drinking I've done since Woolie. I didn't even sip wine that whole time. I thought of myself as chaste—ha-ha—clean. Preggers a fire that through and through burned me. I have him strapped into a high chair now with his chubby red arms flailing, and it seems as if I could stay drunk forever. I've earned it. Earned it and at the moment need it. Mia is with me. Mia and her two children and her husband, Rhuebal Newton, staying in the limestone cottage on the hill next to mine. It's their vacation and Rhuebal has the children. Mia and I have spent the morning getting drunk enough to be able to talk to each other. As if to crown the day with significance, in one hand I hold a letter from Geoffrey and in the other a telegram I'm sure is from Larry.

Geoffrey, Mia, Larry. I was seventeen then, going on ancient. In going back I find my old self still hurtling forward. All those people. All that ground covered. All that time spent getting away from Mama—

1

IT'S NOT AS IF my mother mattered. I tell her I should be spending time on the Lake Street Beaches, not talking with her. I know it's the wrong month, October's not good for anything. But Milwaukee? I couldn't tell her that over the phone. I have always said Chicago. For it not to be Chicago now—she'd laugh. Ha, ha, minimum wage in Milwaukee—you see what I told you? She wants it, too. Envious. I got out. Stick around for what? For a plain man to take care of me? That would be true defeat. What's a man want? Mount you like a horse, children, fixing dinners, wash, the old hi-yoo at night without washing his hands first. Mama got lucky, at least my father's not a pig. A respectable man, honest, loves her even though he has no chance of understanding her. He wants things to work out, the vision of life he gets at church: man wife children farm, all things growing together, reason in the world as dependable as spring rain. He truly believes that—that things make sense. I was thirteen when I first wanted to laugh at him. Mama was getting me dressed up for one of those dances the school sanctioned, girls dancing with girls, the boys standing with thumbs through belt loops or arms folded, surrounding us like a cage, and he came in from chores, the barn smell ripe on him and said, Aren't you Daddy's little girl, and that's when I wanted to laugh. I didn't even know what ludicrous was but even so I knew I wanted to laugh. I didn't, though I think he knew I was capable of that

—laughing at honest intention. I love him with a special sort of pity.

Not like Mama. Mama tells me I did right in getting out. All the men here are the same, she tells me. I tell her men are the same everywhere. It's just some places they expect to pay for it. Men understand commerce. Mama wants drama. On the phone she asks what was it like with a black man, have I had any? I lie to her, say I have. She goes breathless on me, straining to hear each word. What was it like? she asks, what was it like? Like a white man's, I tell her, no mystery. More arch, feels like a snakeskin. They talk more, whisper in your ear, want you to love them. They all whisper, no exceptions. They carry with them their own music; you can hear it playing, I tell her, behind their eyes. White men want the whispers in *their* ears, want to hear your music, want to cry out and groan and die in your arms. They die all right, Mama says, they go right to sleep. She's trying to imagine black men now, her voice full of envy; I ask her how's Daddy and she says, Oh, the same.

I have to remember which lies I tell my mother. Women are so much harder to lie to than men. Men are easy. This job: I started in the coffee shop, answered the newspaper ad for a morning cashier at the Blaisdell, put on my fresh-scrubbed and serious makeup face and Doyle looked me over and said, "Usually we hire mature women for this."

I lied. "I'm nineteen. And mature."

"You ever work one of these?"

I said, "What's so hard about a cash register?"

"You know you have to be here at six, six to three Monday through Friday," and I was nearly laughing but I said, Oh, I'm always up early, and he said okay, but he didn't have a clue as to what he'd hired. He'd just seen my legs and tried to guess the size of my breasts and imagined his tongue sliding between my lips, two perfect red lips, the old fantasy; I'm irresistible, so what else is new? Doyle wanted me. They all

want me. That's why they're so easy to lie to. All I had to do
was pretend without speaking that I knew he'd get me, and so
he hired me out of hope that the shine in my blue blue eyes
agreed with the heat in his shorts.

I didn't even have an apartment yet so that was the next
thing—another section of ads. There were warehouses just
west of the university, nine blocks from the lake to the U and
another five to the scuz housing. For starters I took a second-
floor place a student had rented. It was a house divided into
two flats nestled among those warehouses, ugly, one-bedroom.
I had a futon on the living room floor. Mia was an artist, small
and dark with hair growing from her nipples, wore a thin
cotton halter and no bra. She didn't shave under her arms
either and I thought, This won't last, but I liked the place. It
had a romantic dreariness to it, it was cheap—the hotel paid
just up from minimum—just one block to the bus, and Mia
seemed friendly enough.

I'll show you around, she said, Milwaukee's a good town.
She had no talent, but she was proud of herself and I liked
her for that. We hit a few bars that first night and this older
guy, Robert, he played in a band, hit on me at a club, and
Mia stepped in while he was gone for drinks and said, That
guy's death. True scum, she said, he'll rape you 'cause he
thinks it's owed him. So I said, Why don't we leave and she
said, Exactly. So we did and laughed about it on the way over
to the next bar. You need to watch out, Mia said. If you don't
assert yourself you'll get eaten alive and this ain't that big a
city. It's the same everywhere, I said, and Mia said, I think
we're going to do fine.

When we got home she wanted to change the names on the
mailbox. On a blank name card she wrote *Zolkauer* in a sort
of curlicue script and said, I've left room on top here because
nobody's got a name that comes after mine.

Keillor, I said, I like it better than Brown. Who wants to be
Dorie Brown anyway? And besides, it reminds me of Matty.

Who's that? Mia wanted to know.

My grandmother, I said. She's like me, I think, from the way they talk about her. Still not married.

Who? Your grandmother?

Yes, and she lives with this man, and everyone is so shocked, everyone takes it so seriously. I mean really, so she's sixty—more power to her, it's all still working. And I think she actually likes him, she doesn't have to pretend, she can even get mad at him when he pisses her off. That's really something, I said.

And Mia said, So you want it Keillor, right?

The third afternoon dropping off my receipts is when I met Larry. Larry worked the desk, initialed my deposits, and eventually he got around to asking me for a drink after work.

I'll pick you up, he said.

No, I said, meet me here. I'll come back after I've had a shower and changed. Larry's blond and bookish. The rumors were his wife left him. Perfect, I thought. Nothing worse than a man who's just been left by another woman. For the sake of remnant ego and a warm body at night he will suffer any humiliation.

And later over drinks he told me about his wife, more than I wanted to know, but I ate my turkey club and kept nodding and thought how hurt he was going to be later because all the while he was talking about her it was obvious he wanted us to work out even though we'd barely met, and of course he couldn't *say* anything. He was too busy trying to talk his wife out of his chest, and I was only something soft and pretty for him, someone who would listen. And like everyone, I've found out, whose wives have left them, he was stupidly romantic, hoping the next one would be the right one (not yet done with the last one), as if people came in sizes and so what if the sleeves are too long and it fits badly across the shoulders, a few more drinks and it'll be love. We'll shrink to fit.

"Please let me give you a life home," he said, then caught himself. "A lift," he said. "I meant a lift."

"No, really, I'd rather take the bus."

"But it's cold out," he said, forlornly, so it was like I was letting him down. I felt pity for him then, the first time, it's bad of me. I mean I was determined to get on the next bus and be casual making the receipt deposit from then on, so without talking about it, he'd know it wasn't anything—just drinks and thank you, no. But his nose got red, it seemed chiseled pink, rather lamely hawkish, almost handsome, and I saw how one sock was falling down, a tan argyle. We waited for the bus and then we were kissing, wind rushing past our ears, his hands down the back of my jeans. "Jesus," he said, "you're not wearing underwear."

"Take me home," I whispered and then thought, Stupid, stupid, stupid as he got the car. The bus came right then, I still actually had a choice. But I wanted to get started, feel like I belonged, and taking a man home, whatever you actually felt about him, was one of the ways, wasn't it?

About two I asked him to leave and he protested but dressed and left anyway and I looked at the clock's flopping illuminated numbers, sure Mia had heard us, and Christ, in four hours I'll be there again and later he'll want to say something, and the worst of it is we'll have something to talk about. And suddenly I felt very cold even though I was still warm, still sweaty, from what we'd done.

Larry and I sort of became something. This kind of thing feeds on itself. I pretended not to know that even as it happened. He changed his break time so we had lunch in the back of the kitchen together. Other employees got up to leave us alone, winking coyly when they left. I hated it.

Dorie, he would say to me, Dorie you don't realize how you've changed my life.

Yes, I do, I wanted to say. You say Dorie now in those sentences you used to say about your wife.

That's not true, he would have said, but since I never brought it up, he kept using my name when he meant his wife because I was there and she wasn't. And I ate my tuna fish and drank orange juice and tried to think how I could get away from him which wasn't easy because at the Blaisdell I was making good tips hosting and cashiering. I had my smile firmly in place, and I must've looked like these men's daughters, or better, the daughters of their friends, women whom they'd feel less guilty about coveting, because they over-tipped. I got a share of the waitress money and these private tips besides. "For you," they'd say and leave an extra dollar or two on the counter while I counted back their change. My face glowed and all I had to worry about was lunch and counting out at three and whatever it was Larry wanted to do later, which too often was dinner/drinks/movie/drinks/love as if that string were a single word and for him, yes, he used that word *love*.

"Let's make love," he'd say. "Make it real slow," and then he'd come too soon.

Still anxious about your wife, I wanted to say but didn't. I save that for very late at night when Mia comes home. She has someone, too, an architecture student at the Milwaukee School of Engineering, a soft-faced man with a pug nose and thick glasses, his brown hair curling at the ends. He gets up at three or so to get back to his own apartment, Mia trailing after him, a little whiny, soft, Stay for breakfast. But he big-lips her good-bye and Mia closes her robe, too big for her, a maroon and cream velvet one, and sits at the kitchen table.

I sit by her in a bulky sweater and say, Is it love? and she half-smiles and says, Something like that, and then I say, Larry always wants to stay and I won't let him and you want Jeff to stay and he won't.

"I want someone to sleep with," she says and sometimes I
go into her room and lie next to her. She falls asleep with her
face tucked against my neck and I'm awake for another hour
thinking, How does this happen? It's like we were sisters.

Mia helps me with the lies for my mother.

"I'm supposed to be in Chicago," I tell her. "I don't want
her to know I live close enough for her to visit easily or she'll
be dropping in every weekend like a homing pigeon. If she
thinks Chicago she thinks long trips. She actually has to arrange some things."

"She stays longer," Mia says.

"I need some money to get set up. Mama will send that. I
told her I'd get an address."

Mia goes to her bureau. "Use this one," she says, writing
out an address on a slip of paper. "It's my brother's. He's a
hotshot commodities broker. Anything you get from home he'll
remail here."

"Mia, you're wonderful."

"Yeah, yeah," she says. "Tell it to Jeff."

Doyle does the Blaisdell's breakfast and bar. I was there
two weeks before he said something that didn't concern the
hotel. When's your break? he asked me. We'll have coffee, he
said and came back at three minutes to the hour. No, in a
booth, he said when I picked up my purse (a small makeup
bag, really, with a diaphragm and a tube of jelly in it). You
don't have to eat in the break room when you're with a manager, he said and he ordered a steak sandwich. One for her,
too, he said, but I said no and ordered cottage cheese.

"Like you have to watch your figure," he said.

"Why not?" I said. "You do."

And he gave me a Yeah, so-what half-smile and said, "So
where are you from?" arranging his napkin on his lap and
then offering me a cigarette, which I took, though I told myself I was going to quit sometime soon.

"Oh, nowhere," I told him.

"Nowhere, Wisconsin," he said, smiling, with his cigarette in his mouth like it was plugging a hole.

"What makes you think Wisconsin?"

"Your only other choice is Minnesota," he said. "You're blond enough, but I'm betting Wisconsin because otherwise you'd already be in Minneapolis or Chicago or even Los Angeles."

Doyle has black hair done wet-look like he stepped out of a forties movie with the padded shoulders and skin so clean it shines. He could be handsome, but the end of his nose is flattened like a spatula and one cheek looks lumpy, off center, and then of course there's his body. He looks ill-put-together, like God rolled the clay for his arms and chest too thin, His fingers kneading the chest till it ribbed and the excess clay dabbed onto his belly. I hadn't even seen him without clothes yet, but I'd bet his skin was greenish white, the color of shucked lettuce leaves. He had eyes hard as bowling balls, seemingly as large in the sockets, like he knew everything about you, even things he told you that weren't true about yourself his eyes made you want to believe.

"You used to work at the Playboy Club in Lake Geneva, didn't you, Dorie?" and I made no gesture of acknowledgment but he said, "I thought so. I was sure I'd seen you before and I was pretty sure it was there, one of those tours I make for checking other facilities. 'See how the competition does it, Doyle,' Vaigen says to me. 'I want us to be better than everyone.' 'Yes, Mr. Vaigen,' I tell him, and off I go on another junket. It's quite the life, but what about you?" he asked. "I'm not a generous man, but even I tipped big there just to feel like I was keeping pace, and yet here you are in Milwaukee."

He finished his sandwich, wiped grease from his mouth, then rearranged his napkin. "Look," he said, "you're being wasted here on breakfasts. You've got the looks. As soon as there's an opening I'll have you waitressing nights in the

Green Room. The money's a lot better and you can sleep in. Nobody likes six A.M. I certainly couldn't stand it when I started here. Yeah, I started as a clerk myself, just like your friend Larry. What do you say, wouldn't you rather work nights? Great, I'll drop you off after your shift and pick you up later, take you here so you can see what it'll be like. How's that sound?"

"I could just bus it."

"Buses are a drag. It's no problem for me to drive you. I sort of get into the chauffeur thing."

"Great," I said, thinking at least I had a ready-made for Larry when he asked me out again. He would. It was Wednesday.

"A slow night," Doyle said, "but that's good. I'll have you trail one of the hostesses."

He drove me home after my drop, Larry looking at me like a wet dog, and I a magazine in my hand, Doyle behind me, his coat over his arm. Somehow this is like possession, each of them thinking that. Absurd, but that's men for you. At home I poured him some of Mia's Drambuie. We were sitting in the kitchen, the windows not washed for months, everything gray, inside and out, my Milwaukee I thought, gray November, and then Doyle's saying, no warning, no glance of agreed intent, Take me in your mouth. And I almost hit him, was going to grab him with my hand and twist, let the fingers close around so the pleasure started to run and then do an Indian burn on his cock, but instead I looked at his thing, thin and pathetic-looking like it was abandoned between his legs. He'd just stood and dropped his trousers like we were married. Fifty, I said, and I figured that would make him pull up his pants. Maybe he'd laugh, embarrassed by my shaming him, but instead he squatted, reaching behind him like fumbling for toilet paper in an unfamiliar bathroom, and straightening up, he took the note from his wallet and folded it like a crow you see in kids' drawings. He placed it in an ashtray, nestled it with the filtered butts and broken gray worms of ashes, and I thought, This is what they want of us, then. It's us, not the thing between our legs, the absence of what they have that baffles them, folds pulpy like wilted flowers. No, *us*, all of ourselves to be for them. I was wrong before when I said men paid for it. They don't, they pay for us, even Calvin who knocked me up. If you do, I'll love you forever, Calvin had said, and even though I didn't believe him what was there that was better? I was hot and itchy, wanted to please him, wanted to feel good myself, not something I learned from Mama, no, something older that came from everyone around me.

Mama says, Get what you can get, but I was stupider then, romantic. I even thought Calvin would believe what he told me even as I knew he wouldn't, couldn't. But what the hell, sixteen, he was seventeen. We were sweating and his hands felt cool, chilled me where he touched me, then the heat like dry ice under my skin. I wanted him, told myself to believe that. He was a wrestler, all hard shoulders and forearms. I wanted him. It could have been that first time, who knows? Once we had it became expected. A date was fucking in the front of his pickup so fast he didn't even spread the blanket in back, we worked around the gearshift, my legs dangling, the gearshift a big ratchety thing like a second penis. Whoa, now, don't touch that or we'll go rolling down this hill like Jack and Jill, Calvin said, this half-ton one hell of a bucket. After twice I was already tired of him. What was the point? I'll bet he wondered, too. I saw how he looked at the other girls, hungry, a new conquest better than the steady thing. He looked at his hands a lot, as if for touching me everywhere they were somehow to blame. But we were something, held hands between classes, smoked behind the shop class garage before classes started. Me and Bonnie and Wendy were the only girls, proof of our sexual status, we Did It, wore tops with puckered shoulders, hem cut high exposing our navels, our milky bellies and the sinew of hips. And then I found out he was inside me, growing.

Damn it to hell, I want it out! I screamed at Mama when she talked about adoption, and Calvin avoiding me now that he'd had me and I finally realized what that meant—the guys in a circle in the locker room snapping towels. Yeah, I had her, she was okay and someone making the motion, forefinger and thumb circling the organ, the other fingers curled, back and forth, a pantomime. Yeah, yeah, raucous laughter—possession—*that* was what it was all about, more than bodies, people, the whole person bought and sold. That was the language and it took a baby in me to figure it out. It's *me* he's had, there's no it here. Just me and what he left inside like a calling card. Eyes and hair and shape of the nose and I want it out right now, goddamn it!

And I did. It was July, right before my birthday. I was scraped clean. Only not quite clean. Like when a spoon works on remnant ice cream the carton takes a beating. It wasn't all gone. I felt something had collapsed just below my rib cage. It was all going to fall in. Gushy and disoriented, I lay in the hammock, and Wendy and Bonnie came over, supposedly for my birthday. How was it? they asked, not worried about me so much as taking notes for themselves—Dorie didn't keep hers, will I keep mine when it happens to me? No *if*, I realized, only when, and I knew they would—graduation, marriage and motherhood, and maybe not in that order unless they got lucky, started using something.

Wendy said she did, but if she did she was careless. It was about the time I got fitted for a diaphragm—October. I figured eventually I'd need it, though Calvin had the word out about his manhood, so I was the leper, the under-the-bleachers-and-after-the-game-but-not-in-broad-daylight one. I didn't with anyone, but I wanted the protection for later because I knew there'd be a later, far away from Augsbury. But Wendy was sentenced to the place, the model prisoner. October. She said Danny McCain and her had something really going and it was an accident, but she wanted his baby now that she knew she was going to have it.

What a waste, I thought, and that, more than what happened to me, made me say, I'm out, and I told my mother, I'm going to Chicago.

But you're almost done with school, she said, and I told her, Don't worry, Mama, I'm educated.

But at the Greyhound station—I hitched, left a note for them saying, "I'd thought to wait, but now I've got the jump on everyone. I'll call when I'm settled."—I saw if I was to have any money at all it would have to be Milwaukee and so that first day the job and then the apartment.

"Mia," I asked after we had agreed to share the place, "can you give me a few weeks' grace, until my first check?"

"No problem," she said. "I'm always a week late anyway and the guy who owns this is in Florida. We could probably not pay at all and he'd never notice."

"Maybe we won't then." I laughed.

"I hadn't thought to try it," Mia said.

"So let's," I said.

"Yes, let's."

And now I was back to the crow-wing fifty, Mia at classes. I was looking at it, holding a cigarette, my arms crossed, hugging the backs of my arms. I'm in touch with something elemental—all men will pay for it, outrageous amounts, but a bargain when you think what it comes down to—the me in me taken every time. At least that's what they want, the bottom line, everything about you for a numbered bill. Your mind Indian-burned. They want to wring you raw and hollow. I'm getting ahead of myself, I sorted this out later with Pauline and Nancy, whom I was to meet that night. Meanwhile Doyle's money arrested in flight across the ashes and what? with his little whimpering thing not much bigger around than the amber tubing in chem lab, what would it take? three minutes of me? The equation in my favor, I bent to him, no stamina in these thin ones—that's what I would later think—but he held on, short-breathing, sucking his instructions in over his teeth, leaning back on the kitchen table. I thought the table would crack with his weight, his big panned palms pushing on it. I heard it shudder, but it held. Then the long groan from him, the short explosion, I almost gagged but instead I swallowed and stood back.

I should have thrown him out before. He was pulling up his pants, sheepish and satisfied, as if I'd caught him fondling himself in front of a mirror.

"I'll swing by for you just before eight," he said.

Once he was gone I went to lie down on the sofa. But instead I rolled out my futon and lay on my side, one arm across my eyes. Warm bright southern light in that room, a sort of wash. My other arm bent under me, my fingers touching my shoulder, one knee pulled up, the other extended. Like a dream of one leg dangling from Mama's womb, pushing past the blood outside, cold air on my foot, testing the current of that world. If it seemed okay I'd spin around, drop head-first. But of course I had no choice. Plop! world, here she is.

What a cutie!

Cute? She's all blood and brown wrinkles.

She's going to be beautiful.

I turned out better than beautiful. *Stunning* is the word they use. Only I'm too short, five-four and a half. Why do those women have to be stretched like that? Like Chinese finger traps, up and up. I remember that song, my father had a record of it. *Tall and tan and young and lovely, The girl from Ipanema comes walking,* and I wanted to be her, but instead all my life in a backwater. Life is elsewhere, Mama, and she believed me—more than believed, she knew. After all, what can you do with short beauty? Waitress? On good days in a bad place it's forty cents over minimum tops. Who lives on that? A Revlon lipstick is three dollars. I can go through thirty-five dollars of Max Factor without even thinking. And yet there's no question of my beauty—or at least my appeal. Men have sliced their hands on each other's teeth trying to win what? My esteem? As if the man with less blood on him could slide into my blood, oh happy journey, I want to see you without any pants? A five-ten woman trades on her looks, stares at you from magazine pages, haughty, untouched. Inches less and it's open season.

If I could I'd get even—design clothes for short women. Shorties, I'd call them. Clothes that would make tall women look ridiculous, that would make them look like the gawky sawhorses they are, that would strip them of their grace. Clothes for women under five-five. I should do that. I won't, but someone should.

Mia came in, thought I was asleep, moved around me, turned on the stereo. "Hey," Mia said when I rolled onto my back, the ceiling so far away, one long crack across with tributaries like a river in winter seen from a plane. "So where'd you get this?" The wings of the fifty folded together, pinched between her thumb and forefinger.

"Christ," I said. My tongue still felt coated. I coughed. "You wouldn't believe this morning, like the whole world's my uncle. Between what they left on the counter and my split, I mean we were busy, but these must've been businessmen with Carte Blanche accounts. At two o'clock I cashed it all into that," I said, and Mia said, "Dorie, you ever get tired of that job let me know, I want it."

"You'd have to shave your legs," I said. I rubbed my eyes. Still the river up there, frozen black. She left the money on the table and I heard the shower hiss on.

"Date?" I yelled.

"My Design Two prof," she yelled back. "A bunch of us have been invited to his apartment. He does this every midterm and then he tells us we're all lazy. He left his wife, one of those mid-life things. She still has the house. I hear he's there Saturdays, puttering around." She spat out some water. "He'll be back with her once he's nested down with a few students. He wants to think he can still fuck all night, be the bohemian. I'd almost like to prove him wrong so he'd stop being a lewd ass in class, but he smells funny, like he spilled his wife's perfume on his chest or something.

"You should come," she said. She was out of the shower in the doorway between her room and the living room. I sat up on one thigh. Mia was naked, rivulets of black hair on her legs. "You'd drive him crazy," she said.

"Can't," I said. "I'm trailing tonight."

"Well, la-de-dah," she said.

"Doyle's idea," I said. "He said I'd make even more money hostessing than cashiering mornings, and Lord, to be able to sleep late."

"Good, we can party," Mia said. "We'll hit the after-hours places. Starting tonight," she said and dried her legs. "And in the morning you can put in a good word for me cashiering, huh?"

"Sure."

"Terrific," she said and kissed my cheek and dried her arms, the fine black hair like down. But it looked all right on her, made her look glossy as a seal.

"When will you be back?" she asked, doing the side fastening on a green tweed skirt, green stockings underneath. "I'll call you, you can meet us someplace." A cream blouse next, no bra, a loop of bow at her throat. "Protection from the master," she said with a laugh, tying it. I could see her dark under the blouse, a careful strategy of come hither but no passion. "Well?" she asked.

"I don't know when I'll be back," I said. "Sure, call."

She said, "How do I look?"

"Great," I said. She was combing back her long black hair, her face was white, her eyes gleamed like just-turned loam. "Enticing but . . . pragmatic," I said, hoping that was what she wanted.

"Perfect!" she said. "Maybe I can get an A *without* sleeping with him." She was doing her mouth in the living room, moving her head and holding the compact steady. She looked at me to see if I was smiling or not. "This is yours," she said. "Hope you don't mind my borrowing."

"Take my clothes, too," I said.

"Oh, I'm not that desperate," she said with a laugh, snapped shut the compact and slid it and the lipstick across the table. They nestled the fifty, one wing fluttering, a wounded bird.

"I'll call," she said.

"Fine," I said and got up, turning the lock. Just me in here now, sitting at the table, the edges worn to wood, white paint worried through on the legs and at the crease for the leaves. The compact in my hand now open. Desert Frost, three shades. I remember when I was thirteen looking at them like medicine in the cases at the Gimbels in Appleton, the clerk made up like a cover girl, perfect and beautiful. Her name was Debbie. Ocean Greens, Royal Blues, African Copper, Shimmering Dusts, Sea Pearl, Platinum, Golden Nectar, Peach Sky, Moonlit Rose, Indigo Wine, Amethyst. I wanted something called Plains Song, as if I could be an Indian princess, my hair blond as lemons.

I do my eyes. Arch the deepest color into the seam of lid and brow, fan the blush out to the far ridge of cheek, touch up the mascara. My lashes hold it well. They're like brooms of silk, people arrested by my eyes, men holding their wrists up pleading for the cuffs. I have big lips, the lower one so luminous, so full of honey you'd think it was stored in wet gauze till I was old enough to unveil it. Uncap the lipstick, do myself red, red as fresh blood, red as swollen hydrants, primal red, yes, that color surrounding the black of my open mouth, an advertisement of bold disdain. Ready. Put on the Stones' "Indian Girl" and dance slowly, waiting, change into a different blouse, rhythmic roll of my hips, sensuous, no eagerness. Fuck them all, dancing. And then he knocked. Just a minute, I shouted, the stereo went off, coat and scarf on, mittens, move my face once around the compact mirror—hard disin-

terest—the eyes like glass, the lips closed, inner coldness
and frost. Hello, Doyle. His eyes down me like a drink, with
no emotion. Stairs, door, careful, he holds my forearm, guides
my heels on fresh snow like I needed help, then into the car.
We sit, he pats my hand, his manicured hands on my wool
mittens. His wipers squeegee snow. All the way to work,
snow.

"I'll have you trail Nancy," he says when we get there.
"Girls, this is Dorie. We'll be working her in evenings." The
room's mostly black and leather, Old World, low green accountant lamps for each booth hanging over the tables like
everyone's favorite pastime is balancing accounts without
enough light. Doyle's gone, vanished into the black matte.
People seem separated from the air as if cut with penknives,
cartoons. Pauline and Nancy in strapless black leotards inked
on their bodies, their legs short and strong, crosshatched with
black tights. Bare shoulders and necks white as cigarette
papers. Pauline with the finer features, delicate eyebrows and
chin, sharp nose, heart face. But she's getting old, late thirties, lines by her eyes and mouth like wires or broken spider-
webs. Nancy early thirties, rounded, more water in her face,
blunt but pretty, oval eyes and mouth. Both brunettes, a short
choppy sea of waves and frosted froth. Like sisters with different faces, Pauline smaller all the way around, less to her as
if she'd dropped some weight, worried it off. Skin so thin you
can almost see through it.

"Don't follow me," Nancy says. "Have a drink and I'll be
with you in a minute. Slowsville."

She's right. Seven, maybe eight people are scattered in the
cavernous dark—mostly men, corpulent bodies like irregular
marble quarried in blocks. Late forties and fifties, expensive
suits, big gold rings flashing like brass, lonely and pleased
with themselves, smelling of soap and smoke and perspiration
as if they'd recently washed but the very fabric of their suits is
impregnated. They order loudly, laugh, one holds Pauline by
the back of her thigh while he talks, his rubbery cheeks flap-

ping, sloped head gleaming, someplace toward the back there's hair. Already I can see how I'll hate them all. At least mornings there was the counter between. We wore clothes, the mauve jacket with a lighter skirt, striped blouse, high-throated collar with a bow, fake professional clothing, prim make-believe, but it was something. Here they paw and grin, no clothes or rules, our asses cupped by their hands. Sacri-fices. I order myself a double Scotch.

Nancy places three orders, nods to me, goes away and comes back, slides onto the stool next to me, lifts a cigarette, holding it high, and says, "So you're the spare?" and inhales a long time, looking me over. I kept the Blaisdell skirt on, changed into a blouse with half-sleeves and a boat neck. "Doyle can pick them," she says. "You know about drinks? On busy nights we do our own setups. You know Rob Roys? That's a favorite. Know that and a double-dry Beefeater and that's two-thirds of the regulars. What do you think of these?" she says, blowing smoke out past her thigh. "Used to be we had these mid-thigh skirts with white trim, but now we're in exercise tights. No support for the titties. It's a good idea to get a strapless pushup. You don't need me telling you that, but I like you, you're probably underage. These things are cut so tight half your ass falls out of them. But don't worry, some-body's hand'll be there to push it back. If you like you can slap but you'll get stiffed later and they talk. When I was in my twenties"—a new cigarette, she smokes them halfway down, smiles—"I know it's futile, smoking twice as many half as far." She laughs. "What's it to you when I was twenty? You haven't even seen nineteen yet. I'll tell you, though, it beats most places for take-home. On good nights I'll get what you could in the main room, though they don't get pawed in there, but still they do eight hours and we do six. I'll tell you a secret: wear pantyhose and then the fishnets, maybe two pair of hose if you're thin, and if you've got any kind of hair shave real good, the stubble will drive you crazy but you can't have bush curling out the sides. Doyle wants us hairless as ten-

year-olds. Another of his fantasies. What are you, blond all
the way through?" She leans back, as if to see better. "Just
asking. Look, we stick together—it's us, a few embarrassed
wives, some stiff-assed businessmen and the animals. You
don't want to hear this"—she crushes out the cigarette—"but
who's going to tell you if we don't.

"There's other things, too." She lays her hand on mine.
"We'll talk later," she says. "There's sort of a system for extra
money, but first you better learn the drinks." From behind the
bar she pulls a book—*Bartender's Guide.* "Read this. There's
daily specials, too, on the mimeo sheets in back. Do the
drinks here, see? All setups. On nights like this Bobby'll do it
all. Bobby, say hello to Dorie, fresh meat for the grinder."

Bobby smiles, wrists and hands dunking glasses in milky
water, stocky Irish, came out of the womb a bartender or pal-
let loader, calm and friendly-looking, proud of his work.

Nancy says, "Pauline can go over the prices with you, it's
no great shakes, the machine knows everything, you just have
to punch it up. Most of it is smiling while their eyes fuck
you—are you used to that yet? You're pretty, you should be.
We stick together," she says again, says it no-nonsense as if
she isn't just saying it. She slides off the seat, pulls at the
fabric starting to ride down her left breast. "I don't have
enough to keep it up, everybody getting tit shots when I serve
them." She leans close. "You know I've had fifties wrapped
around room keys slid down there while I changed ashtrays?"

"Do you keep it?"

"Always," she says. "Though if they're really drunk all
they get for it is the room key back and a note saying, Thanks
for the lovely time, and they think then we must have." She
touches my elbow. I'm looking at the pattern of my lipstick on
the Scotch, a smudged half-moon. She says, "You don't have
to, but Doyle— Hello, Doyle, you were just about to get dis-
cussed." Doyle in a tuxedo now, looking like he belonged in
one, hair wet and combed back, very official, a *GQ* reject.

"Have you told her I'm God yet?"

Nancy, still holding my elbow, "Doyle's God, Dorie."

"I'll bear that in mind."

Nancy takes her tray and goes off, moving like the shadows of clouds over open ground. I like to watch her move.

"Tomorrow we'll get you measured—Mrs. Chusek's room, third floor."

"I was there."

He takes my drink, holds it up. "Only this one," he says. "Nothing when you're on the floor. We're very strict about that. You can sneak one, I don't care, but put it in a mug for God's sake. We get spotters, and if Vaigen comes for me I'll come looking for you."

I'm sitting hunched, fingering the glass rim-kissed by lipstick. I'm thinking of those monkeys at the zoo whose cheeks glow red when they want it. Doyle leans close, like Nancy only there's no older brother in him, this is male-in-the-monkey-suit. "Listen," he says, and slides his hand, palm down, next to my glass, "we got someone tonight who wants to be talked to. In the corner to your left behind you." He takes his hand away, dull brass of room key, cut number, *Blaisdell* in script like someone with confidence writes only the last name. Under the room key, money.

"We'll have you splitting shifts," he says. "Wednesdays, Fridays and Saturdays here, Wednesdays and Tuesdays at the coffee shop. A lousy schedule I know, that double Wednesday, but Joyce the old cashier is coming back, and she always wants those middle days off."

"So I'm off till Friday?"

Doyle rubs the nail of his index finger. "Joyce is back Monday. Friday you'll double shift, trailing then and Saturday. Then like I told you. I'll have the schedules up Sunday. You can call in to make sure."

"What if I told you to keep the money?"

"I'd say I thought we already had an understanding."

I say, hating him but seeing how I don't know enough to do more than coast, "I guess we do."

. . .

Doyle, as I come out of the room, is waiting at the elevator. He leans into my face. I made you a hundred, he says. Remember that on my birthday. It comes around often.

Sure, Doyle, you're twenty-seven every week. We brush shoulders. He starts grabbing in the elevator. I knee him a fast one. He folds but grits it off.

Oh, I see, he says, hissing the words, teeth tight together. Then he steps out, the doors start to close. Just remember my birthday!

Mama's waiting for a phone call, I'm in a cab. Pull over here. A phone booth, we're by Lake Michigan. Keep it running, I tell him. Dial collect. Mama, I'm in Chicago and I'm fine. I have an apartment (give Mia's brother's address as mine). I'm a receptionist, Mama. I take people's calls, type letters. I'm doing fine. I'll write you. I don't have a phone yet. Yes, I'm fine. I'm outside. Can you hear the lake? It's snowing.

In the taxi again. A left here, I tell the driver. Three-fifty, he says. We're in front of my house. All I have is this, extending the hundred. What am I, lady? A bank? It's all I have. Yeah, and I'm Nelson Rockefeller. Counts bills into my hand like he was my father regretting a too-generous allowance, only I never had one, allowances sounding like something for nothing. We worked and when there was a dance or a dress I wanted and we had the money, Okay, here's some. But usually the third degree for money and I was the lucky one. Mama didn't like Tommy or Scott; they'd get half what I'd get. Girls need more money, Mama said. She favored me, still does. She'll send money. She paid for my scraping, lied to Daddy about it. She needs new contacts, she said, and I got those, too. You know what a girl in glasses has for prospects? Mama told Daddy. You think anybody wants a four-eyes? To

me she said, You start using something I don't care what,
there'll be no bastards in my house. And this cabbie like a
disgruntled father. Here's something for you, I say, giving him
five. I'm an Indian princess capable of presents.

Snow reaches my ankles. I'm wearing open-toed shoes so
there's this diamond of cold at the front of my foot. I need to
buy clothes. Up the stairs, stamping off the cold. I want to be
warm. Inside I start tea. The clock's swept around to eleven-
thirty, early yet. Pouring water over the stainless steel tea ball
the phone rings. Mia? Yes, I'd love to. Where's that? Okay,
I'll change. Sloppy or dress up? Fine, I didn't want to anyway.
Music to change by, Joni Mitchell telling me about ladies of
the canyon. I step out of the skirt and slip. I shiver. The
thermostat's stuck at sixty-three. I bang on it, push it to seventy. I want to wear shorts in the apartment or run around
naked, air on skin, delicious, but it's always too cold. Wash
myself, fresh panties, that guy's gook's going to drip out all
night. A quick pee gets some. I feel better, cleaner, I don't
want to think about it. I put on a blue flannel shirt, one of
Daddy's, no bra, I could get away with never wearing one but
I fought so hard to get to, that impulse hasn't died yet (Mama,
will I ever have them like you? Pray you don't, Dorie, they get
so sore and droopy). Instead I've got a man's athletic T-shirt
on under the flannel. I love the look, small pink-nippled
breasts rising under the ribbed white cotton, soft blue flannel
over that left unbuttoned, blond hair loose to the shoulders,
jeans and white sneakers. Still with the makeup, men will kill
for that, eyes drool desire, talk loud to impress me, make up
stories with themselves as heroes. Ha, ha, you hungry fools,
$140 plus change rides in my front pocket, not on my hip, the
square of folded money a distraction. I want the eye-popping,
heart-breaking curve of my ass unbroken, and I'd sooner
break your fingers as let you touch me.

2

NOT EVEN THE HOPE of light yet and the 5:00 alarm sharp-
edges into my sleep, my two hours dreamless. I have time for
a shower, light makeup, instant coffee and the bus. Mia
stretched out with her professor. I go from bathroom to
kitchen and back. Shower/coffee/makeup. How'd we end up
here? Oh, yes, the party. Moved to someone else's house, big
warehouse thing, naked mannequins, plaster of Paris figures,
bare floors, unframed paintings propped against walls, others
hung with wires from the ceiling. Even a band, The Widgets
—kids my age leaping about, frantic energy, like paddleballs
snapping frenetically on rubber bands—everyone else moving fluid or herky-jerky, dense pack, greased to fit with their
own sweat. People against the walls looking cool, one leg up,
knee out, posed nonchalance.

Beer's over there, someone says. We head that way. Mia
introducing me in quick shouts, one ear to the other. Neither I
nor the other person hears the name but we nod and smile,
the women seeking flaws, the men looking as they do, the
sizing up less critical than a woman's but then they're looking
for different things. Sometimes you can almost see it stiffen in
their pants. I want to pat them there, Easy, Tiger, and watch
them turn blue. I smile at one and he turns away, knowing
that I know he's going to jerk off later in the john, mouthing
my name.

We get plastic cups, I say thank you to the curly-haired
redhead who makes a gallant show of pouring us beer. He's

wearing glasses, gold wire rims as if it's still 1970. He touches my wrist, cocks his head toward the frenzy.

"Dance?"

"Only when I'm alone," I say, and move off to the room's far end, near where we came in, and stand next to the water pipes, Mia on the other side, like we're bookends for the pipes. Someone mentions that—human bookends for inanimate objects, he says. I lean my cheek against a pipe, curl my fingers around it. Warm. Someone sitting on the radiator next to Mia. Here we are, I think, huddled for heat, cold drafts when somebody else comes in, stamps their feet as if saying farewell to the outside air. There's another woman in this group, Connie, tall and anorectic, and three men. One of them the professor. Of course, I think, he'd be the one passing out joints like spearmint sticks. He's a little heavy, but he used to be in shape, has a block chest, all black hair, tufts arching out his T-shirt, head balding but he doesn't do anything stupid about it like paste five hairs into place. His pate's smooth, the hairs combed straight back, proud to recede, his scalp glistens with sweat, his voice coated with asthmatic authority, a wheezer. He hands me a joint, lights it, the lighter dropped into his jacket pocket, satisfaction on his face. His hands stay in the tweed coat till he needs them. So worldly in his Harris. Anxious and smug. I take the one puff, why argue, and pass it on. I keep passing it on the next few swings. The professor's watching me.

"Temperate, are you?"

"Transcendent, thanks."

"Transcendent, is it? And where would you get a word like that?"

"My dictionary."

"You just flip through it looking for good words?"

"I read it as a little girl, because it was more interesting than most of the people I met. And meet."

More professorial bemused smiles, his eyes glassy, his arm around Mia. He says, "She's very talented, you know."

Mia looks embarrassed, then hard. Her eyes shift from me to him, calculating. I can almost see the numbers run through her head: net worth, one fuck with drunk prof. She drinks her beer, laughs. The other boys are nothing. They're standing in this group as hangers-on and they know it. After I say, Not interested, thanks, to whatever they propose—outside for a drive, a walk, some coke, whatever—their attention shifts to Connie, Mia already spoken for. Connie looks at me and lights a cigarette. I already have one in my mouth so I'm occupied when the joint comes by again. Connie's pale as moonlight, pencil thin, looks like she survived something and isn't sure she wanted to. Full blackness in her hair, eyebrows like thick washes of charcoal, huge round eyes bulging. She knows about death. Death has worked his fingers through the uncombed hair hanging down her back, he whispers in her ear, he sits on her shoulder grinning. She looks at me. I smoke my cigarette. She knows she's next, is unsure of herself, should she follow my lead and say no? What if she's missing something? The shorter one will go home with her and she'll wake up in the morning, desperate, feeling hollow all day, wondering what it was that caused her to say yes. Death gnaws at her crotch. In her head she's doing the eeny-meeny-miney-mo for the agent of this night's destruction. At least when you have a name for it you know what's happening.

One swallow left in the cup, which I leave on the radiator to be knocked backward, the spill on the wall like dog pee.

Come, I say to Mia and we tromp off for the bathroom, not that I need to go, but to break the circle, it was all so damn cozy, like someone had poured gelatin around our feet and we were afraid to move or muck up the floor. The stall's institutional, gray metal dividing wall, a toilet on each side, one with privacy and one without. Mia leans against the wall, her feet out bracing her. She smokes a cigarette while I worm down my pants. We're on the private side. I finish but we stay that way talking.

"Men like you," Mia says.

"Boys," I say. "All boys." I start my own cigarette. "So what's with Professor Tweed?"

"He's just drunk. I hear one more thing about his wife I'll scream."

"I thought he left her."

"He did, but he's pretending she forced him to."

"So he wants a sympathy fuck."

Mia exhales at the ceiling. "Exactly."

"So are you?"

Mia runs her hand through the blond waterfall spilling over my ear, tucks it back, her finger following the ear's curve, then the finger down in front along the lobe, along my jaw, she holds my chin between her thumb and forefinger, the cigarette up in her hand.

"Depends on how drunk I get."

"Mia—"

The door bangs open, music pours in, liquid, a bottle breaks on the tile, green shards shoot under our stall. A man's voice.

"I see feet. Who's in there?"

Mia pokes her head out.

"Women's is it? Two of you? You're not doing anything else, are you?"

Mia says, "What's it to you?"

"Nothing, I say. Nothing. Any port in a storm. But if you're doing blow I want some." I hear the thunder in the sink. "Load off my mind."

Mia says, "I'm sure." The door bangs again.

"Who was that?"

"Nobody."

"So what about Jeff from MSOE?"

"Jeff's married."

"Oh."

"He tells his wife he works late at school." Mia starts another cigarette. "I always wondered why he washed himself before he left. At lunch today he told me. So," Mia says, breathing deeply. "Lately I'm O for two. Not that I'm keeping score. But shit," she says, "two married ones in a row— well, one and a half." She holds her glass up to the fluorescent light as if she were looking for sediment.

"I'll need to get drunker than this," she says.

Three men offer to take me home. Their mouths work at their lines, their attempts cast into my placid blue eyes, under the surface there must be fish. Lunkers! They want me to mouth their bait, follow it to the surface, rise, till my eyes light up, Yes, and I'm theirs. But their attempts are too pathetic to take seriously. When I was fifteen they might have had me, I was stupider then, willing to be the notch on someone's bedpost, this was like love, wasn't it? But not now. No emotion even in turning them down, no condolences.

I don't get drunk, because Mia has. In a strange way I feel responsible. This is my first act of kindness for her. Prof. Tweed has draped himself on her. Twenty people are left. The Widgets are doing a slow sax shuffle, eyeing their equipment, eager to pack and go. Tweed has Mia embraced into his shoulder. I see how this is going, should have seen before, but I felt protective, wanted to do the motherly thing. I'm calling a cab, I say, my speech dropping in between their chests like a wedge. They both straighten, arrange themselves.

"No need," says Tweed. "No need." He fumbles in his pockets, comes out with the bright ring of keys. "Exhibit A," he says. "The prosecution rests."

We go to his car, a Saab. They walk like welded twins. At home I get the bathroom first, scrub out the aftertaste of beer, wash my face, put on my father's flannel pj's, blue with royal piping at the collar and cuffs. They are fumbling on the bed, not even under the covers yet, as if that were too much to manage. They're working at each other's clothes as if at Chinese boxes, pushes and tugs and pulls. Somehow his shirt buttons have disappeared. Tweed has her blouse tails in his hands as I cross to the living room. He pulls the fabric apart and up, buttons spitting off like cherry pits. The bed creaks back under their weight, two long sighs—fatigue—twisted as harmony, but then no more sounds. I had steeled myself to hear the rocking of someone else's sex, my lullaby for sleep, but they are already gone and I feel more awake for not hearing it than if I had. I hear one breathe and then the other, systems slowing down, the rhythm of shared breath like two trains, a marriage of respiratory systems. I wonder whose heart adjusted to whose? I finally sleep when I realize that if you're drunk enough you can be happily married to anyone.

So it's morning and I confront the mirror, do my eyeliner delicate as painting a miniature, no false strokes, and in comes Tweed, tousle-headed, graying, a little belly like bread dough rolled in flour, still wearing his underwear and socks, his walk stumbling into a crawl. He hugs the toilet as if he's not seen it for a long time, retches, realizes my calves are attached to the rest of me, turns his wan, stubbled face upward, blinks from the harshness of the vanity light, and is struck dumb.

"Good morning, Professor."

"G'mornin'." And regaining his upright balance, he weaves to fall back into bed where Mia rolls away from him, still asleep herself, but even unconscious, astute.

The gray sky lightens, I walk in hiking boots to the bus stop, my loafers in a plastic bag over my shoulder. No one's moving yet, mine are the snow's first prints. It's still pretty, but at four the ugliness will have come back, seeped in with the traffic. Snow made slush made sludge. I think again, you could be married to anyone.

I have sixty dollars in my pocket, the balance balled into a pair of dirty tights at home, bottom of the closet, next to my heels.

. . .

Mia's making soup when I come home, lentils with lemon. The first soup of winter, she says, sprinkling cumin. She sniffs and stirs. Steam has made her hair curly, the strands even thicker, black waved into black like brambles. Her cheeks pink, her pores open.

"You're beautiful," I tell her.

"Not everyone thinks so," she says, gesturing with her head. On the table is an opened box, half a dozen long-stems. "The delivery boy said they were from the professor. I didn't even look at the card till I'd gotten them in a vase."

"To Dorie," is on the envelope. Inside, "As soon as I saw you in a man's flannel pj's I wanted you. Maybe even before."

I ask Mia for paper, something heavy. She pulls a sheet loose from her sketch pad. In charcoal pencil, smudges of black dust like litter, I write, "Dear Professor." I'm talking as I write for Mia's sake, too. "Dear Professor, As soon as I saw you hugging the toilet bowl, perhaps even before, I knew I didn't.

"Have you got an envelope?"

"Here," she says, and tears loose another sketch sheet. I fold the one into quarters, put it inside the other folded in half, tape shut the edges, address it—what's his real name? Harris Vandersol?—to the U, Art and Design Department, put on three stamps—the thing is huge—and away it goes, an oversize kiss-off Valentine. Of course, I think, and with a red grease pencil I draw a child's crude heart as big as the envelope. The roses go under the sink.

"We'll eat in an hour," Mia says, putting on the lid. "I want everything to cook in." She sits down. "It's funny, you know, we were just next to each other for those five hours—he was gone by eight—and I don't even think we did anything."

"You don't remember?"

"I remember we didn't." She gets up and pats the cabinet under the sink where the roses are as if she keeps an animal there with the cleansers and scrub brushes. "He probably remembers that, too."

I change into fresh faded jeans, not worn yet to chamois thinness, the cracks in the coloring like rivers, tributaries of bleach and resistant fabric, and over that another plaid flannel. Oversize men's shirts make me feel safe. They can't touch me if I've got their clothing on. Switching, I become the stud, they the skittish mares, their eyes wide, nostrils flaring —Easy, boy, easy. I pat them on the back, apple in hand. I mount them with my indifference and ride them till I want to get off.

"It's the lemon that really makes this soup. Wait till later in the week. Nothing ages like soup. Pizza hardens and milk goes sour, but soup—soup resonates!"

I leave the soup on my upper gums and let it slide back as Mia tells me to. "Taste that?" she says. "The lemon. Only wine goes back like that."

"Beer, too," I say.

"Peasant," Mia says. "Beer is for men. Women drink dry red wines."

"So last night we were one of the guys."

"Exactly. And tonight we're women"—she touches my cheek—"and with our soup and fried zucchini we'll drink red wine—"

"And become delirious."

"Exactly."

Mia rolls herself a joint after dinner. We feel insulated, warm. I sit on the rolled futon smoking a cigarette, shake my head when Mia offers the joint, look out the window. Mia says we should just fuck everything and move to Greece. "Let them wonder what became of us," Mia says and shrugs her shoulders, as if people were already wondering.

Lights are on in neighboring buildings, random yellow rectangles. People move in the windows. I watch a couple embrace, multiple baby kisses on cheeks and neck, the woman throws her head back, the man feeds on the exposed neck. The first thing I wonder is, Are they married to someone else?

I've undone the buttons on my shirt, the cloth was bunching at my waist. The tails are pulled out now. Like a triptych, Mia says. You know—shirt, flesh, shirt—three panels, she says, touching me just below each shoulder and on my sternum between. Mia says I'm beautiful. I try to think of anytime I wasn't. I think of myself in comparison with Mama. I'm not big enough for lobed cleavage. Instead, two softly rising swells of skin, soft down of blond hair between. Mama says, Good, you'll last longer. I raise the cigarette to my lips. Three panels, I think, like modern or ancient art: shirt, flesh, shirt.

"I'd like some coffee," I say and Mia gets it. She settles down next to me, kneeling, haunches on heels, touches the middle panel again, her finger centered on my chest. Have I ever?

No.

Would you like?

No.

I thought—

I don't.

Mia twists around, sits with her knees up, her back slouched. "I didn't mean anything. You don't think, I mean, I just thought—"

The light is yellow, a low-wattage bulb. I lie back. The ceiling's water-damaged plaster bulges low like a woman in early pregnancy. My cigarette is my friend; smoking it, I don't have to talk. Mia puts on *London Calling*. Cigarettes. My third since Mia's silence.

"It's not that I don't think about it, it's just I don't want to."

Mia's head nods with the music, violent dislocations of neck, her lips pouting. "It's easier than with men."

"I'd have to want to and I don't."

3

WHAT'S WRONG? Larry asks me. What's happened?

We're in the hours off between cashiering and hostessing. Larry's taken the bus with me. He hopes to stay too late for the bus back, and then get to spend the whole night, and Saturday breakfast, too, as if he were home with his wife. I've yet to tell him I have to go back, our shifts will be different, my time with him less regular, the clock providing explanations for me. We can drift. Time an ocean putting me blissfully on a different shore. High waters between us. Wait for the tide, Larry, spits of land you can walk across but during these hours only. And then I'm gone, the fog's come in, I can't see you. Hurry back to your own peninsula. This is a small isle here. I can only support myself. Hurry, the moon is full, the water's coming back, it's rising. Go back, Larry. I'm gone.

Instead of this I say another truth: mail from Chicago routed here. Mama's coming. Only she thinks I'm in Chicago. She thinks I have no phone. I want her to believe I'm there. Chicago is safer for both of us.

"Why don't you just not answer?"

"She has an address. She'll come anyway, street map in hand, asking policemen in intersections Where is this? Am I here? My daughter lives in a brownstone."

"How did she get an address?"

"I sent her one. Mia's brother."

I dress. Earlier I shaved my crotch, lathered with soap and peeled off the blond fur close to the crease of my loins. I was careful for nicks. Mrs. Chusek, when she went through the tights bin for my size, clucking because I was a funny size ("You've got too much shape, dearie," is what she said), told me, "Careful where you shave, dearie. Down there you'll bleed something terrible." Now the flesh-tone pantyhose, also from Mrs. Chusek, everybody's overweight, printed-house-dressed aunt. Then the fishnetting. My flesh holstered, cargo.

I've told Larry too much, he shouldn't know me, but I need his car for Chicago, need him to haul me down there— Mama's cargo shipped so she can meet me at the wharf, intact goods, safe. Mama, don't worry, I'm safe. And then get hauled back north—Mia has to go along—and somehow ditch Larry, maybe a long sullen fight on the drive back. Or better, just get him to lend me the car, please, Larry, please please. Just Friday night and Saturday. You'll have it back Sunday. I'll clean it myself, vacuum the flooring, pull out the candy wrappers and McDonald's packaging, wash it with my tits like that woman for Paul Newman in *Cool Hand Luke*. I'm not big like her, but you can watch me anyway. I just need your car. Thank you, thank you, I'll have it back on Sunday.

"But where are you going?"

"Work. I waitress three nights a week now."

"Since when?"

"Wednesday."

"But we won't see each other much."

"It's more money, Larry."

"And here I thought you were putting that on for me."

"I have to go."

"How long's your shift?"

"You have to go, too."

"I couldn't wait here? I'll go down to Hooligan's and come back when you're back."

"I'm going to be really tired, Larry."

"We'll just sleep."

He doesn't say it, but I can hear the words behind his glasses, emphatically waving their hands at me as if he were left at the station, the train pulling out—My car!

Okay, I say.

I come home that night at three, two hundred-dollar bills under my arm, tucked into my bra's side strap. Larry has the futon out, the covers down. He's asleep, cradling my crumpled pajamas to his face. Smelling me in his sleep.

We sleep like old marrieds. I let him keep the pajamas. I sleep without clothes, he puts his leg between the two of mine. If not for that he probably wouldn't know I am here, he could mouth endearments into my flannels. In a way it's all the same. He wakes up once when I do. I feel stiff. My right arm has gone asleep, has gotten under him. It holds the small of his back like I'm guiding him, holding him in line. Surely not affection. My hand stays there because it's cold, it wants bulk and warmth poured into it. Larry is thin and courteous. He wants to be in love with me and so says nothing as I move my hand from under him. He pulls in his lips, smiling, a pucker of skin. He's embarrassed. I am only going to hurt him, but he pretends it's the other way around. We sleep. Sometime later he touches me in sleep, finds the spot between hair and belly, all my warmth there. He sighs, connected. I am awake, almost want to cry. Larry Fields, I want to whisper to him, Larry Fields, you don't want me but you want someone for in between and you're embarrassed. You use me this way, a halfway house for your heart, and so to you it's love or something like that. But this will end when you get your reason back, when you stop thinking with your cock alone, when the ache is gone. But it's okay for now, Larry Fields, because you don't know what you're doing and I don't want you to. You are puppy-love-struck with desire and you think of me as a gift, manna from a just God.

I curl in closer to him. There is no God, Larry Fields. I'm only seventeen and I know there isn't justice. People buy only what they can't steal. Then out loud I say to him, I got fucked by two men tonight, Larry Fields, and they paid me for the privilege.

I'm leaning over his chest, talking. He's on his back, by his ear the ball of my pajamas. The sleep of the dead. Larry Fields, I whisper to him, Larry Fields, you don't know anything but you're very special. I sit on my haunches, move back and forth till I'm wet enough and take him. It's seven A.M. He moans my name.

I watch his face—a hatchet, nose and jaw and chin sharp-edged, eyes deep-set, under the lids the eyes squirming with what? A dream? The last wet dream I had was when I was fifteen. It was a dream that I had to pee my pants. I was at a crowded park and couldn't find a bathroom. Near me was a wading pool, one of those yellow double-tubed things for toddlers, with two children in it. I upended that, the children spilling out with the water, and I kneeled behind it, holding the pool at arm's length like a lean-to, my jeans rolled to my ankles. I sat back just a little, felt the warm urine down my thighs, the hamstrings washed in pee, it felt so good. On and on I peed, and finally stood up. I'd done it through my panties. There was the lifeguard, classic in his pith helmet, whistle, ribbed athletic T, all muscles and tan, tapping in his hand a policeman's riot stick. He looked at me with compassion, raised the club across his body, poised for the backhand that would kill me and I felt the rush of a come—but it's Larry. I had closed my eyes and for a minute I was back there, fifteen, wet-dreaming the lifeguard. I look now, Larry's eyes rolled in terror, in great joy, guttural sounds twisting his mouth, hands grabbing my thighs. I'm lifted up by his hips, a swell like a roller coaster about to plummet down, he's deep in me, good, deep against my stomach, yes, and he's crying, Oh! and Oh! and Oh! He bursts inside me crying, Cynthia! Oh my God Cynthia! and I find myself coming, too. In my ears Cynthia! Cynthia! I have stopped being me.

He can't look at me for a long time. I get up to wash and come back to find him rolled on his stomach, still crying, a bird fallen from the nest, wings and legs broken. He'll be curled forever, sniffling, a baby. I grab his cock. Fuck you,

Larry, I came, too. He sits up, suddenly happy, everything forgiven or forgotten, his life a strange song. I can think of nothing to say to him but crawl in beside him and we sleep for two more hours. He makes love to me again when he's awake. He remembers my name.

While he spreads the paper across the kitchen table, Mia and I shower. First Mia, then me. Mia dries her hair in the bathroom so we can talk. "I let him in a half-hour after the bars closed," she tells me. "He was knocking and said you said he could stay. I was too tired to argue."

"It's all right," I tell her. "It was sort of agreed."

I start breakfast, Mia makes coffee. We plan our trip.

"I've already spoken with Doyle. He'll accommodate me. Another something I owe him."

Mia says, "Fine, I'll just skip Friday."

"That won't be necessary," I say. "We'll leave late afternoon. Mama's bus won't be in till nearly seven."

"But we should be settled. It should look like we live there."

"And your brother will let us?"

"Aaron's never there. He lives with his girlfriend. He keeps that place for show, a second home. His safety valve."

"I'll have to bring him something."

"He's already got a better one of everything."

"Wine?"

"A civilized red, yes." Mia laughs, all mouth. I like her in her delight. She says she loves conspiring. "And thank you for the car," she says to Larry.

"Yes, Larry, thank you." My hand with the cigarette touches his wrist. For him this means something. Connection. I tamp out the cigarette, swivel in my chair to keep speaking with Mia.

Larry's hunched over his plate, hugging his arms, happy to be on the edge of belonging. It means he's important, he still counts for something. He laps up what I am for him—a woman he can be with. He feigns experience. His wife left him and so he knows about love. Poor Larry Fields, I think. Someone should tell him something.

Larry is a lost jigsaw piece from a puzzle no one's doing. I have another cigarette and Larry looks at me. We will never make love again and, knowing that, I let him stay all morning reading the paper. When he leaves he kisses me tenderly on my cheek and strokes my hair. He says he'll call. I never want to see him again except I need his car.

4

MAMA CAN TELL right away it's a man's apartment. Who had we been trying to fool? She bursts in, it seems like we had been there waiting for her, rabbits waiting to be skinned, though we had gotten her at the Greyhound station, driven back with her, pointing out sights as if we knew where we were, blasé as old residents, containing our own excitement. Yes, that's the Sears Tower, that's the Commodities Exchange, Mia's brother works there, has his own seat. Isn't it weird, all the els like unfinished dinosaurs?

On the elevator I start answering Mama's unasked questions. Oh, Mia's a decorator, I sort of got lucky, hooked in with her, she wants to put aside money for Europe. Then Mama's in the front room, she seems to precede us, as if we are attendants. She looks around. "Beautiful," she says bitterly, the same voice she uses when correcting Mia, who says "Thank you, Mrs. Keillor" and Mama stares at her and says, "Brown. The name's Brown."

And Mia says, "Oh, I thought Dorie—"

"So Dorie's using my maiden name now. I'm flattered. Brown," she says, lighting a cigarette. "It sounds awful even out of my own mouth. Amanda Brown. Amanda anything-but-Brown." She shakes the match out, pinches her cigarette between thumb and forefinger as an old man would, pincered just ahead of the filter, cutting it nearly in half. Her hands shake, she'd probably drained her purse flask on the way down, sitting in the back on the toilet, nips at each railroad crossing, each package stop—Addison, Slinger, Richfield, Lannon, Sussex, Union Grove—every pull, every draw getting her ready for me.

She goes straight to the phone, picks up the receiver. "When did you get a number?"

She turns around. "And the number is?"

We haven't even thought. What was I after except a postponement of this? Mia tries to cover, looks at the ceiling, as if drawing the number from memory, which she is, and of course that finishes it. She starts with the area code.

"You don't even live in this city, do you?"

I look at Mia, abashed and powerless.

Mama sits down. "Is there a drink to be had? Do you know at least where the alcohol is?" Mia gets out the liquor. I get ice and glasses. We sit on the couch opposite her.

"It's not that I mind you lying to me. Lie to your mother. It's good practice for your husbands. But now what? We're here in this beautiful apartment—whose is this, your brother's, Mia?—and where should we be?"

She eyes both of us, but really me. Mia is an accessory, an audience. Mama will never so much toy with someone— whether Daddy or the boys or me—as when someone else is there as witness.

"Come now, where?"

"Milwaukee."

"Milwaukee. And what are we doing in Chicago?"

She knows. Knows my reasoning clearer than I. Dreamed it before I could: the abandonment of what you know. Everywhere the same, but there are other places with the promise of being different, surfaces at least that aren't what you know, have grown up knowing, and that, at least, is something. In getting away, you confirm what it is you know, the strata of similarity, the geology of sameness, but at least you're away.

"I had said Chicago, Mama. I didn't want to disappoint you."

Her glass flies over my shoulder, cubes hitting the wall,

Scotch on my face, my forehead. Amber and cold. Sticky.

"You're lying!"

She has me by the shoulders, shaking me. My face snaps away from a backhand. I feel it coming, the disturbance of air, my cheek stinging and numb. When I turn back, she's in my face, hissing, "You were afraid, weren't you? Afraid I'd come see you, afraid I'd be there, follow you too much. Is that it? Is it?"

"Yes," I say.

She sits down, settles into the overstuffed leather easy chair, the chair green like an avocado. She strokes the arms. "Lovely," she says. "Everyone should have lovely green chairs into which they can sink and sink. They just take you, swallow you up. Like you and me," she says, looking at me. "Get me a drink," she says and Mia, like a good servant, gets her a fresh glass.

"I want my own life, Mama."

"I want my own life, Mama," she whines, mocking me. "I want to live and live," still in the whine, pausing for a long drink, neck bent, leaning forward, meeting the glass halfway, ice cubes a logjam against her upper lip, straining the alcohol through her teeth. "You little fool," she says, calm now, giving herself up to the chair's depths. "What have these years been *but* your life? Your father's life, your brothers'? Everyone's but *mine*, except as I scratch one out, hiding it from everyone. Did you know I took a studio apartment in town that I go to sometimes just to pretend it's mine? Do you know what I do there? Can you imagine? Can you even pretend to know?"

Mama's face is puffy, blotched red like dying roses. The flask she'd drunk on the bus, these last two drinks as well—all that alcohol in her has detonated, fuse to powder. I imagine the warmth going through her, distributed through trunk and limbs, her elbows tingling, everywhere the warmth. She's close to crying, the heat inside her, oh blessed heat. My aunt Rose isn't the only one with arthritis. My mother's hands are curled, gnarled and bumpy like the nibs of tree roots before the ground swallows them. Alcohol gives her freedom. Her stomach radiates thin blood. The marble of her stretch marks glows pink. Liquor is her sacrament, a miracle.

"Again!" Mama cries. She pushes herself to her feet, sways there like dead wood still green. She gets another drink for herself and turns around.

"Your brother's apartment," she says. "And where's he?"

"He shares another apartment with a friend."

"A woman? Be frank. I hate a lack of frankness between women. Sisters," Mama says. "Let us say we are sisters. And we keep nothing from each other, nothing whatsoever. Wouldn't dream of it. The frankness of sisters." She settles into her chair. "I like that." She lifts her glass. "To the frankness of sisters!" Her eyes narrow, black agates in fat. "A woman?"

"Yes."

"Well, that's cleared up. You see? We're straightening things out. We're getting it all arranged. Now, you're in Milwaukee."

"Yes, Mama. I said that already."

"And you drove here to meet me."

"Yes."

"Because you don't want me where you actually are, in Milwaukee?"

"Yes."

"Your own mother," she says. "Sister, oh frank sister," she laments, going into her drunk country preacher mode, "you needn't be so emphatic with those yeses. A simple nod of the head, please. No need to speak your heart so loud."

"I don't want you in Milwaukee, Mama." I sit with my hands folded between my thighs, watch her gulp her drink, throat yo-yoing the liquor as desert travelers do water. She's caught up in her own theatrics, Mama a vaudevillian, only she thinks she's doing high tragedy, soap opera at least, heavy melodrama. She wants me to run to her sobbing, pull her close, press her belly to my cheek, plead, Oh, Mama, Mama, and she's the wounded matriarch saying, There, there, we are still family, after all. Only she's into her old gunfighter voice. The glass bangs twice on the counter. She isn't aware she found it the first time. Her old-gunfighter-looking-for-the-showdown voice. In her eyes she sees young Henry Fonda, me, telling her to move along, old codger, move along. At forty-one I'm a codger, eh? she thinks bitterly, and she says, "Town isn't big enough for both of us, eh? But Chicago you'll see me in? Chicago's okay?"

"I just don't want you here all the time."

"What all the time? When am I here?"

"You'll keep coming, Mama. You won't stop."

"Of course I'll keep coming. You think only you've ever wanted to leave?"

I say, "I'm gone, Mama. I'm history. I'm the one they'll say about, 'She went to Chicago,' as if it were Africa or Polynesia."

"I'll tell you something," Mama says. "I tip my hat to you." She tips an imaginary hat, takes pains to settle it back on her head. "We shall continue your little charade. To everyone, I have a daughter in Chicago. 'Dorie? Why, Dorie's gone to Chicago. Yes, I'm going to see her.' You see? My end of the bargain. Your father, everyone—you're in Chicago. And we meet here when I say so—that's agreeable? A safehouse for you and me, the old and the young among us. Mia's brother willing."

She's winding down now as a tethered ball will, wrapping around the pole of herself. She wants someone to say Amen! so she can go to sleep. Her glass is empty. She shakes it to resettle the ice cubes, then puts it down.

"I've had a long trip," she says. "I can still feel the rattles and bumps."

She goes to lie down in the big bedroom, kicks her shoes off at the bed's foot but doesn't remove her coat. With her arms spread wide she can barely touch the sides of the bed.

She's afloat, a snake still in her skin, too tired to move, drunk, my mother. I put one arm at her side and fold that side of the spread over her.

"A nap," Mama says, someone asleep talking inside her. "A nap and then dinner."

When she wakes up we're gone.

We argue about it on the way down in the elevator.

"Why'd you do that?" Mia asks.

"It's useless," I tell her. "We'll get an evening out of it, isn't that enough?"

"She'll get your address anyway," Mia says. "I bet she waits there till Aaron eventually shows up, and she'll ask for my address and phone number, and then what are you going to do?"

"We'll call your brother," I say and drag her over to the lobby's pay phone. "Call him and tell him under no circumstances to give out your number or address."

"He's probably out."

"If he's such a hot shit he's got an answering machine, right?"

She gets his answering machine. She starts, "Look, Aaron, Mia here." And while she's telling him, more convoluted in describing what has happened than what has happened needs, halfway through his machine clicks off and the message starts again. I think about the evening ahead of us, laughing.

"She's like that," I say. "Hysterics and then sleep. Once, more than once, she'd drink all afternoon, I'd come home from school, and she'd be in the back hanging up laundry—that was when the dryer was broken—and shrieking, just positively shrieking."

Mia leans on her knuckles, pelvis moving as her palms push away from the wall. "You sure it wasn't singing?"

"Sometimes it was singing. Real throaty," I say, and

burst into song myself—'Trolling for Jesus in the Great Lake of Life'—and stuff like that. But usually just out-and-out wailing."

"Like what?"

"Animal noises."

"Come on."

We're in the street. Volvos, Saabs and Mercedes parked in orderly rows like grade-school students at their desks, hair slicked into place.

"I'm serious. Who would hear her? She could scream like a banshee and no one would know. They'd think we were butchering a pig. It made her feel better. Later she'd go into the house, I'd be changing into my chore clothes, and she'd lie down on the sofa, a drink on the floor and a washcloth on her forehead. I'd get her awake before Daddy came back for supper."

And then this place we go to, for which we aren't dressed, Mia in a loose cotton tank top and a pleated skirt, white anklets and pumps, a black leather jacket, me in blue-white Calvins and an oversize man's short-sleeve dress shirt with a thin red-and-black rep tie, the shirt sleeves ballooning about my arms as if I'm an aging math teacher. I'm sitting on my coat. Everyone else dressed as props in a liquor ad—men in business suits with the ties properly dimpled, women in executive navy wools or raw silks, white high-necked blouses, exchanging phone numbers, debating IRA options, discussing with voices as decorous and squalling as birds the wet towel of life they seek to wring dry.

But we brazen it out. Find two stools at the bar's far end and order vodka tonics, staring down the bartender who considers carding us.

And then this big square back bumps me, a deep laugh coming out the front. A whole group of them laughing. I blow cigarette smoke deep into the man's gray-suited back, then angle the smoke up past his ears as if I'm a humidifier. The man turns, square-jawed, tortoiseshell glasses, the lenses so clear you'd swear he's only wearing them for the look of it, his sunburned eyebrows arching like caterpillars, his green-flecked tie quietly alive with flying ducks.

"Well, excuuuuuse me," he says, Steve Martinish and predatory, doing the up and down on me as if it's a professional privilege. What follows is a pointless conversation, complete with his gesturing toward the bartender and producing for me another vodka tonic like this is a magic trick. He touches my cheek. "Beautiful skin," he says. "I know someone who'd like to photograph you."

"Everyone knows someone who'd like to photograph me." My hair is pinned to one side, exposing whispers of blond hair and the oystered length of my neck. This guy is talking into the skin below my ear. I turn to Mia.

"Do you ever wish that the guys who just come right up to you and start talking weren't such perfect assholes?"

Mia nods, then swivels her head, leaving me to him.

The guy on my neck has one of those early-thirties-going-to-seed bodies, the chest that'd been worked up in college settling, the stomach swelling, content with itself. By forty the waistband of his trousers will have turned inside out, he'll switch from suspenders to belt to keep that hidden.

He asks me about tennis, which I don't play, and he admits he only plays enough to stay in shape, patting a freshly sucked-in stomach, as if I've only just looked. And then the inevitable barrage: what do I *do* to stay in such great shape? Swim? That's terrific. Here's my card. I'll call you, if you don't mind. We'll get together at my club. What's your number?

This guy is standing as a farmer would at dusk, the planting done, crows flying, three deer in the lower field.

I slide away from him, hoping to catch Mia, who's disappeared off toward the john. But the stalls are empty. Two women sit at the vanity, one rubbing her earlobes.

"I'll probably get an infection," she says to the other

woman, who's kissing air while she turns her face from side to side, checking her blush and working her cheeks hollow. In the stall I balance the tonic between my thighs, and drop Mr. Suit's card into the toilet.

"I told you to get hypo-allergenics."

"But these were perfect!"

"Except, dear, your lobes are swelling."

"I'll switch to these onyx drop ones."

"They'll look awful with your blue suit."

"They will, won't they?"

I wait long enough for that guy to picture me gone, but when I skate back through the crowd, men eyeballing me (I can tell from the arc of tension, the women pulling up stiff), there's Mia sitting shoulder to shoulder with what's-his-face.

My lips go up close to Mia's ear. We talk like two children with tin cans and string. What's-his-face waiting for a chance to speak, which we won't give him. Mia telling me about this guy who out of the blue invites her to the parking lot. "He was making nose gestures," she says. She says he's gorgeous, a hunk. His chin's dimpled, his mustache is rusty yellow, his eyes are blue. I say, "Lucky you," and she says, "No, lucky *you*." She says he wanted to find out about me, and that she gave him our number and said that we were only down for the weekend. "I told him we just flew in from Greece. Pretty slick, huh?"

"Great, he's probably phoning my mother."

Mia reaches into her purse, gives me the guy's card, where-upon the other guy gives me his card a second time, says he wants to call me, really, can I please give him my name and phone number, and I do. Lotte Lovic, I say, and rattle off some numbers which I say is a Skokie exchange, which he dutifully writes down, very smug and stupid, and then he goes for the good-bye kiss, grazing my cheek as I turn it, his lips wet on my ear. I roll my eyes and Mia holds up the two cards as if she's inspecting photographic negatives. "Collect 'em, trade 'em," she says. "Sometimes I really hate you."

"So what am I supposed to do with the card of someone I've never met?"

"Save it," she says, her mouth close to my ear, though it needn't be. "You never know when it'll come in handy."

"This really is stupid," I say. I turn my ear to hear what she'll say, but instead her lips touch my ear, her tongue quickly running the upper furl, down the lobe, which she pulls by her teeth, her tongue again behind my ear. I shiver in spite of myself and pull away. Mia smiles, her eyes bright as stars. She takes my hand and squeezes.

And then outside the cold. I button up my favorite coat, a long farmer's jean jacket with a corduroy collar and a plaid flannel liner. Oversize, it comes below my ass. The sleeves are rolled back. I think of Mama, still sprawled as if she's given herself up to the bed. Mia and I have dinner, a little Japanese place where they constantly nod at us until we feel we've acquired the tic, too.

And then dancing. I have to convince her of this. She wants to go to someplace quiet, have coffee and talk, but I don't want to. She insists on holding my hand in the car. She seems preoccupied with pleasing me, reassuring me it's all right, really. We dance. I feel people watching us. No, I want to say, it's not like this. I dance for a while with a black man who works his groin in slow circles on my ass, one of his hands on my waist, the other working the cap off a vial balanced on my shoulder. I think of Mama in here instead of me. Mama all heat and thunder, grinding her crotch on a black man's knee, matching him grin for grin. Mia and I stumble out later, swaying into each other for support.

Just after midnight we go back to the apartment and find Mama dead drunk in front of the television, her face swollen and changing color with the TV light. Gin and soda water bottles lined up like communicants by her chair. I imagine her first waking up and us not there, all around her the darkness without sound, trying to remember where she is, the bed, the apartment, her purple overcoat crumpled like a robe. She'd turn on the light, adjust her scrunch-eyed vision, go into the dark front room, feeling along the wall for the next switch. Reorient herself to the track lighting, the plants, the white-painted brick and dark woodwork, the green leather furniture, the purple Levolors, the black and chrome stereo, the original artwork, slashes of mauve and lavender on white canvas, the white lilies in the crystal vase on the glass-top coffee table, the pots on the wall in the kitchen, the butcher-block table. We get our bags, leaving her there, and sit on the front stoop for maybe forty minutes trying to think sober. Let's go, I say, and Mia follows me.

We drive past row upon row of sturdy brick townhouses. Past the bay windows, iron-railed balconies, roof gardens. I think about Mama, clinging as she is to those vestiges of high school beauty that had kept her popular and envied. So she told me when I first started to bloom at fourteen, late. Mama said, That's good, you'll hold it longer. I'll teach you makeup, too, she said. Make it stretch for as long as you can, she said, meaning beauty, as if someone allotted an amount to you and you had to give it back later, timed payments, but with cosmetics you could juggle the books, pay back less than you owe, refinance your face. I think of Mama as being on her second mortgage, loans due soon.

I think of her, too, in her rented studio in Augsbury. Steel-legged kitchen table and chairs, the couch, twin bed and nine-inch black-and-white. Maybe a radio. Plant cuttings in jelly jars on the windowsill over the sink. What does she do there? Long hours of bottles and cigarettes. Splayed in her chair, the soaps going. Do men come? Mama with no top on in her window, gesturing at the men having coffee in the front booth at Leeman's. A vision of sloping breasts pale as celery, two long loaves of bread dough set with brown penny nipples.

Who sleeps with Mama on dead air afternoons? I want to know their names.

. . .

That's when Mia first asks me, Why Chicago? It's like
salmon, I want to say. Yes, like salmon, leaping and plunging
and arrested by gravity, their gills bursting, tails flailing till
they lie bruised and exhausted, pulverized by water and rock.
That's Mama, chasing her childhood. And if she catches me
she'll eat her own spawn. Do salmon do that? No matter. I
have to stay ahead of her, have to keep her farther than arm's
length. Even if that means leaving upon arrival, the weekend
cut short. No Museum of Modern Art for Mia, no visit to the
Lake Street beaches for me. I want to imagine myself there,
bikinied and brown, blond hair bleached white, skin gleaming. Even though it's November my mind will see summer,
will see the empty khaki sand populated with the others like
me, but not like me because they lack my beauty. But waiting, too, to be plucked like a ripe peach for whatever it is
you'd call a destiny. I have it figured out. I know enough to
wait till summer.

Business cards, I think. Two to play with. Even the
schmuck has a photographer friend. A phone call and a fast
drink will tell me whether it's anything I'll want to get caught
up in. They stick to face shots, no room for length, and maybe
things will happen. *Playboy* is in Chicago, right? All those
women probably plucked right off the sand. And short, too.
On the stat sheet all of them five-one and five-two. The only
problem is that those women probably have to take their
clothes off forever. Like you're invisible with clothes on, a
nobody without your body naked. Skip that, I think. My face
is plenty. I check my face in the mirror to see if it's true.

And then the bad weather comes and I keep busy with my
plans, Mia still miffed about the aborted trip. "But it doesn't
matter," I try to explain and then give up explaining. "It was

a game and we got caught but we slipped away, and she hasn't called, has she?"

But then she does. Or rather, in late March, Aaron calls, says he has a telegram for me, it'd come down there and he thinks it might be important. We're getting ready for Mia's spring break. I have time off from work. We're going to drive to Florida, nonstop, two Amelia Earharts in a Mustang. Mia says we're practicing for Greece. She says we have to be properly tanned. She shows me pictures from the *National Geographic.* "See?" she says. "Florida's just like Greece only without the limestone mountains and the men are younger."

And then this telegram. YOUR FATHER'S SICK.

Mia says, "I'll go with you. You might need a hand."

"In our family nobody needs help from anyone." But she comes anyway. This is her road trip. I have my own car now, and Mia and I are traveling north to see my father; this is not something I would do for Mama. Leftover heaps of bone-gray snow litter the ground like abandoned clothes, ragged and pocked with dirt and gravel. Corn stubble stands like tipsy soldiers. The fields are the wet brown of smeared shit. Rolling hills. Muddied cows like scattered tombstones.

"Everything here is so fucking brown," Mia says.

When we started, Mia asked how many men it had taken to pay for the car—a Mustang convertible, new, blue as cobalt, blue as barn swallows. Let's see, she said, paper out, pencil in hand, but I plucked the pencil from her and snapped it in half. It doesn't matter, I said.

One can be shut of them. Nancy told me that. We were at her house after work one night, the three of us, Pauline, Nancy and me, drinking whiskey-sodas, no ice, warm as radiator water, and Nancy said you just had to draw a line angling from Adam's apple to ass and say, I'm outside myself, outside that parabola of tits cut to crotch. Let them feed on you like blind puppies, she said. You're elsewhere, counting horses in a field, playing Scrabble, throwing your I Ching, smoking a cigarette, worrying about your son's junior high where it seems everyone carries a knife.

I don't think you can do that, Pauline said. I know I couldn't. I'd know the whole time.

Know what? Nancy said.

That I wasn't outside myself. Nobody can do that. Ramona certainly couldn't.

Well, Ramona— Nancy said, gesturing impatient indifference with her cigarette.

Who's Ramona? I asked.

Nobody, Nancy said.

Somebody always inside herself, Pauline said.

Nancy said, Baloney.

It's true. The whole time she was with you.

With you? I asked.

Nancy's eyes stayed on me. She wants me, too.

I am desired by men and women equally.

Fond du Lac. We're going past the lagoons fronting the Evinrude plant now, a low white building with manicured grounds as if the executives drive golf balls over the water hazards on their lunch breaks. Just past noon now, the sun bleaching the buildings a painful white, the road a lighter-than-air gray. Mia's hair is blowing across her face. She's let it grow, has to rake it back, tangled as kite strings, her eyes blinking in harsh light, lips tight and dry in the wind. We like the windows open, the air smelling of gasoline and wet earth swollen fertile.

"Why'd you need Chicago?" she asks me.

For what *did* I need Chicago? This question has cropped up at odd moments ever since the trip itself. The first time she asked was during the drive back, when we saw the golden spires of the Polish churches in South Milwaukee, the next time during a blizzard, when we were snowed in, had enough warning to stock up on fruits and vegetables, soups and crackers, and we watched the snow beating upwind on the windowpanes like salmon spawning. I didn't answer her. I just called her attention to the snow and the fish. So she asked it again later, not put off, while the two of us were shoveling out, and later again. I never answer satisfactorily.

Mia has clear answers. Paths, courses, routes of life all plain, self-evident. In her world where nothing connects, one lies as necessary, erases the past, moves onward. She marches through the events of her life, a snowball eating the gravel in its way. You get bigger as you go. I try to tell her that everything touches everything, and her eyebrows arch like peaked hats.

"You must be kidding."

No, I tell her, nobody ever gets lost. Everything's connected. Accounted for. It all comes back to you.

Mia laughs. "Or you come back to it."

"Yes," I say, "if only for a weekend."

Mia's drinking wine from a boda, the wine splashing her chin and chest as the wind pushes the arc awry. "You really should think about Greece," she says. "Blue and white and blue—that's a damn sight better than brown and brown and brown, yes?" She has the Greece issue open on her lap and she holds it up for me to see. I nod my head yes. I've stared at the magazine and daydreamed being there, too. It's not like I don't think about it—the photographs seem as real now as if they were our vacation photos, not just something from a magazine.

Mia's doing bennies and gin with orange juice out of a glass quart bottle. Mia's the independent witness. She's eager, curious for the freak show. Lou Reed's telling us about his street hassle—Mia's got that turned way up, head nodding.

The blue sky and brown earth are folded like two fabric swatches unevenly sewn together. I'm driving barefoot, worried about Daddy, a plantar's wart on the ball of my right foot my only flaw. I know how I got it. Professor Tweed has a studio downtown, in the Blaisdell's shadow. An open-roof deck with an iron railing, a third-story walk-up, dead plants in planters, big picture window so even in winter he can work. But this was February, a thaw, so warm you could be outside in shirt-sleeves. In our neighborhood they were playing basketball, by the U, tennis, everywhere joyous defiance of the month itself. I was in a towel, white skin stippled, as Tweed (Mia told me his full name once, Harris something-or-other, but I promptly forgot, it seemed an impediment) plied his brushes, cooing like a child. I was his coup for the winter. He was back with his wife. That meant nothing to me, but he offered me twenty-five dollars an hour to stand around in a towel. This was the second week; until then we'd been inside.

"Now drop the towel," he said.

I pulled it tighter, tucked the flap in a little deeper.

"Fifty an hour," he said. "Just for while I get this done."

I was standing without the towel, roof grit chafing my feet. I wondered if anyone in the hotel was looking. I'd been in those rooms. I knew what they could see. I set my face harder, twisted, my hands on the railing, my body chilled but my face warm, haughty.

"Perfect," he said.

I thought of it as practice. Later they'd be photographers and I'd have this down, the careless pout, the radiated knowledge of immaculate, untouchable flesh. I said nothing to Mia about it. She would be upset. She was anyway, when she was painting my toenails and discovered the wart. No doubt from some fungus in that roof grit. She wondered how I got it, as if she was as bothered by an imperfection in me as I would be. She administered drawing salve and picked at it with a tweezers, had me soak my feet at night in Epsom salts as if I were an old woman. She rubbed my feet as if better-moving blood would help me heal.

"What did the doctors say about your father?" Mia asks. She shakes her head to keep her hair blowing off her face. She's pretty far gone now, lubricating herself till everything is either funny or tragic. She is overcome with her own mortality, and needs the simplest things re-explained to her.

"There's a mass near his elbow," I tell her. A mass near his

elbow. I think of the priest in the white chasuble shot through
with gold embroidery, the servers in black and white (my
brothers? it's hard to think of them as religious, but they're
young enough yet, would still do that, reluctantly, grumbling,
but still some sense of awe, of mystery), the solemnity, the
arms raised, the chalice held high. My father sitting up in
bed, wondering why this is happening. A mass near his
elbow. If I explained it to Mia she'd fly into hysterics, would
laugh until she couldn't breathe.

I shift my foot over. A hot wire sears through my foot every
time the wart pushes down on the accelerator. I'm driving
with the right half of my right foot, which tires my ankle and
my calf. In a short time we'll be there, the farm laid out below
us like a foreshortened aerial photograph, the long fences disappearing down one hill as the next hill rises up, taller than
the first. My stomach is queasy; I will admit to fear. Mia's
gone to sleep, her mouth slack. I think again about salmon,
knowing nothing about them but their leaps. Do they really
try that hard to get back home?

5

MAMA'S SITTING behind the house in the Chevy, one of those two-tone '57s, the ones with the steering wheel so big you feel you're on the deck of a clipper ship or something, only you're sitting down. One of Daddy's presents to the boys. They'll know how to take it apart and put it back together, cleaned and oiled, before they're old enough for licenses. It's up on concrete blocks now, the tires off, looks like something abandoned after an invasion. The engine itself is in the shed, rings and valves and pistons spread out on a torn paisley sheet. A cat is curled on the open hood nurturing, it would seem, the squashed plus-sign logo. Mama's on the passenger side, a plastic cup with ice and her Teacher's on the glove compartment shelf. She looks up as if she were waiting for us.

"Mama—" I start and she just laughs, waves one hand, her forearm catching the door, as if gesturing toward the house for us to take it.

"I should have known," she says. "My father dies of cancer, my husband's got it." She reels her arm in. "Maybe we're carriers," she says.

"Where's Daddy?"

"In the barn or someplace. Haven't heard the tractor start up since he went out there after lunch. 'Course I wasn't listening. Maybe he's having a drink himself."

Mia and I put our bags on the back stoop next to the cat's milk bowl, kittens scattering, and we walk down to the barn. Daddy's not there. The tractor either. But the scabs of straw and cow flop left like a candy trail over the rise show where he went. We walk down there, up one sandy rise on the rutted cow path and then down, where a gully spotted with scrub oak and brown, matted tussocks cuts the field in uneven halves. Daddy's on that far side, the remnant third of field too wet for anything but corn or giant sunflowers (last year it was sunflowers—Wendy and I heard you could catch a buzz from them, we pulled down a plant, two feet over our heads, and tried to dry the seeds and eat them, but we were misinformed and nothing happened). The manure spreader's going like sixty, throwing up clots of shit as if in jubilation, the way a water-skier leaves a wake of spray, this arc of shit and chaff, like birds gathered against the sky, throbbing and pungent. I feel the old thrill, like when Daddy kept me on his lap while he manured or plowed or disced. Even on the tractor he wore cologne, shaved before breakfast. I could smell him in my hair when I was little. That was when I thought the only thing you could be was a farmer.

Later I helped on the wagon, wore blue jeans and a white T-shirt, gloves on my hands, pulled the bales off the chute as they chugged back to me and I stacked them, Tommy and Scott too little then to be anything but in the way. Dust and rivers of sweat and beaded blood mingling, the cut ends of straw sharp as used razors, my forearms sliced, fine scratches like cuts in crystal, little spikes sifting into my gloves so my wrists got crosshatched red. The slivers would work into my fingers to fester, as if the bales could lay eggs on my hands. I'd be days getting them out. And Tommy and Scott sitting higher on the oat straw pyramid, three and then two, a pattern, repeated until the wagon got full and then you had to improvise. Panting, I'd heave up the last few higher than my head—the things weighed sixty to ninety pounds depending on how wet they were—and Tommy and Scott would yank them onto the very top, leftover bales like extra bricks. And even with the dust in my nostrils and the acrid smell of my own sweat and my own blood I could smell his cologne. He'd

put it on extra heavy during haying season. We'd do the alfalfa first, then the oats, then alfalfa again, maybe even a
third cutting if the weather held. And then, I don't know,
puberty, I was fourteen and he was yelling. It was just hard,
dirty work and the cuts weren't like badges anymore. Tommy
and Scott did more. When a bale broke or crashed on my
head and I was responsible for the hook, he'd shout, C'mon,
C'mon! like I'd done it on purpose, and around about then I
decided a greasy farmer wearing cologne, dabbing it in the
thick coils around his neck two or three times a day, was
pretty ridiculous, even if he *was* my father.

We're just standing there, watching Daddy set one brake so
the whole rig, linchpin and PTO and spreader, pivots at the
corner like a baseball player rounding second, tight to the
inside of the base. As he comes around, I see the triangular
white sling on his left arm.

"This is nice," Mia says, meaning everything.

"You never had to work it," I tell her.

Daddy had help, of course. The place is too big—three
hundred and twelve acres, one hundred and sixty-some cows
—for one man and three children, one of whom is a girl and
no longer around anyway. Years ago he'd hired Harmon Dill,
Clete Noyersdorff and Frank Broom Cloud. Harm, Clete and
Frank—one cloth. Tall, sharp-featured Indians, gangly,
given to lots of dirty talk, but strong. Seasonal. Daddy paid
them better than Everfresh Canning or they'd have been over
there with the migrants (Wendy worked there one summer
with her mother and said all the instructions for the equipment, even the labeling machines, where it was only white
women, were in English and Spanish, too). Harm and Clete
and Frank came each May like some three-headed beast and
Daddy set them to work—so many acres to plow and disc and
drag and seed and then spring-tooth around the young corn.
Fencing. Those cows to milk, dawn and dusk. Something
always broken. Besides our own three hundred acres, Daddy
rented another hundred eighty. They'd stay till the third week

of September, living in the shed Daddy had set up as a bunkhouse, with a stove and tables and two dry sinks, and then
they'd head over to Door County for the cranberry harvest.
Where they went in winter I don't know. Daddy said the reser-
vation, but then why didn't I ever see them in town during the
winter? Daddy never explained it. Drifters, I thought. They
traveled all over, went someplace warm come winter, south,
picked oranges and their skin turned coppery, brown as bark.
Daddy wouldn't tell me because I'd get ideas. Harm and Clete
and Frank: they would take me with them. I was stupid, and
Daddy kept us separated anyway, always had them working
the rented acres or the far back fields. He kept us near the
house and wouldn't let us near the shed at night. I went down
there anyway.

"Girlie, girlie," one of them said. It was Harmon. He was
the tallest and skinniest, his arms like muscled rope. "Come
here or get away," he said. "You got to make a choice."

"Leave her alone," Frank said. "She's only twelve."

"Eleven," I said, as if that were important. I didn't know
what I should say.

"Eleven," Harmon said. "Get on. Scoot." He gestured like
I was a lazy springtime fly. "We throw you back," he said.
"Fetch your Mama."

"Harm—" Frank shot his eyes like coals, very white and
black.

"I'm just funnin'," he said.

Clete was asleep in his bunk, newspaper draped over his
face.

I went back to the house and didn't tell anyone. But I kept
thinking their life was both better and worse than mine.

"He'll be a while," I tell Mia. "May as well go back to the
house."

Tommy-and-Scott (they had always seemed like one person,
too, like Harm-Clete-Frank) have been sundered: each has
his own room now, Tommy having claimed mine. Mama's rattling pans in the kitchen. I know enough not to go in there.

The first thing now that she's up will be the accusations. So, you've brought someone home! she'll scream, not even recognizing Mia. Just bring them here without warning, and I suppose I'm supposed to wait on you, she'll say. She'll continue, At least I called. Not that you'd acknowledge that, no. One trip and you hightail it out of there the very first night, leave me to my own devices in a strange city. I had to call a cab just to get back to the bus station on Sunday. Yes, I stayed till Sunday. And let me tell you something else— and she will. She'll go right on telling me, keep going because she has the audience and because we've not exchanged two words since that night in Chicago. There are scores of scores to settle. Mama has them filed away and she's waiting.

But she looks at Mia and says nothing. She looks around the room like there should be a granite outcropping from which she can pounce. She'll find it and wait, and then when I'm alone—

"Where do we sleep?" Mia asks, still holding her bags like someone waiting for a train.

"We can each take a couch. One in the living room, one in Mama's sewing room. Or we can kick the boys in together and share Scott's room. Or—" I'm thinking, turning over in my head the possibilities, the likely scenes and scenarios. "Or we can steal some wood from the shed, clean out the bunkhouse and stay there."

"Oh, let's!" Mia says. "It'll be like camping."

Mia is hopeless with a saw. I show her how to set it, how to pull and push in long smooth strokes so the gathered branches can become kindling, and instead she rasps as if using a file.

I'm splitting the larger pieces with an ax when the boys come home, loping with the sideways steps farmers use, at once boisterous and a little shy. They come up and offer to help almost before they say hello and hug me home. They back up the tractor and want to show me how to run the splitter, a metal channel with a machine-driven wedge at one end, which they attach to the power take-off. They're dropping in logs as fast as the recoil allows. I don't trust it. I don't trust anything attached to a power take-off. A log once shot up and caught Daddy in the stomach, knocking him down and backward into the tractor. Alongside his backbone he had a chain of bruised welts like a second spine.

"Just let me split it my own way," I say, taking the ax back from Tommy.

"You'll kill us all," he says, and yanks it back.

They're like this: eager to help but in that belittling way of theirs that takes the joy out of whatever it is you are doing. It's like Mama had me, then waited to see if it was worth going through it again, thought, Oh, hell, and boom, boom, the two of them. And it's like they sense they were afterthoughts, and they make up for doubting the desire for their existence by talking too loud in voices that've just started to change, their chests still adolescent but their arms like college fullbacks. They're hard to tell apart—fourteen and thirteen, each of them spindly, eating at full steam so they can flesh out the frames they find themselves in. Tommy's older, but you can hardly tell. Maybe it's his eyes—blue like mine but frightened. They move back and forth like he expects someone to hit him. So he's loud to make up for that, the fear in him that keeps him looking small even though he'll top out at six-something or other. Scott's going to be smaller, but he looks bigger now. He grins more. Maybe it's his size—that he can give Tommy a run for his money, that Tommy can't lord anything over him. I don't know. But they're my brothers and I hardly know them.

Tommy gives me back the ax and off to the side I chop up a pile of kindling and quarter logs. Tommy and Scott with the machine have two or three times as much done and they're satisfied, sweat glistening on their arms, and their dark flat bangs plastered to their foreheads (their hair! It's like we're two different families. I came out blond, all light and haloes, and they came out auburn, steeped in dried blood and dark clay). Scott's missing an eyetooth and he whistles through that, a red-winged-blackbird whistle, two shrill blasts like a factory at quitting time.

"You look good," Tommy said. "You almost got muscles." He pinches my bicep, his chapped fingers on my slicked skin like Mama tests cucumbers. "Gosh, that *is* a muscle."

"Lifting weights," I tell him, shrugging it off as if I were an older brother, too, not the sister they can't begin to fathom.

Lifting weights: Larry's idea. He had a slip of a body himself, shaped like a lower-case *i*. All the substance of balsa wood. In November he took me aside. "I've started something," he said. "My life is going to be different."

In the hours between his shift and mine we went to the Ninth Street YMCA. He'd taken out a membership with the men's because they had the older building and everyone (men included—what was the point of working out if you didn't meet women?) was flooding to the newer women's building on La Salle, leaving the men's virtually deserted. I was Larry's guest. The first few times I sat in a T-shirt and shorts straddling the bench press. I smoked cigarettes and watched him suffer. He'd put more weight than he could handle on the bar that looked like a lazy W and he was obliged to lessen it. He went around to all the stations and I just watched him and smoked cigarettes. A crew-cut behemoth came in and told me not to smoke. Why not? I said, the air in here couldn't get any worse, and he just sniffed like what I'd said had given him a cold. Larry lifted until he was red and shiny as a newborn. Then he wanted to do free weights, so we tromped across the hall and he lifted in that room until he was satisfied with his exhaustion.

"They've got a swimming pool, too," he said.

"And a beach?"

"We can do laps."

"I don't do laps, Larry."

"You should. You should do these, too," he said, sitting down on one of the red vinyl benches and hoisting a dumbbell up till his fist and shoulder met, counting under his breath as he eased the weights down, his bicep jumping like a rat in a blanket, like there was something actually there. "I was married once, you know. You'd be amazed how fast my wife lost her body tone, got as rumpled as laundry. They say it's only men who lose their shape once they get married, but women do, too."

I was stunned. It was the first time he had referred to his wife leaving him as something like a distant event. There *is* hope for you, Larry Fields, but he was already on to something else.

"This would be good for you," he was saying. "You're firm, but this'll keep you that way." Out of his duffel he fished a two-foot stick of bamboo with a length of quarter-inch rope wrapped around it. He took a five-pound weight, threaded it with the rope, and cinched a knot so the weight hung suspended from below his outstretched arms.

"Like this," he said, rolling it up to meet his hands and then unrolling it.

He handed it to me. I crushed my cigarette under my sneaker and did as he had done. Even just those few times he had me do it I felt the pull along my arms, the quivering underneath my biceps, the tension under my rib cage, as if I was really working at something. My forearms and belly and even the undersides of my breasts felt tight and firm. Strong. When he said, "Enough," I was truly tired. Larry smiled, pleased he'd been able to show me something.

"They've got a Universal at school now," Tommy says. "I didn't make the varsity this past winter, but I will this next one. I'm going to work out during study hall."

"Which team?" Mia asks.

"Wrestling," Tommy says proudly. You can practically see

his head tilt back and his sheet-board chest swell. They can go out only for winter sports because Daddy needs them spring and fall.

"Bet I make varsity my first try," Scott says.

"I bet you do, too," Mia says and Scott whistles by accident, embarrassed.

We spend the afternoon cleaning the bunkhouse. Daddy comes back at dinner and pokes his head in. After hugging me, he says, "Good, now I don't have to at the end of next month." I look not looking at his arm. "Nothing," he says. "It's going to be better than new. You watch and see."

Mama serves spaghetti and says she has ironing to do. I was going to show Mia the back fields and the ravine, but a swarm of clouds come up and I tell her the best thing would be to scoot into town quick for beer and munchies and do the real sightseeing tomorrow. I change into a black miniskirt and a white Fruit-of-the-Loom V-neck with HUMAN stenciled on the left breast, one of my own designs from around January. I'll be back in jeans and a sweater after the trip, but I want to show them something at Buss' Foods.

The store is cold, all those open refrigeration units throwing it out like dust. Our pores rise like moguls, the hairs stiffening. When I was a kid and they talked about the energy crisis, I remember these folding metal plates they put over the freezer section and heavy opaque plastic sheeting they kept over the meats and milk. You had to lift all that up to poke around for what you wanted. When Mama wasn't looking I'd rearrange things, do something like a shell game with the ground beef and the cheese and the yogurt. The next person to look wouldn't know anymore what section she was in, even with the signs telling her.

We walk up and down most of the aisles hugging our arms. Friday's the day they straighten and replenish the shelves for Saturday's onslaught, so there's a small army of them out, fifteen-to-nineteen-year-olds, all lapping us up as we cruise by. Cans fall in our wake. Most recognize me and are speech-

less. I'm the one who did it but didn't keep it. The one who
went away.

In the chips aisle we're deciding on Doritos or PretzelThins
when Kevin Netley confronts me. He grabs a box of bagged
unpopped popcorn from the shelf in front of him so it looks
like he's there for a reason. But the wire basket is already
full. They look like discounted artillery shells.

"So you're back," Netley says.

"Visiting."

Netley's one of those pimple-faced blonds, as if his face
were littered with maraschino cherries nearly submerged in
bread dough. He's tall, with wiry arms, like some great bird.
With his black frame glasses taped at a joint and the ten
yellow wires on his chin he insisted was beard, he'd have
been laughed out of school. But he got beer for the toughs,
setting a case out by the bottle pickup in back of Buss' when
he was supposed to be sorting Coke bottles. He learned to
swagger as much as any of them, thought of himself as a
leader. He was tolerated.

"There's a party tomorrow at Pankow's. Next week, too, if
you're staying. Bring your friend."

I take a second bag of Doritos and Netley follows us over to
the beer display. Cases are against the wall, flats and six-
packs stacked on the floor up to over our heads. Everything is
advertised as the Everyday Low Price.

Netley says, "So. Chicago, eh?"

"Chicago," I tell him. Netley nods, taking this in. He looks
at the stencil, too, like the word is there as an advertisement
for my left breast. "Human," he says. "Cle-ver." Then he
offers to drop a case out back for us, we can swing the car
around after we pay for the Doritos. I tell him no, we've got
plenty of money. Mia rubs her nose. She's standing in front of
the Schlitz. We look at each other like the legend lives on.

"Is that how you're known?" Mia asks back at the bunkhouse. "As the one who went away?"

We're drinking beer and have a fire going in the stove.

"Went away. Got away. Took off and left," I say and feed the fire with splits big around as my arm. It starts drizzling and then comes harder. We can hear it on the roof, first the splatters like paint dripping on newspaper, then the incessant patter, its own rhythm and music. A complete orchestra of rain and gullied tin and randomly exposed tar paper.

"Your brothers are cute."

"Yeah, we're all fucking adorable."

"No, really."

"I suppose they are."

"You suppose," Mia says.

"Okay, so they're cute. Our whole family's cute. What are you going to do about it?"

"Nothing," Mia says and giggles. "Cuteness is its own reward."

We're each of us on our bunks; a third bunk's farther back, tucked against the wall. But these two look like a pair, flanking the wood stove as if it were a night table.

"I wish we had a radio," Mia says. "Was it always like this? No music and the rain?"

"What, are you kidding? Daddy's got a tape deck in one of his tractors. Conway Twitty and Willie Nelson till you want to throw up. I had a stereo in my room—Tommy and Scott've claimed it since I left."

"I mean in the bunkhouse."

"I was never here except for a minute or two. I remember when this was the toolshed. I spent more time here then."

"But did you ever imagine it like this?"

"Mia, what are you talking about?"

Mia's on her back with the can poised on her midsection like a daisy. "It's just so peaceful here," she says. "If you didn't love it, you'd go crazy."

"Well, I never loved it, okay?"

"Don't get angry."

"Who's angry?"

Mia turns her head to me with a look of something like pity.

"I wanted to see how you lived," she says.

"It's not much, is it?"

"I don't know," she says, turning back to the ceiling. "I haven't seen that much yet."

"The rain'll peter out by morning."

"That's not what I meant."

"I know what you meant," I tell her. "Don't worry, you'll see all there is to see. We're geeks, every one of us. Cute, but geeks."

Mia gets up for another beer from the flat of Old Style we ended up buying. She grabs a handful of Doritos, offering the bag to me as well. "Why do you keep seeing Larry?" she asks, sitting on her bunk now, alternating nacho Doritos and Old Style.

I sit up, too. I've put on a loose sea-green and sea-blue V-neck argyle sweater over my T-shirt. I feel like there should be a 1950s engineering student coming by soon to take me to a sock hop.

"Larry..." I begin, but I can't think of anything after that. "Larry's taught me about weights," I say, thinking about the sixteen-pound sash weight he keeps at his apartment, one of those modern apartment complexes with the railed balcony off Wisconsin Avenue and Twenty-first. The sash weight is roped to that bamboo pole he had before, and in his living room instead of a couch he has a weight bench. I discovered this in early December when I started going over there. Easier to leave, I decided, if *I* did the leaving. Even with the bus or taxi home it was simpler. Better the inconvenience of waiting on the street than that caused by an overanxious lover, one who just won't go home. But then Larry found another sash weight in our attic, took it out of a nailed-shut window, actually, and with a length of doweling from the closet I had one, too. I could come home and roll up the world on a string till I got tired and let go. Then a long bath, my skin red from the heat, hair up in a towel, the blood thick in my forearms and breasts.

"Big deal," Mia says. "Larry could be replaced by a Jack LaLanne record."

"It's more than that."

"You still pity him, don't you?"

"It's more than that, too."

"Convenient pity," Mia says. "You can see Harris or anybody and yet keep your distance. 'Oh, I have a boyfriend,' you can say. It makes me sick."

"What, Tweed?"

"You don't still call him that, do you?"

"It fits."

"And yet you see him? You despise the man and yet you see him?"

"It's an imperfect world."

"And what about Larry? Don't let me get sidetracked, Dorie. We're into this now. I want to find out. What is it with Larry?"

"It's nothing with Larry. I like him. I mean, I like him as much as anyone."

"Who else is there to like?"

"No, I'm not just talking leftovers, Mia. I mean I really sort of like him. I'll tell you something"—I glug back some beer to give me time to think of what I'll tell her—"Larry's not like a lot of guys. He's like them in lots of ways but he's sometimes sweet, too."

"Oh, brother."

"No, really." I'm sitting up now, my legs crossed as Frank Broom Cloud's would be if he were into solemn story-telling. Sometimes he liked to pull that. His Indian act. Frank'd start off serious, talking about the old days, but by the end of his story he'd be talking into his beer bottle about copped feels and women begging for him to fuck them. He'd get morose and trail off, finally smile at his bottle like his story had leaked out of him and he was embarrassed to have started it in the first place. Unlike Frank, I'm energetic. It's like I really have to stick up for Larry Fields here, though he's totally on his own and I don't give much quarter when there's the two of us, him and me trying to pace off the boundaries of our relationship. "Let me tell you something," I say. "I'll tell you about Larry Fields. Once I was shaving my legs before work and he was watching me. Sat on the toilet seat right next to me while I had the one leg on the tub and I was doing it all the way up. Long streaks of Foamy bunching up like fabric. And I get to my crotch, see, and I'm really concentrating, but I know Larry's concentrating, too. I can hear him breathing, almost like each breath depends on that razor inching up a little more, the fine blond hairs and stubble whisked away clean, and him breathing like that, intense and obscene. Reverent. And I look at him looking. How he has the towel wrapped like a native—he'd just finished his shower, too— and even with the weights there is this ring of belly flesh like dough waiting to be worked into something, like a raw muffin poked by a finger, and his legs so white below the towel and he's sitting there hunched and pathetic watching me shave my legs like I'm an artist or something. Then our eyes catch and he realizes I've been looking him over, sizing him up, the legs not really muscled yet with their black web of hair and the limp handles of his waist. And he turns away. He looks at the sink as if the porcelain is a picture tube and I think, My God, he's embarrassed about his own body."

Mia gets up and sits on my bed, shifting her body around till we are facing each other, me cross-legged, her with her legs over the bed's edge, her feet on the floor. She leans her face close to mine, her sparkly brown eyes clouded, her voice earnest. "Dorie, you're just letting him weep all over you."

"You want to hear something funny?" I push myself so my back's against the wall, my toes almost touching Mia's leg. "He wants me to go to Minneapolis with him."

"Don't be absurd."

"Who said I was going?"

"But to be thinking about it, even a little—very bad, Dorie, very bad of you. It means you're susceptible."

"And what about Jeff?"

Mia leans back and brings her legs up so she's again looking at the ceiling, a side-by-side mirror image of myself.

"Jeff from MSOE," I say, as if she needs to be reminded. "Jeff with his wife who doesn't understand him."

"Oh, Jeff," she says, shaking her Old Style can as if dismissing him. "That's just a little self-destructive tendency I have. I'm always falling in with people who aren't good for me." She rights her head, her chin tucked so we're eye to eye. "Or people I can't have."

"But you're still seeing him."

Mia is up and furious. "Yes, for chrissakes, I'm still seeing him! What do you want me to do—sew myself shut?"

"Mia, I just meant—"

"We get along, don't we? The two of us? All the people we're with whom we couldn't care less about, or they us, and yet we get along and we're not even sleeping together!"

I get her to sit down on her own bed again. "Maybe it's exactly that, Mia."

Mia sets her can by her feet. There's a collection there, all variously kinked according to her nervousness, the last can crushed flat. "I doubt it," she snaps, striking a match for her dangling cigarette, a fresh beer squarely between her splayed-out feet. She takes a long drag and adjusts her feet pigeon-toed. "The professor thinks he has you on a string," she says. "Why do you let him think that?"

"Why? What's he said to you?"

Mia's calm now. She can talk about these hurts to her exposed heart as if she'd heard about them happening to someone else. When she's not frenetic I admire her more than anyone.

"He keeps telling me what a discovery he's made in you. 'Imagine,' he said to me once. 'The Venus de Milo with arms.' I wanted to throw my coffee in his face."

"He actually said that?"

"I think he takes a great pleasure in telling me about you.

Like I owe him something because he never dipped his wick."

"And I told him not to."

"Not to what?"

"To talk about me in front of you. I told him it would be cruel."

"It *is* cruel. Why do you think he does it?"

I reach over to take the last drag of her cigarette. "He's getting an earful when I get back."

"Like he's really going to care."

"Let's stop talking about him."

"Hey, you're the one who's seeing him. I just have to take classes from the bastard."

"I'm not 'seeing' him. He pays me as a model."

"Everybody pays you for something, don't they?"

I hit her across the mouth hard. I have a ring with three tiny emeralds in it and my backhand scrapes three parallel lines of blood across and above Mia's upper lip.

She reels back and looks at me hard. "If you think I'm going to apologize, you're wrong," she says. Her tongue explores her damaged lip and then her middle finger taps the bloody flesh gingerly. "Fucked me up good, didn't you?"

"I'm sorry I hit you." From the ice chest I take two watery cubes and wrap them in paper toweling. Mia's lip is already starting to swell.

"Is it going to scar?"

"No, of course not."

Mia sniffles, breathes in from her nose. "Bullshit. I'm going to have white lines like somebody cut me." She sits down, turning her head from side to side. "Have you seen my cigarettes? I can't find them. I had cigarettes around here somewhere."

I sit down next to her and with my forefinger wipe tears off her cheek. "I'm sorry."

Mia winces and grins weakly. "Every great love leaves its mark."

I take her head in my hands, examine her closely. "Really," I lie, "it's going to be nothing."

"Nothing," Mia says, lighting a cigarette. She puts the filter end right under her cut lip. "Dashing, huh?" Her eyes brim over again. "Shit," she says, shutting her eyes and turning away from me.

"Could you just leave me alone, Dorie?"

I go sit on my own bunk. We're like that for a little while, me with my hands between my thighs and Mia smoking, her face turned, looking down at the floor beside her foot.

"Mia, would you like me to stay with you?"

Her eyes come up from the floor and rise into my eyes. "You wouldn't like what would happen," she says.

b

I WAKE UP, can't remember the dream that woke me, but I have to pee. Sitting then, I shiver. Mia's asleep in her own bed with her torso tilted and arms raised in surrender. I touch myself. I'm amazed at how cold I am. Like death. No life in me. So this is how I sleep.

7

THE NEXT NIGHT we tour the rooftops. We keep away from Mama all day, not such a hard thing when she's holed up with her bottle in the destroyed Chevy, sitting in it like it's a boat run aground in the backyard. I tell her I have things to show Mia and she waves us off as if we should just go about our business. Daddy's already in the fields, has been gone probably since six or six-thirty, as he always has: lots of work, breakfast (made by me when I was home, and I'd have today, too, except we overslept), and more work till late, eating the lunch Mama makes and puts in a cooler so he doesn't have to come in till six or so. I see the dishes in the sink, rinse them and put them in the dishwasher since Mama would let them cake over without even thinking, and I remind myself to make it up to Daddy, to have something really good waiting for him tomorrow A.M. With that idea I shower, change in Tommy's (my old) room, look at what he's got for music, mostly country rock and hard rock bands—Head East, Marshall Tucker, things like that—and then Mia showers and changes, too, her lip's still swollen, and then we're ready.

We drive around and I show her all the neighboring farms so she gets a feel for the area. I'm eager for her to like the place even though I can never see myself actually living here and would deny it if someone asked—me? No, I'm from Milwaukee. Once from the road we see Daddy, and I think for a second I can imagine him there forever, and I wish I were a boy, or again at that age when being a girl didn't matter, so I

could help him. From the road his bandage doesn't look so
bad, he seems to be managing okay. He will eventually sell
the farm to Tommy or Scott, or both, and someday it will be
them bumping over the ground, breaking it clean, but in that
I find no comfort.

I say to Mia, "I'll show you what there is to Augsbury."

It takes maybe twenty minutes. The back streets, the saw-
mill, the Kafka Feed Mill, the railroad tracks, the Everfresh
Canning Company, the toy factory ("They make casket handles there," I say to Mia. "I once dated a guy who had that
job"), the wire works, Main Street and Roosevelt, police and
fire station and library all yoked together, and behind them
the town hall, where my grandmother Matty still works, then
the hotel on the lake, the bottle shop next to that, the elementary and high school on the edge of town on the way back to
our place, and finally the cemetery and the golf course.
"Something for everybody," I say and Mia laughs and lifts the
wineskin. We're picnicking in the cemetery, food laid out on a
flat Quinnleven tombstone, our seats getting wet through the
blanket, the grass not yet dry, and then I say, "You should
meet my grandmother Matty," and after we eat we drive over
there.

Matty looks up from a ledger book, her eyes tight behind
her wire-rim glasses, her face freckled and peppered with
wrinkles, her orange hair almost without color now and cut
like a boy's—bangs in front, blunt-cut in back, the strands
drifted into each other like a tangle of pickup sticks.

"I heard you were back," she says, as if I'd gone for an
afternoon perm in Menasha.

"Mama told you?"

"Everyone told me. Grace Bauer saw you at Buss' Foods
last night. 'Painted like a harlequin,' she said. I think she
meant *harlot*. And Mrs. Miller stopped in later to tell me what
Grace had told her." Matty gets up to cup my face in her
hands. "Bad stereo," she says. "I hear everything twice. And
distorted, too." I kiss her wrist and we hug.

"Grandma, this is Mia," I say.

Mia says, "How do you do?"

"Oh, I do all right," she says. "But everyone's just gotten their assessments, so there's hell to pay every time the phone rings. The town board upped nearly everyone's except their own. I sort of let that slip a few times in conversation, so now there's going to be a general hearing. I told Frank Buss having his brother as the assessor wouldn't do him any good, but he just smiled like everybody's going to lie down for him since he's on the board and owns the supermarket. Politics," she says. "Petty men waving their arms so everyone can see them puff out their chests and crow, cock-a-doodle-doo, and feel better." She smiles. "Like you want to hear this." To me she says, "Have you shown her anything yet?"

"This morning, Grandma. We drove around."

"You can't see anything from a car," she says, offering us two bottles of Grafs root beer she keeps in a small refrigerator behind her desk. "Are you showing her anything on foot, or have you wiped the dust of us off your sandals?"

Mia takes a bottle and I shake my head and say no thanks.

"Tonight we're climbing the water tower," I tell her.

"There's a church key on that string by the door," Matty says. "The water tower," she says. "Of course." She looks at each of us, sizing us up. "I suppose this is the required visit-to-grandma then? The 'She's moldering to death, but we should drop in on her once while we're here' visit?"

"No, it's not like that, Grandma."

"Then stop by the house one of these evenings and actually spend some time. You do have some of that, don't you? Time?"

"Which house?" I ask, referring to her and Luther.

"Mine, of course. Which one did you think?"

"Oh," I say, passing it off, "I heard Luther Kraike—"

"Stories," she says. "Idle gossip. Hardly a lick of truth to them." She opens the bottle I didn't take and fills a waxed

Dixie cup, offering me what's in the bottle. She gestures with her cup. "We'll talk about that later, too," she says.

"You can't tell me what I already know, Grandma."

"What you don't know would fill a book," Matty says. "Two books. What your mother doesn't know would fill one and a half. And both of you thinking you know more than me." To Mia she says, "She does do that, doesn't she? Acts like she knows something?"

"Pretty much," Mia says.

"Finish your soda then," Matty says to me. "And go show Mia the bowling alley or something." She gestures at me like I'm still ten. Mia and I back out. When we're in the hallway already Matty calls, "And Dorie? Be good to your mama. This business with your father is hard on everyone."

In the afternoon we walk fence lines. Like I want to show her the wire boundaries of where I grew up. "See how tight these are? Daddy does these every spring, comes out with the wire stretcher and the boys. They wear heavy gloves and they get these wires to hum." We walk through the wooded grove that catches the spring wash and come to three bluebird houses nailed to three fence posts, one, two, three. "Tommy made these two years ago for a shop project. Scott's was a gun rack." Mia nods like I'm telling her something important. "It'll be three weeks yet till the asparagus shoot up. People stop by the road then to pick them. Sometimes they'll march right down a side fence, too, like it was their backyard they were in. Daddy always sent us out early in the morning and again when we got home. He said the only way to discourage people was to make sure their pickings were slim. We'd pick so much of it Mama had to freeze bags and bags of it. Did you know asparagus can grow three to four inches a day? What's too short at seven A.M. is plenty tall enough by four-thirty." Mia looks at me like this is exactly what she wants to hear.

We cross to Hulley's side of the fence at the creek bottom. Years before he'd cleared all the brush out, the willows and scrub oak, and our side is just a tangle, good for rabbit and deer and grouse but hard to walk through. We jump the creek and cross back.

"Strange, you know. Daddy showed me once on a map how this water eventually runs into the Mississippi and beyond. Into the Gulf of Mexico. I couldn't imagine it, how it could go that far from here."

Mia says, "I'd think as a kid you'd want to believe anything."

"I was very skeptical." I hold the fence for her to get back on our side. "Something I picked up from Mama. Daddy wanted us to believe."

"In my family it's my mother who's religious."

"I don't mean just that," I say. "Christmas presents, crops coming up, children dressed as ghosts at Halloween—everything's a miracle for my father. See how on this hill all these pine trees have sprung up? Cones got blown here from those woods. To Daddy that's a miracle. Everything is."

"Doesn't he ever get disappointed?"

"He's married to my mother, isn't he?"

At the hilltop our farm looks like two tilted planes, one sloping under our feet down to the creek, another rising away from it, the house on a level patch far, far away, the V in between ten shades of brown and ready to explode. You can see the two greens of the Chevy and I wonder if Mama's still inside. Wouldn't she be at her room in town? Or is the Chevy the room she imagines, the room of her own she wants? Until I see the room I'm betting it's the Chevy.

"This is the best of it," I say to Mia. From here we can see the silos and the blue-tiled or sheet-metal-roofed barns of neighboring farms. Rolling ground and room for everything. Fence lines so the chaos of land looks ordered, sewn together like God's great quilt. I turn to Mia, pleased with myself, and Mia has my face in her hands. We're kissing. The air is cold and the sun hot on my neck. It doesn't occur to me to pull away. So this is what it's like. Exactly the same only it's Mia and not a man. When we stop Mia looks ready to cry. She says, "You're beautiful," and, smiling, her eyes brim over. We walk down the hill and up the far one without talking, loosely holding hands. In the cow path we stop to pick the brambles and wet seeds from our socks.

That evening we cut each other's hair and drive toward Augsbury's rooftops.

"How come we never do this in Milwaukee?" Mia wants to know.

"It never occurred to me anyplace but here." We're on the high school's roof. The brick was easy to climb; a tipped-sideways chevron of concrete rectangles gave us lots of toeholds. We're wearing heavy navy blue sweaters and jeans. Ankle-high sneakers, like the black kids in Milwaukee. Giggling commandoes. I'm carrying a sack of loose Old Styles that clink and sound like they're about to break. "We should have bought cans," I say to Mia and she says, "Oh, indeed," giggling. The roof is a tar-and-pebble surface studded with air vents. We find tennis balls hit from the courts below and throw them into the elementary school playground as far as we can, green and orange-brown lobs losing their color in the dark. When cars go by, we duck down, smiling at each other like eight-year-olds.

"Let's try some other buildings," I say. "We'll go to Main Street, there's an alley with a fire escape we can climb up."

We park in the Lutheran Church lot and walk over. In the mercury light Mia's hair shines like black water. I've cut it for her so she can comb it like a boy's, short around the ears, longer in front and on top, slicked into waves and short curls like breaking surf. Mine she's cut into irregular spikes, which I gelled up like blond candles. We had gotten started, cutting here and there, and then the hair was falling in a frenzy, we didn't even know why, as if our heads were stuffed with feathers and they'd broken open. We shrieked, sheaths of hair from collar to midback just gone. And after the damage was done we said, All right, now what? and set to shaping it.

The boys had seen us, a ratty towel around my shoulders, Mia working on my hair, just cutting into it so it looked like planned savagery, and they had said, "Yuck," as if insects were falling from our heads. "Why did you do that?" Scott asked. "You looked pretty when you had long hair."

"And we don't now?" Mia asked.

"You look different."

"That's what we wanted."

"I bet you didn't want to look *that* different."

"How do you know what we wanted?" I said.

"'Cause you always seem to know what you want," Tommy had said.

"Right now we want you gone."

"Yeah, right. As soon as we tell you what we think, you want us gone. Come on," he said to Scott. "Dad wants us to pull that back lot of hay forward."

"Why is it they think we know what we want?" I asked Mia once they'd gone.

"Don't you?" she had said.

I hand Mia the Old Style sack, upend a trash can and pull myself onto the lower rungs of the Buchardt Funeral Home's fire escape. They have a *B* done in ironwork on the back windows, which I've always found funny. Who'd want to break into a funeral home? Mia hands the sack up and tries to follow but she can't. She struggles and pulls, but her feet come back down on the garbage can with a hollow booming that echoes in the alleyway like artillery. "Come on, Mia, it's just a few feet." "I can't," she says. "I don't have any strength." "Pull," I tell her. "You've got the build for it. Just yank yourself up." It's a silly thing, but I don't like her just now. I lean over and pull her up myself, catching her helpless wrists and tugging while she keeps her elbows tight to her stomach. Her forearms get scraped and she yelps. We sit on the landing, catching our breath and splitting a beer. I pour half of it over her arm to wash off the blood. Really, I think, she's weak. I scrunch my face. As if it were the beer that left a bad taste in my mouth.

"What's wrong?" Mia asks me and I can only give her a half-smile. I can't bring myself to say to her, "You're weak." It's just a physical failing on her part, what do I expect? Yet it had been easy for me and so there it is, between us.

"Are you ready for the rest?" I ask. She stands up and I smack the rust off her ass. We leave the bottle behind the *B* grillwork. They live on that second floor there. The bodies I think they do in the basement. We had a joke in school that the Buchardt children ate a lot of liver. This time Mia goes in front of me and I carry the sack. There's a boda of wine in the car for when we do the water tower. A half-floor above us on the fire escape is an attic window with another landing, and from there you pull yourself onto the roof. We get tar smeared on us like chocolate. The roofs tilt. At one time all of Main Street had different facades, different heights, but a few years ago a consultant came in and under his direction everything got a mock third story and matching facades that sloped back to just a crawl space in back. As distinctive as a suburban shopping mall and people were pleased that things had become so regular.

We run the length of the street (the new regularity helps in that you don't have to jump from roof to roof, but I sort of miss that, and now the trick is running as if one foot is shorter than the other) and as we run, I call out the buildings beneath us: Coast-to-Coast, Maggie's Bar, Jim and Nancy's Landing, Vemhagen's Bakery, Morley's Insurance, Poacher's Inn, Erndt's Meat Market, Avco Plumbing Supplies, Everfresh— the front office, Natalie's Antiques, and then the block stops and Main Street is only houses again. I run back, all the way to the bowling alley, whose roof you do have to jump onto, and pause just long enough to pull off my sweater and drop it next to the beer sack. And now I'm running in an athletic T, running back and forth like a shuttle race, the night air cool on my arms and tops of my shoulders, and I'm free on Augsbury's rooftops, trampling the town under my feet. Is Mama's room underneath me? I gulp in great bites of air, the roof of my mouth cold, and run nearly blind, seeing the rooftops' end by the glow of a street lamp at one end and a traffic light at the other, and then comes the drop-off to the bowling alley, which I take in a leap, air moving up past me, coiling in my armpits, moving up past where my hair used to be. I love it, love it, delicious. Damn you, Mama, for trying to spoil this for me, for having a life under where I'm running.

Running like we did in high school, on top of the world then, too, throwing water balloons and then escaping. Clayton Jones, Augsbury's lone cop (except for Bud Willers, the deputy, who didn't work nights), waiting for us in back. And so we jumped the eight or nine feet onto the bowling alley and again the other ten feet right onto Main Street, six or seven of us running past the now-vacant police station. Someone would break the window for good measure and then we'd be scattered among the houses on the far side of Main, running through backyards and along the nearly dry creek bed and we'd meet up again. I'd be the only girl (even Wendy couldn't keep up, she'd run for her car and drive home and call me later to find out what happened. Nothing, I'd tell her, the usual stuff. Oh that, she'd say and giggle), and we'd meet at the culvert on Jackson Street, a block up from the Everfresh plant, and we could hear the machinery going there, hoppers and chain belts and blanchers all whining and clanking and wheezing away like old men fumbling with themselves just the other side of the bushes. And then I'd be over there with Calvin, gravel from the rail embankment on my back. I could hear the other guys snickering, probably trying to get up the courage to say something to Calvin. Hey, Cal, how about a little pass-around? But nobody did because they knew I'd claw their eyes out. I had that in my face even as I was running with them and they were thinking about the possibility of later, say if Calvin blew me off or I him and all of a sudden I'm Miss Available.

That seems like a long time ago and it's just me running now, Mia's sitting with her arms locked about her knees and she's looking across the alley, at the two churches and the cemetery. I sit down next to her, feeling good in my sweat, and we each drink a beer and kill the last one together.

"Why do you run like that?" she asks me, as if it'd been distasteful, and I tell her it's what I've always done up here, run as if I were on a great open plain, the boys zigzagging up to the facade tops to pee over the edge, as if they had something on everyone down below for their being up higher. But that's what we did, I explain, we ran back and forth and tossed water balloons at each other as much as at the cars on the street.

"What were you, fifteen, sixteen?" and when I say, "Yeah, about that," she says, "Well, you're not fifteen anymore," and I realize my freedom isn't her freedom. Hers is the stationary kind, the kind you savor in one place, and mine is the kind you get by being in motion, and since she is here to see what I'm like, I'm going to show her a thing or two about mobile freedom. Let her see it all, I say to myself. I stand up and say, One more expedition, Mia, and I lead her back down, coaxing her on the final drop from the fire escape. Come on, Mia, it's only four feet, I tell her and then we're in the car and I'm driving us to the back of the cemetery (Here's what you get for being stationary, I think) and I park where the water tower rises on splayed legs like some metallic beast.

"Let me ask you something before we start. Are you afraid of heights?"

She says no and I say, "Good. The climbing isn't hard, they've even got a cage around the rungs, but even so you're up quite a ways." She says she understands.

She doesn't. Her eyes follow the long cage up and she

flinches involuntarily. Her shoulders shudder back with her head like she can't believe it.

"It's no big deal," I say, but she looks at me like she doesn't believe that, either.

I swing the boda onto my shoulder and position the car right under the cage so you can stand on the car's hood and squeeze between the cage's bars and be inside. You can't get in from the bottom since they put a padlocked grille there. I prefer doing it the boys' way—yanking yourself up like doing a chin-up, the delicious pull across your chest that says, Hey, these are my arms. That thrill of being inside your own body that women are taught to be afraid of, and when you've pulled yourself so your neck's even with the cage, you swing your legs, your sneakered toes feeling air for metal. Usually the first time you drop back and try again, your toes only hitting the cage, not getting the hold, but then the second or third time you catch, and then it's your calves and the front of your thighs all tense, holding you while you pull yourself up from below, amazed your body can do that, too, and squeeze yourself in between the bars of the cage, or if you're small like me, in between two rungs, eight inches apart, the boys calling, Watch your tits, but they glide over too, I'm small yet, and then you're inside and what else is there but what's above you?

"Climb on the hood and in," I say to Mia. I don't like leaving the car there. Usually we park back in the cemetery or, better, in the golf course parking lot, and then walk over. The car under the cage is like sending up a flare. Jones if he comes by has only to wait, the ticket already written. But Mia won't go unless I lead, which she doesn't say but doesn't need to.

There's almost no moon, just a fingernail slice already pretty low to the south. Good.

"Up we go," I say and start going. I want to scamper but don't want Mia to get resentful. I do it like I first learned and over my shoulder I tell her the same. "Take every rung. They're puny steps for a ladder, you could skip some if you wanted to, but take each one. You'll feel better."

"How many are there?"

"Not that many." One hundred and sixteen, if she wanted to know, but she doesn't. She'll count them herself anyway.

I feel better once we're going. I don't not like her so much. I was afraid my first time, too, but it was easier. Those boys, Paul and Calvin and Larry Cooners, all egging me on, daring me I couldn't do it, laughing that I'd freeze halfway up and they'd have to pry my fingers loose and lower me like I was a tied sack of potatoes. Because I'm not a man I can't use that tension with Mia, can't say to her, "I dare you," whereupon she'd think, Fuck you, and climb like a monkey. So we go slow, not talking, hand over hand, easy does it, the houses spilling away below us, passing up through the levels of trees, the cemetery looking like a file cabinet in a dentist's office, all those teeth standing at attention, the golf course looking curvy and green, as if it were calm water. You could dive from the top and the dull green sod would swallow you whole, no ripples, not even a murmur.

Mia's about five rungs below me. She's resting her chin every few steps, the cold steel keeping her going, and she has that look of someone who's counting. Not seeing anything but the numbers, and not even numerals, but written out— *eighty-three, eighty-four,* passing through her mind like storm warnings do at the bottom of TV sets until you forget what show you're watching. I feel bad doing this to her, she seems an inch away from terror, so I tell her, The view at the top is spectacular! Really, it's marvelous.

I don't want to tell her it'll be worse going down, there's that certain blindness of your foot, your toes wiggling at ten inches instead of eight, each rung seems terrifyingly mis-placed, even though you're counting them again. It doesn't seem you're really moving, the increments down don't have the changes in perspective you had going up. It's easier to lose count, and the only thing you're certain of is that the ground is still a long way away.

But Mia keeps coming, determined now like I first was and the pleasure's in my hands, that feeling of old calluses come back to life. The ache in my shoulders from reaching and pulling and with a quick burst I put another ten rungs between us. I say to Mia, "Hurry, the view is wonderful," and I take delight in being the strong one. With everyone there's that imbalance of strength, always, it seems, tipped in my favor. Fine, except with men I resent it, as if they aren't holding up their end, and when they do it's all or nothing their way, never any hope for equilibrium—like with Doyle or Tweed, they want me to coo and spread my legs. With Mia I don't know. I don't feel settled. All this is too new for me, like a child with a new toy. Do I share it or keep it for myself? That's how I feel about my strength. It's not fair of me, I think, even as I'm exploiting my advantage. You just want to see how much you can control things, I say to myself, and here you are where it's easiest to do exactly that, not like with a man where it's expected, even required, if you don't want to get buried alive.

I wait for Mia to catch up, wait for my own breath to come back regular. Above is the water tower's round, dark-silver bottom, like a hole in the center of the sky, and outside the curve are stars. It's like climbing up the esophagus of that beast we saw as we approached, climbing the open thorax, cartilage you can wrap your hands around, and up we go into its brains, to wander around and peer out of its eyes.

"Why are you stopping?" Mia breathes up from my feet. "I don't want to stop."

"We're almost there. Another thirty feet."

"Go on then. I don't want to stop," she repeats. We're whispering, as if we don't want the head up there to know what's coming. Sweat's running down the small of my back. I can smell it under my arms, too, leaching from the stubble to

run down my side, a stray trickle detouring under the rim of
my breasts. I love the smell of my own sweat, especially in
spring, when nothing else is in bloom yet. I'm the only flower.
A man's sweat, too, when he hasn't tried to pretty it up with a
Mennen Speed Stick or something. It's clean and the salt
tastes good. Delicious. I lick the droplets on my upper lip, as
good as any frosting spoon, and finish the climb, pushing
back the diamond plate cover with an effort until it clangs
against its collar, and I hoist myself onto the open ledge,
made of iron grating and surrounded by a double pipe railing.
The crack of my ass is wet. I lean down to help Mia, watching
her count the final rungs aloud—"One twelve, one thirteen,
one fourteen, one fifteen—there's a hundred and sixteen of
these bastards!" she says, angry at the cage but happy she's
up here to have counted them.

"What a stupid number—a hundred and sixteen," she
says and wipes her forehead. She's slick as a seal, and it's
cold and a wind's blowing. "Clammy," she says and pulls at
her jersey top as if to shake loose the moisture. We're sitting
with our backs against the tank. Still exhilarated. We tip the
boda for long drinks each, lukewarm red wine that tastes a
little flat. We swirl it around our teeth, gargle with it, start
laughing and half swallow and spit it out. Our mouths wine-
coated and happy.

"Now what?" she says.

"Depends," I say. "If you're a boy the first thing is to
piss. Piss and get a photograph of yourself doing it. Like
you own the thing and you can do whatever you want. From
the football field behind the high school"—I point north
and east—"you can see the flash cubes going off here and
everyone there knows someone's getting it all on film. As
for us," I say, taking the boda this time and having a regular drink, arcing the wine back till it gurgles in my throat,
then offering it to Mia, "we write our names and the date,
of course."

Mia starts looking at red and black markered names and

dates, written as crudely as if they'd been carved into a tree trunk. "Where's yours?"

"On the other side. I only put my name up the first time, though much later Calvin and I came up, just the two of us. I got a red mark across the middle of my back from the railing. I had my back out and his legs dangled over this catwalk. It was the most carefully abandoned fuck of my life. Over here he wrote it." I get up and show her. Calvin had written with thick and precise red letters "Calvin and the Door fucked their brains out" and the date, as if the bright aluminum tank were a historical document, a sexual declaration of dependence. I'd taken the marker then and crossed out "their brains out."

"The Door," Mia says. "That's funny. Like he'd gotten himself stuck in a keyhole or something."

"It wasn't that funny."

"Hey, come on, Door, it must be now. Why'd you cross that off?"

"Because it wasn't true. Hard to let yourself go when you've got your eyes scrunched tight and it's just open open space and the only thing holding you back is a quaking length of pipe. All I could think about was the railing giving way."

"That would've been something."

"Anyway, it wasn't that much fun."

Mia says, "With men it never is."

"That's not true either." And then the standoff: we're leaning on the railing, supposedly looking at the view from ninety-some feet up, but what we're really doing is arguing without words, trying to stare the other one into agreement.

Mia laughs first, dismissing the whole thing. "Don't be angry," she says, touching my face. "I could show you."

"Don't touch me," and I step back, my face flushed, the rest of me cold except under my limbs. "We're going down."

"But the view—"

"It's just some lights."

"Are you afraid?"

The old dare. To show I have no fear I've done any number
of foolish and terrifying things: leapt from a train trestle into
(what I hoped was) eight feet of weed-choked water, climbed
the outside of this water-tower cage, never looking down that
time, rode Calvin without his raincoat—looking down the
whole time, watching his face contort in what I hoped
(wrongly) was agony—the time I got caught. It would have
been easier to fall from the water tower, those six weeks of the
stranger in me, wanting it, because how could you not, and
yet hating it, hoping the very fibers of me from which it fed
could somehow snuff it out, poison it so I could be quit of the
whole thing, not bring all those other people into it—doctors,
Spread your legs and say ah, the looks from nurses, their little
clucking sounds, Miss Brown (yuch, what a name), why do
you want to quash your egg? Why should the doctor turn it
into an omelet? Mama hating the necessity in all of this but
robbing Daddy for the money anyway. She didn't want to help
so much as to have something on me.

And now Mia saying, *I dare you,* only politer than that,
almost pouting. Was she concerned or mocking me? I didn't
know and that's what kept me on the railing. Curious and
strangely passive. I let her do things to me, didn't bolt down
the rungs like I could have. She touched me all over. Absolutely cooing to me and I felt like I did sometimes with a man,
my knuckles clenched white, not from fear of heights but from
overwhelming confusion. I held on even as she got me going,
my breathing hard and short, as if there were pain under my
ribs or a great weight on my chest, my eyes focused on the
dark over her shoulder, at the bare trees way off by the Wolf
River. Mia feeding on me. Coaxing. All this silver-painted,
graffitied iron and our two bodies, clothes worked up or down,
the open band of white-hot white skin, knees to neck, the air
cold. We're shivering and sweating, hot with goose pimples,
fire beneath the frost. Our animal smell sharp and solid,
something tangible. Metal prints on my back. For a moment I
consider clasping her hard and rolling us both into oblivion

—wouldn't that be something? Yet it's almost as if I were perched on the railing, separate from all this, steadied by my hands, watching the two of us with the detached curiosity of someone much younger watching two strangers.

"No better or worse," I sigh into the stiff clipped hairs behind Mia's ear and she sits back, hurt to the point of tears which I did and didn't want to cause.

"Let's go down," I say and she acquiesces—I've always loved that word, *acquiesces*. It sits in your mouth like chocolate, like something sweet. I acquiesce, she acquiesces, we all acquiesce. Something wonderful inherent in the word if no one tries claiming a victory. But something sad, too. Small losses. Always that small loss when you find yourself with someone else. For Mia it's that we get our clothes back on and in leaving this ledge it could be we'll never speak of these moments again and they truly will be lost, forcefully ignored by me and so lost to her, too.

Maybe I only love the sound of the word, the slithering of it on my tongue, or when it's someone else acquiescing to me. Does the word count as a command? Acquiesce! Is that a victory anyway? Mia's eyes cast about as if she's looking for something to grasp, as if the height has suddenly gotten to her. I squeeze her hand. My breath is almost back to normal. My nostrils still hold the smell of us and of the water tower— both the salty, musty warmth and the rusty odor of chlorine. The day after tomorrow Daddy will have his operation and I realize everything is going to be different. I squeeze Mia's hand harder. "Let's go," I say, and she looks at me with what seems to be understanding. We drive home with the windows open, as if everything outside were welcome inside, the chill air drying our faces. But she doesn't understand, not really, because after we shower at the house, tiptoeing about, everyone asleep, she settles herself into my bed, the overhead light very bright on her satin teddy, and she looks at me expectantly.

"Mia—" I explain, my hands indicating my loss for explanation—how can she know when I don't?—but she goes back to her own bed without a word and we both breathe, expecting to see our exhalations though the stove is throwing heat, and we stare at the ceiling we can't see until we give up thinking and betray ourselves into sleep.

8

FRIDAY I ARGUE with Mama while Mia hovers in the background. It starts in the morning when Mama hands me a list. "You're home," she says, "and that entails certain responsibilities."

"Such as?"

"It's written out very clearly for you." Her list includes getting the laundry room clean, which has generations of leftover socks, scattered lint strips, abandoned shirts and hosiery and a layer of crusty towels from when the pipes froze and broke three years ago; cleaning out the rotting and sprouting vegetables and fruits from the root cellar; papering the kitchen cupboards; washing the screens—all the things Mama's put off doing and probably wouldn't do at all except I'm home to pawn them off on. I rip her list into tiny pieces. Mama cracks me one across the face.

"How dare you!" she splutters: not nine-thirty yet and she's already into it pretty heavy.

"I'll cook and clean, Mama—"

"It's about time for that," she says.

"—but I won't do your nigger work."

"Your father, young lady, is going into the hospital tomorrow."

"New paper in the cupboards or a bushel less of wrinkled apples isn't going to change that, Mama."

"You can still pull your own weight."

"But not yours, too, Mama."

She grabs me by both shoulders. Suddenly she's shrieking, her red nose and watery eyes large out of all proportion. Mia's retreated to the bathroom. "I hate this life!" she screams. "I hate it! Do you understand? I hate it! I hate it!"

"Me too, Mama." Very quiet. I expect a truce; Mama goes like that, from the screaming meemies to tearful apologies. But instead she pulls herself together, arranges her blouse as if it'd gone awry. "Ha!" she says. "What do you know?"

Mia flushes the toilet. Mama shakes her head, tilts it sideways and says weakly to the ceiling, "God, we must be an eyeful." She pushes her hands down the front of her too-large jeans, tugs at the fabric of her blouse again, as if Mia had left the room because Mama wasn't dressed right. "I'll tell you what," she says. "If the two of you do the root cellar, I'll do the cupboards and the laundry room. Make things nice for your father."

Mia says, trying to be helpful, "That's fair, I'd like that," and I tell her, "Mia, you've never seen a root cellar."

"What could be so hard?" she says and Mama says, "It's a deal then," and she makes a show of clattering down the cups and the Burger King glasses and the everyday plates and setting them next to the coffee and sugar and flour tins on the counter, which is littered with flour dust and coffee grounds and sugar grains, a beach of spilled foodstuffs.

As we're sorting through boots and overalls in the mudroom, Mia says to me, "I didn't even know you *had* a root cellar."

"More precious than jewels," I say to her and lift a finger to my lips. "If word got out—" and we both laugh.

"It's an adventure for me," she says. "Though nothing to compare with last night, I'm sure." Again she's got that expectant look. Not pleading like Larry, but uncertain, as if it's within me to offer confirmation and she's waiting for that.

"Hmmm," I say and tug on Scott's boots. "You'll have to wear Tommy's boots, seeing as how you're bigger than me."

"Do I get to get into his pants, too?"

"A boy's dream comes true."

"If he were a few years older, you know. It'd be fun, toying with an adolescent."

"You have."

"I don't think of you that way."

"Obviously. Here, put these on. They're Tommy's, too."

We trudge down the steps, awkward in black rubber boots with yellow trim that are too big for us and the gray overalls we have to roll up the bottoms on. The boards give under our weight and I pull the light string.

"Wow, like a dungeon," Mia says.

"That's what I've always thought, only we keep a cat down here for the mice. Here, kitty-kitty," I call and a black cat with green eyes slinks under the open steps. "Too bad they don't eat spiders."

The air has that damp cool dark smell of thick forests. I point out what's what, though it seems pretty obvious. "Potatoes all along that back wall, reds and bakers, sorted by size, in the center red and green apples, all your basic varieties—Macs and Red and Golden Delicious, Winesaps, Granny Smith's—plus radishes, turnips, carrots, squash, and onions alongside the wall. Daddy loves carrots. All going to rot with infinite patience."

"The floor's wet."

"Everything's on pallets, see? And the floor's cut with a center trough maybe four feet wide. The apples sit over the trough and underneath them water condenses. Things stay cool. Too bad over the winter the fruits and veggies dehydrate. They get wrinkled, and the pallets and the baskets soak up moisture. Along about now everything on the bottom starts turning to mush. That's what we've got to clean out. We dump these baskets into empty ones and pick out all the bad stuff, which is now on top. Then the wet baskets we hang on the wall to dry, all those hooks on that pegboard Daddy put up."

"That doesn't seem so hard."

"You ever put your thumb through a rotten potato?"

We begin gingerly, upending the bushel baskets and picking out the mushy potatoes, holding them between our thumbs and forefingers, under the skin the meat a blackish white like dying teeth (I wonder if Daddy's arm is like that under the bandage, wet with decay, or is it hard and cracked, like old carrots?). "The wrinkled ones with eyes we put in burlap sacks," I tell her. "Those are seed potatoes for this next year."

Mia says, "That seems to be most of them."

The baking spuds are nearly sorted when we hear the door upstairs slam. I scramble to a sand- and dirt-grimed window to see Mama in cuffed white pedal pushers, baggy at her thighs, and a red blouse tied at her stomach as if she's knotted there, a puckered wrinkling of belly visible, as white as a potato, advertisement of her age, get into the Chrysler. Gravel dust hangs thick after she peels out and Mia's there at my ear, a long exhalation of her perplexity. We look at each other, knowing we've been had.

"Well, fuck this," I say and we spend the afternoon getting stoned and baking cookies, oatmeal chocolate chips we gobble down before they're set. Toward dinnertime we make a potato salad, too, rescuing some spuds we peel and cut into quarters and boil. We start the grill for bratwurst though it's too early for cookouts, but we're not even attempting reason. "Cookout!" we shout and dissolve into laughter. The ice on top of the Weber steams, and water runs underneath the ice skin and then the cap slides off and shatters. We step back, alarmed and laughing.

Mama comes home then, looking smudged and not at all focused.

"I thought we had a deal," I say righteously and Mama just laughs.

"Please, Dorie," she says and pushes an eyebrow back up with the palm of her hand.

"I suppose you went to town," I say and Mama says, "No,

dearest, I went to Chicago," and she laughs again, laughs so hard she has to lean with one hand on the wall and the other holding her stomach.

"Dorie," she says, "Dorie, you're just Mama's little girl, you know, aren't you?" and she stumbles back to her room and locks the door.

Daddy comes in then, his face floured with flakes of wind-chafed skin. He starts undoing the scarf wrapped twice around his neck, using the one hand so it looks like he's trying to hang himself. Daddy has a clock on his tractor so he's back at the house pretty close to when the school bus gears down opposite our drive and the doors flap open and the boys spill out like two fish poured out of a live well. They check for the paper and mail and then race up to the door, using their free hands to push each other back, to interfere or gain leverage.

"What's up?" Daddy asks and I think to myself, You poor man, you haven't got a clue, but then I think, No, you do probably know, have known, in fact, for a long time and this open-faced naïveté is just another way of getting by.

"Mama's locked herself in her room," I say, as if the room weren't his, too, and Tommy looks disgusted and Scott looks away, red-faced. Mia puts her hand on Scott's shoulder and he shrugs it off. But Daddy just nods and says, "So what's for dinner?"

And I say, "Daddy, Mama's locked herself—"

"I heard you," Daddy says and kicks off the mud-caked and cracked boots, the toes curled as if he spends all his time walking tiptoe or sitting on his haunches. He shrugs off his coveralls, flapping his one arm to get past the bandage. I help pull the sleeve off for him and feel like this is the first time I've looked him in the face since I've been home. Leotis Brown, my daddy. His eyes all crinkled in, like there're triangles of dusty aluminum foil worked in under his lids, and his face is fleshy, with deep creases ringing both cheeks and running below his chin, long pleasant jowls as if a capital *U* had been pushed into the flesh. His smile almost always uncertain but quick, as if he's rolled with so many punches he's a little slaphappy. He just nods, silly, and figures if he's going to be hit anyway he may as well look amused in the meantime. But why does he look sometimes, like now, that he's really enjoying himself? So your Mama's locked herself in her room again? he seems to be saying. When she gets tired of it she'll come out, though, won't she? And she won't say anything for a while, she'll be sullen, but she always smiles later, doesn't she? A sheepish smile like I've been a bad girl? You just watch and see.

And Daddy sits down on a wooden kitchen chair with the varnish rubbed raw to wood and he runs his hand through his Brylcreamed hair, hair shiny black with the grease, even the sideburns to his earlobes are trimmed and greased, like he's just stepped from the shower, only there's the indented ring from his feed cap and you can smell the heat steam off him, the brown paisley shirt sweated right through, a heat the coveralls hold in, made of human juices and diesel oil, a burnt-gasoline and clay smell—almost like exposed river bottom on a hot August afternoon, death ripe and fetid. I look at his arm like it came from there, the white gauze and taupe sling grimied a blackish shit brown, his hand coming out the one end like it really wasn't connected to the rest of him. You can't even see the arm, I have to imagine it like the other one, stringy and strong. When I was young, he'd swing me up to the ceiling and I'd look down the long exposed white meat strips of his inner arms and scream Daddy! and he would let go for an instant. I'd part with him. I'd be in the air totally and then coming down I'd be caught, his hard brown muscles snapped to attention, and I'd be giggling, safe.

Truly perplexed, he says, "What's for supper?" And I realize I didn't cook for him this morning, either, like I'd promised myself I would. Another day wasted. I'm ashamed for getting hazed this afternoon, and my offering isn't going to be good enough. "Potato salad and brats," I say and he looks pleased. But it's stupid, it's like buying him a scarf so pretty he won't wear it and in that way you can get it back, or like when Scott bought Mama a first baseman's glove for Mother's Day.

"Just like summer," he says. "Too bad it's colder than a witch's tit." His eyes gleam, having used that word in front of me. He's pleased and a little embarrassed. He knows I've got them.

I want to show Mia an unblemished father. Never mind the dirty gauze wrappings on his arm, that will be better soon enough. I want him perfect for her, though, even to rooting out the blackheads on his nose. I want to explain to her, You're seeing us at a bad time, as if if my father washed his face and used Nivea on the dry spots and scrubbed the yellow calluses on his hands with a pumice stone, we'd come across better.

It has always been a bad time. I have always been embarrassed. I had wanted the two of us to laugh at this quaint old life of mine as something horribly rude and unkempt—it really is ridiculous when you think about it—but now my eyes plead with Mia's to tolerate, to not laugh. Her eyes register nada, a blank, which has me nearly frantic, but at least she's not looking at me with pity. Pity I couldn't stand.

We eat outside even though we're in jackets and our hands feel chapped and the butter on the corn niblets stays hard. Daddy insists on this. "Summer food," he says. "You got to do it right." He's poking fun at me, but we go along, pretending it's a picnic. The wind has our noses dripping and our foreheads cold, but he says he wants the coffee out here, too. He sends the boys down to start the milking and says he'll be along directly. Mia's clearing the table and I'm closing the vents on the Weber. We're on the deck he built last summer. He wanted a place to sit outside "of an evening." It's been dark nearly an hour now and he's flicked off the light we ate by. I'm holding the mustard jar and the ketchup.

"Sit," he says. "The dishes'll keep." He lights a cigarette, shakes out the match that flares his face amber and locates the ashtray in front of him, his middle finger tapping ashes. He's crossed one leg over the other and his bandaged arm rests on his thigh, that hand holding the cigarette half a foot from his mouth, his other hand cupping the diseased elbow, his body hunched forward, a certain tightness even in his relaxing.

"What is it, Daddy?" I shake out one of his cigarettes and two orange glows mark our positions. I've got my farmer jacket on. I've rolled the cuffs down and they nearly cover my hands to the second joint of my fingers. Still, I'm shivering.

"Your ma and me . . ." he starts and shakes his head. The smoke's hot in my mouth. My lips feel chilled, as if they were rubbed with an ice cube. I'm waiting. I remember once when I split my lip. I must've been seven. We were coming out of church and in running to the car I tripped and gashed myself on the walk, and on the way to the hospital Daddy held an ice cube to my lips. When he took his hand away for the doctor to make two stitches I saw this watery red all over his hand and the white cuff of his best cotton shirt which Mama always complained about ironing and I thought, "That's me on him," and I was strangely thrilled. Even more so when he told the long-haired intern (his hair tied back and a tiny gold hoop in his ear) who'd pulled Emergency Room duty, "Make the stitches tiny. I have to kiss those lips forever."

Daddy's not going to say anything else. It's been an effort for him just asking me to sit with him. I wonder how often he comes out here to have a smoke and sit quietly by himself in the dark, Mama off somewhere herself.

Almost daintily he pecks out his cigarette. "Can't have Tom and Scott doing what I won't," he says and uncoils himself. He's forty-two and moves like a tired man, the enthusiasm gone out of him. I'd like to say he's stiff with cold, but cold doesn't bother him. His hands will chap and his face flake white and he'll seem not to notice.

"It's gonna go fine tomorrow, Daddy."

"I know," he says. "Heck, I'm just gonna pack my toothbrush and a change of underwear."

I follow him inside. Mia and Mama sit drinking coffee, ladies in waiting. Mama's eyes look blurry, sullen.

That's it for tonight, I want to announce. Everyone go home. I want to leave the dishes unrinsed, the dishwasher unloaded, and pull the covers high over my head and dream I'm breathing in a collapsed tent. How can they sit there like that? Not having a conversation, just taking each other in, silent osmosis and measure. It's scary.

"How about pie and ice cream when we come up?" Daddy calls from the mudroom. You can hear the splatter of mud shards as he claps the boots together before putting them on.

"Sure," Mama says. "I'll just conjure up something in the next twenty minutes."

"No hocus-pocus. Isn't there two-thirds of a pie left from Wednesday?"

"I'll have to look," Mama says. The three of us around the table, some kind of coven, Daddy in the other room, the long zip of the overalls sealing him in.

"There's pie, Mrs. Brown," Mia said. "You brought an apple and a peach when you came home from shopping."

"Amanda," Mama says. "Let's cut out this Mrs. Brown shit." She pulls at her cigarette and wipes her eye, circular motions like the thing is loose in its socket and has to be settled. She sniffs. "You know I used to bake? Pies—custard, apple, rhubarb, lemon, peach, pecan, you name it. Even Key lime from the Betty Crocker book. Cakes too. Your father loves German chocolate cake. Myself, I can't stand it, all that coconut in there like field dirt. Now I don't even remember buying a damn pie or not." She yells to Daddy, "Leotis, you'll have your pie."

"Back soon," Daddy calls. We hear the two doors open and then the matching thuds, the first like it's on air brakes, a sort of whoosh, then a hollow and muffled bang from the screen.

Mama sighs. "God, I hate this place."

She smokes while Mia and I clean up. "More caffeine," she says and gets it from the kitchen where we are and then in the dining room we hear the clink of a bottle on porcelain and I mutter to Mia, "Rum."

Mia rubs herself just below her collarbone. The fat of her breast starts there. It's as if she's reminding herself of who she is. Mia Zolkauer of the short chest and slightly heavy, slightly conical breasts.

"I feel sorry for her," she says.

"She wants everyone to feel sorry for her."

"Bullshit," Mama says. "I just want a plane ticket out." She's come in holding her coffee in front of her and her cigarette at mouth height. Drunken housewife as Statue of Liberty. She's leaning with her head against the cupboard and her hips on the counter, her torso sort of swaying over the empty space between, twisting slowly as books say the bodies of the hanged do.

"You think you've got me figured out," Mama says. "Now *there's* something I pity you for." She sets her rum and coffee on the counter. It moves when she sets it down, the short jitter of an unsteady hand, and then she wipes her hands and she's gone outside, too.

I don't even look. "In the Chevy. Beached. Lapping it straight from the bottle without an audience."

But she's not. Or at least not the whole time. We drink coffee and smoke cigarettes. Discover the pies and heat them and set out plates and forks. Paper napkins. Serious dessert. Mia goes to the window. "They're coming back."

"Mama still in the car?"

"She's with your father."

"She must've gone down to meet them."

"He's got his arm around her."

I'm at the window too. The boys are in front, jogging like puppies, cuffing each other in the intense way boys show affection and count coup. Frank told me about counting coup. It amazed me, the innocence of those Indians, that in battle they would seek to strike an opponent without injuring him, the humiliation of being struck injury enough. I'd count coup, too, but I'm not sure who I'm keeping score against.

Mama's in the shelter of Daddy's good arm, and they've got their mouths open, teeth shining white in the dark. Laughing. Perhaps it's hysteria. I push up the kitchen window and listen. Laughter. Mama counts coup, too.

"I wonder what went on," I say.

"Who knows with marrieds?" Mia says. "My parents used to do a nightly slow burn and I'd sit at the head of the stairs with Aaron and my sister and we'd wait for the shouting to start. And sometimes instead we'd hear these sounds, like fish being slapped together and slurping sounds and my mother crying out like she was in pain but she liked it. Aaron crept down the stairs once enough to peer over and he sat there awhile, hunched, and then he came back and whispered, 'They're doing it.' I didn't know what doing it was, but from the roundness of his eyes I figured they weren't fighting anymore; it had to be something even more terrible. Aaron tried to stop me but he couldn't without our parents hearing us tussle on the top of the stairs so I got to see, too. You know it did look awful."

"Everybody looks silly when they're about to come."

The boys are in, stomping and loud. "We heard there's pie," Scott says and starts whistling the Oscar Mayer tune. Mama and Daddy are still outside. Kissing. Daddy's clumsy with the one arm he can't get free to hold her until he shakes the sling loose and then it's like a goddamn prom night. Mama even lifts one leg coyly behind her and stands on tiptoe, her calves tense as if an electric current pulled her up short.

"So what are you looking at?" Tommy asks, shucking his overalls like old skin.

"They're like teenagers," Mia says.

"Temporarily."

"Well, leave 'em alone," Tommy says. "You like it when somebody's watching you kissing?"

"Depends on who I'm kissing," Mia says. "For instance, if I were to kiss you," she says and grabs for him, pulls him close and plants one on his astonished puckered face.

"Christ," he says, pulling away.

"Or I could kiss Scott," Mia says, but he's already backing away. "Or Dorie. What would you say if I started kissing your sister?" She has her arm around me, a buddy pose.

"Mia—"

"Weird," Tommy says. "You go around kissing everybody?"

"It's what we do in the city. You meet someone on the street and this is what you do." She steps back to face me. "Daaaarling, it's been ages!" and she throws herself at me, pecking both cheeks and making smootchie sounds. And then she's at both of them, saying, "Daaarling, it's been ages," and kissing them, too, on each cheek, and though they check with their fingers for any traces of Mia's lipstick, you can see they're thrilled. They wish they were older and could take advantage of Mia's teasing. They are more familiar and strange to me than ever before.

"Got the pie ready?" Daddy says. He and Mama are in the mudroom. Mama tosses his overalls over the banister of the landing and they come up, Mama in front.

"You wouldn't believe it," Scott says. "Mia showed us how they kiss in the city."

"Eye-opening, I'm sure," Daddy says. "What about the pie? Did you make one or are we suffering through a store-bought?"

"Something wrong with store-bought?" Mama says.

"Well, used to be a man going into the hospital could count at least on having homemade pie his last night."

"Used to be a lot of things, Leo."

"Okay, so store-bought is fine. The coffee's real, though, isn't it?"

"Look, you just shut up about it, Leo."

Daddy's winking at us, pulling Mama's leg. "The milk for the coffee's not powdered, is it? I mean, we got the cows right outside—"

"Shut up, shut up, shut up!" Mama screams.

"Amanda, I'm just—"

"I don't have to listen to this," Mama says and she slams her fork down and it bounces and then she's gone, out to the Chevy to sulk again, I figure. But no, we hear the Impala start and the lights arc through the living room and we see the cone of light swing to the right, toward town.

"You kids wait here," Daddy says and wipes his mouth and goes for a coat and then he's gone too.

The four of us looking at each other. "Marrieds," Mia says. "Go figure them."

The bunkhouse seems particularly damp. Without talking, we cleared the table and put away the dishes and the boys followed us down. I get a fire going, the wet wood smoky at first and then snapping through the air pockets, cracks like a car backfiring. I like this wood the best, it sings its own consumption. The boys sit with us and we let them each have a beer. I wasn't going to let them but Scott says, You aren't old enough either and when I say, Like that's going to stop me he says, So why should it stop me? and I realize they haven't forgotten my age, even if Mia and I have. "It's just an argument," Mia says but the air stays hollow after she says it, and we alternate looking at each other and looking at our beer cans and at our knees and feet and sometimes we smile but those are sheepish, like we're in the doghouse and we know we're equally responsible for being there but we don't know what we did exactly that landed us here. Scott tries whistling awhile but stops when Tommy glares at him. He goes to the window and says, They're not back yet. Yeah, we know, stupid, Tommy says and swigs from his beer and stands up and says, Well, nothing's happening here, like it's old hat to him, drinking beer with older women. Mia says, You want another one? Naw, Tommy says. Maybe tomorrow. He puts the can on the floor and says, Come on, Scott, and waits for him to go out first. See you guys in the morning, he says and leaves himself.

Mia stretches out on her bunk. "It's too bad your brothers aren't older. They'd be fun."

"Yeah, they're okay."

Mia gets up and starts undressing, pushing her pants down first, then sitting on the bed to take off her shoes. "I think Tommy likes me." She has clothes hanging on a hook behind the door and takes down a translucent teddy, one of those flesh-tone things that hang like gossamer drapery. Off with her sweater and she rubs her released nipples. "You know we have to get back Sunday, don't you?"

"I'll have to see how it goes," I tell her. "I may end up staying longer myself. See how it goes," I say again, letting the sentence trail off. The evening feels like this, like rope you find in the shed, a loose tangled mess.

Mia's sitting on a wood box facing the mirror on the one bureau. She's combing her hair as if it was still long and needed patient brush strokes. She's still naked and looks at me to see if I'm looking at her. She sighs and slowly lets the teddy slide down her arms. Shadows cover what I'd been seeing—the crease of belly from where she bent forward, the unflattering hang of her breasts, the black cotton tuft of belly hair.

I leave my panties on and add a T-shirt. Underneath the covers I take off my socks. Mia stops combing her hair and gets into her bed, saying, "'Night, love," as she arranges her covers, keeping her arms outside the blankets once she's settled in.

My throat feels swollen, my nose is stuffed up. Even with the fire I feel the lingering chilled damp that makes me shiver even under the blanket and quilt. I'm looking at the ceiling and without looking know that Mia's looking at me. I turn my head the opposite way. She's still looking at me. The fire's going down to embers, a rubble of hot coals. It's like it's watching me, too.

Mia says, "I love you, Dorie. I really do."

I want to tell her, like she's Larry or anyone, Give me a break. But I don't. I pretend I'm already asleep. Neither car has come back. I can feel the dark pressing in on the shed from every side. I don't want to think about them, about Daddy's operation or about Mama and Daddy driving off separately. Or about Mia and me and all that, or about anything awful and immediate that will keep me from sleep. So instead I think about Ramona, who exists in a distance that barely touches me. She's like a bedtime story, one of those spook stories that makes you feel more relieved about yourself, better. Ramona, whom I've never met.

It was between Christmas and New Year's. One of those slow times at the Blaisdell. Nobody wants to be in a hotel at Christmas. The bar stayed busy, though, lots of lonely people wanting alcohol, free with their money and mouths. All three of us on, two of us covering for the third. After closing one night we were at Nancy's. She and Pauline shared a place, a second-floor flat in a big brick house off Washington, close enough to the lake so you could feel its white glow filling up the room at night, even with the drapes closed. We were too tired to do anything but smoke cigarettes sullenly and drink iced Scotch. We called it that so it sounded harmless, like tea. "Another iced Scotch," Nancy would say, shaking her glass as if Pauline or I would jump to fill it and when neither of us did she'd say, "Christ, my back," and go to the kitchen to fetch it herself.

Ramona. Her name kept getting mentioned. Nancy would say I reminded her of Ramona and I'd say why and she'd say, "Oh, that was before you started," case closed. But this time I settled in next to her on the couch. She liked that, it seemed like she was getting attention. Pauline in an easy chair by the fire, which kept threatening to go out. They were feeding it scrap lumber left from when the landlord replaced the basement stairs. The wood had no substance to it, would burn as if reluctant to make itself flame, a pouting fire that Pauline shoved and rattled with another board fragment she'd eventually lay on top of the others. The damn thing couldn't breathe but they didn't seem to care if it did or it didn't. They watched it not burning with the same attention you'd give a late-night movie.

"So what about Ramona?" I said to Nancy, and she stretched her short legs out, and her arms, too, spiderlike. Nancy the spider-woman, I thought, a black widow, only her husband left her; she was thirty-two and had a fifteen-year-old son (Pauline was thirty-six and had a five-year-old grandson, her own daughter was twenty-one). Nancy said, "You want to hear a ghost story, do you?" And she told me about Ramona, starting with the parallel between us. Precocious, she said. Both precocious. It gets on my nerves, she said. Everyone going faster than me.

"You wouldn't say that if Tom hadn't left you," Pauline said flatly.

Nancy turned to me. "You have to ignore her sometimes. She gets these feelings of superiority from time to time because she left her husband before he left her."

"At least I don't talk about him all the time like you do about Tom."

"I don't."

"You do, too. You talk about everybody."

"Ramona," I said, and the two of them sat back in their chairs, as if they'd been called back from a false start and were skittish; they were waiting for it to begin again.

Nancy took a long drag on her cigarette. "Ramona had started the previous spring as a receptionist in sales. She had a foul mouth, thought nothing of saying *fuck!* on the phone to whoever was calling. Her upper lip was thickened, as if it'd been split or beaten. The scar tissue looked pulpy, upper and lower lips shiny with a clear gloss. Or she kept running her tongue over her lips, a nervous habit. God, I loved that," Nancy said, and stopped talking to think about it.

"I'm going to bed," Pauline said. We watched her go.

"Jealous," Nancy said after the light in Pauline's room went out. "She thinks the only thing you fuck should be men." She went into the kitchen and came back with the Dewar's and a tray of ice and poured liberally for both of us. "Once we had a bunch of people from work over and there was a waitress then, Clarissa, and we were back there"—she pointed in the direction of the hallway—"kissing after Pauline had gone to bed, and Clarissa was going to drive somebody home and then come back, Larry Fields, I think it was, and when we came back into the living room Larry's eyes were so wide you'd think he'd seen a ghost—he's like Pauline that way." She put the Dewar's on the table and screwed the cap back in place. "It's funny what some people think," she said. "Larry probably had it figured Clarissa was going to bed with him and instead all he was getting was a ride home."

"How do you know she didn't go to bed with him some other time?"

"Because she was living here with me then. That was after she found her boyfriend in bed with someone else."

"And Pauline moved in later?"

"No, the two of us have shared this from the beginning."

"And Clarissa?"

"The fool moved back in with her boyfriend. They had one of those fights that end with somebody getting punched, you can guess who, and the next thing, Clarissa said, they were making love. The sap." Nancy shook her glass. "I need ice."

While I got her fresh ice from the tray, she lay on the couch, her hands folded on her stomach, a sort-of smile creasing her face. Waxlike. Death gets the grins. I took what'd been Pauline's chair. Nancy looked at me and sat up.

She looked at me stupidly, as if she couldn't remember who I was.

"Ramona," I said.

Nancy's eyes snapped back into focus. "Ramona," she said thickly. "Ramona. Never wore a bra and always with three buttons, never just two, undone. Drove the straight men crazy and kept the gay men amused. These champagne glass tits of hers always popping out. Beautiful. Like she didn't mind if everyone had a free look-see. But she'd get exasperated, too, like nobody should notice what she was showing."

"What did she look like?"

"Oh, taller than me or you. Long-legged. She always wore long-sleeved blouses and long, tight skirts. When you actually saw her limbs, saw her naked, that is, it looked like she was entertaining the idea of anorexia. Like this," she said, holding her thumb and forefinger in a circle.

"She had beautiful hair, though, fine brown hair that she flounced off her forehead and that fell straight back behind. Yummy. You know what gave her away, though? You know how I found out she was younger than the twenty-two she claimed? She was horrible at makeup. Like a little kid. Foundation caked on her green skin, blush not the same shade on each cheek and too thick, and she used this purplish brown eye shadow that made her look cadaverous, like she'd been punched out and left for dead. A pretty face, but my God, with that makeup job she looked like a mistake from embalming school."

"So what about her?"

"I suppose I haven't told you anything, have I?" Nancy took a drink, pursed her lips and pulled them into her mouth, something she did often. "She was just this waif saying fuck this, fuck that all the time. Always irritable. And *she's* the receptionist for them down there. What can I say? She was attractive, and she certainly didn't like the men, and someone should show her how to put on makeup. . . ."

"On dates she'd smoke like a fiend, wouldn't drink, though I always got drunk. She ate like a horse and she talked non-stop. Everything was distasteful to her. I loved it. She hated everything." Nancy lit a cigarette. "And these were just friendly dates, mind you. I thought she was a little slow pick-ing up the signals, but I finally figured she was talking so much about nothing—her apartment, her car, winter, men at work, the meals, the weather—she hadn't noticed any signals at all. I practically had to drag her to bed. After that she kept talking, but now everything mattered. I heard about how she hated her father, her brother, her father's friends, her mother, on and on and on. Everyone she'd ever known either fucked with her or condoned the fucking. What do you mean fucked with you? I asked. Nothing from her. You mean fucked you? Is that what you mean? I asked how old she was and she said, Seventeen, and then I got all the specifics. Her father slept with her, her older brother slept with her, friends of her father slept with her. Sometimes they just took pictures of her, other times they'd beat her up and all have her, then leave her, nearly unconscious, near the river where her parents kept a house. Once friends of her brother tossed her in the river to wake her up and they had to fish her back when she didn't move. She showed me her four-year pin from AA. She'd eat a pound of M&M's at work and throw it all up during her coffee break. And you know what's sick? Other than getting her to see a doctor about her throwing up I fucked with her, too. I wanted her like a drug."

The end of her cigarette fascinated Nancy for a minute. Then she looked at me over the glowing tip and said, "Like a drug."

"Could you keep it down out there?" Pauline called from her room. "I've heard this already."

"Shit," Nancy said.

"I'm trying to sleep."

"Eat shit, Paulie dear."

Pauline's in the doorway. "I'm going to the bathroom and I

want you to play quiet. No loud noises, Nance, I'm tired."

"Tired," Nancy said. "Like you're the only one who's tired."

"I hate it when you get weepy like this, Nancy. You look horrible, dear, you really do."

Clearing my throat in the endless silence, I asked, "What happened to Ramona?"

Nancy said, "Oh, she finally did end up in a hospital. It was what she wanted. One of the secretaries found her throwing up in the women's room. But she didn't come back to work after that. I visited her and she said she was and that's what everyone thought—that after a week or two she'd be back. They were even holding her job open for her, using those temporary people. But the next time I went she had checked out and she'd changed apartments. I keep thinking I'll run into her on the street or in some bar like the Safehouse doing the beautiful bit, but I'm just kidding myself. Women named Ramona never have good lives." Nancy sighed. "Like I should talk."

I turn over in my bunk and out loud in the long silence I say, "Women named Ramona," and Mia, half-gone, says, "Whaa?"

"Nothing," I tell her. "Go back to sleep."

9

I'M DRESSED and at the house early. Mia's still clutching her pillow. She's hugged it so it looks like me. I move about the kitchen with a sense of purpose, cracking eggs, frying bacon, brewing coffee, even squeezing fresh orange juice till my fingers smell of it. The toaster pings and I'm buttering toast. I knock once and burst in on them. Daddy's on his back. Mama's got her one leg draped over his groin, her mouth slack and ugly on his chest.

"Daddy's breakfast," I announce and sit near his knee, the tray in my lap.

Daddy sits up in jerks, going from his side, rising gingerly by pushing off on his bad arm and rubbing sleep with his other hand. "Thanks, honey, but I can't eat anything this morning. The doctor said."

"I can eat," Mama says and swings her feet out of bed on her side.

"It's not for you," I say and our eyes lock in a stare-down.

Daddy says, "Thank you," and hands the plate to Mama. Mama's eyes are all I-won-I-told-you-so. I sit for a moment and then get up, one hand on the doorjamb keeping me in the room.

"When do we go?"

"Mid-morning."

"Surgery's at eleven," Mama says, chasing egg with a triangle of toast.

• • •

The boys have chores. Mia sleeps in, says she wants to read. It's the three of us driving into Appleton. I'm sitting in back. I have this feeling like I've done something wrong, like I'm back here as punishment, only this is prelude, not the punishment itself. "I see, Doris, that we're going to have to call your parents in on this. Sit down there and wait." Trying to be light, Daddy says, "Be playing softball with this wing in no time." Mama nods grimly. I look out the window. Brown mush like a bad soup.

Leo and Mama do the signing-in bit, Leo deferring to Mama on insurance numbers and medical history, and they put Leo in a wheelchair. "We do this with everyone," the nurse says and they wheel him off. Daddy—Leo (if I think of him as Leo he won't seem so close, it'll be someone else and maybe this dull weight near my heart that I shouldn't have will disappear)—looks sadly smaller. Sitting down, he has no size. A chair with wheels doesn't do him justice. Get bigger, Leo. Throw out your chest. Stand on those two bandy legs of yours, the legs you passed on to me—Mama's tall and lean for a woman—and howl. Let them hear you angry, Leo. Show them how thick and tan your forearms are. Squat and then stand up so they can see the power in your thighs, and the thick band of muscle across your back. You're bigger than they think, Leo. You can show them.

"We're going to remove some tissue and do a biopsy," Dr. Cleggwell says. He's been introduced and talks with Mama. She keeps nodding and I close my ears. Who wants to hear what they're going to do to him?

For hours all we do is read magazines. Mama turns pages rapidly—*McCall's, Family Circle, Ladies' Home Journal, Redbook, Woman's Day*—two or three issues of each, goes through them with the thoroughness of deciding which clothes are going to Goodwill, as if the faster she turns pages the faster time itself will move, as if speed and success were connected and her heart could stop pounding so high in her chest. In my chest.

I find one raggedy-paged issue of *Mademoiselle* from January and stare at each ad, projecting myself into it, but not as
the woman in the ad. Rather I'm an observer, inside the
frame, and what I see is real. People *do* live like this—expensive black clothes or woolly tweeds with leather finish-
ings, staircases larger than lots of houses, casual clothes with
colors so bright you should need a permit to wear them. In
one ad there are no clothes at all. The model is maybe twenty
and she sits on her heels, nude, her smooth torso turned
three-quarters away from us, her arm bent in a V, vaguely
Egyptian, a perfume bottle on her open palm as if she were
blowing a kiss. She's mostly shadow. The photo's black and
white, the light full only on her thigh, hand and forearm and
cheek and side of turned-up nose and one clear-lighted
breast, her perfect stark white nipple—the whole point (I pun
to myself) of this or any ad (how much did she sell half a
bosom to them for, I wonder, the other half gone as if it didn't
exist, the one-breasted woman—is there a market for that,
too: one-titted woman needed for profile shots, those without
perky firmness need not apply?). And then I see her full fron-
tal, I've stepped around the picture. I see the other breast
really is missing, radical mastectomy, the rubble of flesh left
is like gray-white clay, and there are lesions festering on the
side of her away from the camera, on her arm and rib cage
and the other thigh. The photographers work as if nothing is
the matter, adjusting lights, positioning the umbrella, taking
her chin between thumb and forefinger to get the desired tilt.
Of course she's ravaged, what did you expect? they say
matter-of-factly. Look here, and a crusted hole is where her
other eye should be. My breath comes in short and catches in
my throat. I close my eyes, afraid one might get loose if I
don't, and the magazine slides off my lap. Every picture is
going to be like that—whatever isn't showing is diseased,
ravaged, as if you took a fork to putty.
    Hours later: "You can see him now." As if they'd soaked
him in lemon juice and just now had decided to hold him up

to a hot light. We are led down white and green corridors. Grandma Matty is with us, must have been in the waiting room for some time, too, though I don't remember that, and she keeps saying, "He'll be fine, he'll be fine," a statement of belief and prayer. Mama lights a cigarette which a nurse says she has to put out. Mama grinds it into a litter of tobacco and paper scraps against a wall. The nurse sweeps it into her hand with a three-by-five card.

Doorways are open I can't look into. When I do it seems people sit around the tilted beds as if the person swaddled there is going to bless them or disintegrate entirely. They look afraid of either event.

Outside Daddy's room the doctor says, "I should explain what we've done," and he talks very quietly, very calmly, to Mama and Matty. I could listen but I don't—don't want to know the technical things they've done. I'll see for myself soon enough, and to know ahead of time just gives my imagination time to roam, to picture things far more awful than they probably are. The doctor gestures with his hand high up on his arm and the color goes out of Mama's face like dropping mercury. Matty pulls her breath in hard and nods. Mama sits in a chair in the corridor and her shoulders collapse. Matty's hands massage the base of Mama's neck. I haven't heard a thing. There's a buzzing in my ears loud enough to drown out speech. I look at the doctor, at Matty, at Mama. They must be lip-syncing and the sound track is shut off. There's only the hum in my head and a fluorescent green wash over everything. It's numbing to find myself in a hospital corridor with my mother and grandmother.

Daddy's room is semi-private. We're ushered past a screened-off bed around which I see a nurse's white hose and white squeegee shoes and other feet in street shoes, shuffling foot to foot or rocking back and forth. Feet in waiting.

"Hey there." Daddy's voice has the barely-there weak cheeriness of someone who's really not prepared for company, as if he needs to consult notes and is stalling for time. His face is the frightened green of blanched peas and they've got an oxygen clip on his nose. His late-afternoon stubble seems longer than usual. His eyes are a watery brown, river water with pink blood in it. His hair is mussed. Daddy, who's always had a comb with him on the tractor and would occasionally remove his cap to work his hair into neat rows again, as delineated as furrowed corn, now has a rooster tail coiling up from the pillow and another tuft roiled near his temple. The first thing I do is comb his hair. "Good as new, Daddy."

"Almost," he says.

Mama and Matty have both pulled up chairs. There's a doctor at the foot of the bed holding a clipboard, and the nurse with him pulls the curtain around us. The doctor starts to say something to Daddy and catches a look from Matty's eyes and then doesn't say anything. Mama and Matty are just looking at Daddy. I'm looking, too, but only at his face. It's Daddy's face, even with the oddities of stubble (he even shaved on Saturdays) and the mussed hair and the nose clip, as if he were ready to go swimming.

"I never believed 'em," Daddy says and tries to keep talking, his lips moving, they tremble and quiver, but it's not even a mumble. Whatever they've got inside him, the anesthetic or whatever, has him bleary and speechless and nodding in and out of sleep.

Matty's moving her hand up and down his cheek as if to say, There, there.

Mama's got her mouth working as if to sob, big hunks of air she takes in and can't get rid of. Finally she explodes with, "You bastard!" and I'm not sure if she means the doctor or Daddy.

Daddy bites his lower lip and tries to think of what to say. He nods off and then comes to, but he's still off someplace even with his eyes open. Like his watery eyes are here but the rest of him is just receding and receding. "Cleaner than if a corn-picker got it," he offers, but the little bit of voice he's got breaks on the last two words and then he's sobbing, his

cheeks a floodplain of loose salt, and Matty wipes at the tears
and cradles his head. "You don't have to be brave," she says
and then he lets go, long whimpers as best he can, like there
isn't even strength for a full-out wail and Matty holds him, her
son-in-law. I'm just standing there, helplessly and stupidly
still holding his comb. Mama's kneeling, her face pressed to
his limp hand, the one without his wedding ring, the ring
itself on a little tray from where I picked up the comb. I see it
now, the fat band that used to be on the blunt ring finger of
his left hand, and with Mama muttering into the knuckles of
his right, "You bastard," over and over it finally hits me.

They took off his arm.

There's a massed winding of gauze and adhesive tape like
shoulder pads and a sort of splint with IV tubes running into
that, but everything just stops above where he should have an
elbow.

They took off my daddy's arm.

The nurse and doctor sort of back out of our enclosure,
quiet and sheepish like they know Mama and me are on to
them. I'm going to follow them. I'm going to demand his arm.
Where have you got my daddy's arm? I'll ask. You put it
back. It's not yours.

I find myself sitting on the floor next to his bed, in a corner
with my face on the cool green cinder block. Mint. I feel
weak. I don't remember getting on the floor or placing cheek
to concrete or curling knees to chest and chin to knees and
hands to ankles. There was that moment when I was next to
Daddy, both of us sick and semi-conscious and then I wondered if I should sit on his bed. Would any more weight make
him uncomfortable? And then the room seemed terribly hot
and my neck was sweating and my head was light and I had to
sit down someplace and then I was in the corner, curled and
crying. It seems like a long time later.

"He should rest," the nurse says. She doesn't seem to have
a nose, just two nostrils set below large blue, sympathetic,
knowing eyes, eyes I'd like to slice right open, if only I could

stand up without swaying. The razor blade held aloft, How do *you* like it, Miss Know-It-All-He-Should-Rest?

And then I'm in the car with Matty, Mama sitting in the back seat. "We'll drive back and get your car when we see him this evening," Matty says over her shoulder. Mama nods.

Matty says to the boys at home, "We're all eating dinner at my house." She takes Mama and the boys in her car, Mia and I follow in mine. Mia doesn't say anything when I tell her. "What can I say?" she says. "Something," I tell her. "Anything at all." She takes my hand in the car and holds it in her lap. I pull it away. "I'm driving," I tell her.

Luther Kraike hugs everyone badly, figuring this is the thing to do though he doesn't know how to go about it. He even hugs Mia, wondering who she is. Luther is my grandmother's lover. He's large, with wiry black arms and receding hair, a flat face given to great tenderness and cruelty. He's in his late fifties and is just starting to show a gut. My first thought when he hugs me is why is this bastard so healthy? In the crush I feel his arms around me, both of them, and when he lets go, my own arms still feel the strength of his. I hold up my arms to remind myself they're still there. Seeing everyone with two arms is suddenly strange, as if we were freaks of nature to have turned out like this. Look here—the elbow is pointed and the forearm oblong. Downy hairs cover it topside and there are creamy green veins visible on the underside. The hand is hand-shaped, as it should be, and grows from the nub of wrist like a mobile map of Wisconsin. The fingers bend, the knuckles apelike, or maybe the apes' hands I've seen at the zoo look remarkably human. Whatever, there it is—my hands, left and right, the palms marked with lines as if they were aerial photographs of a many-rivered land. I marvel at the engineering of my own arm. All the places it can bend and twitch. The muscles rise and fall as if alive in their own right. And I've got two of them, a goddamned matched set: Incredible!

So how in hell is it that Daddy's only got the one?

Matty takes the boys aside and in a hushed whisper ex-
plains to them what the doctor did. She ladles out a bacon
and potato soup for all of us and the way she gets us to bustle
around—Luther, get an extra chair there for Mia, Scott, set a
place for her, too, you know where the bowls are. It's not like
you've never visited me, everyone pulls their weight, I expect
you two to help with the dishes—you can tell she doesn't
want us thinking—Amanda, pass the bread, Tommy, I need
you to pour the milk, who's going to want coffee?—but we eat
with faces down, the pot roast and the cooked carrots and
small onions and the radishes and Cheddar cubes and scal-
lions on the salad going into our mouths mechanically.
Mama's the worst, packing her mouth as if it were a suitcase,
more clothes than room. Matty says, Amanda! Mama looks
up, her cheeks bulging, her eyes wet with tears.

Enough! Matty says. He's going to be fine.

"Hell," Luther says, pushing his chair away and methodi-
cally lighting a pipe with an old-fashioned Zippo lighter (he
keeps fluid and flints in the glove compartment of his truck
the same way Mama keeps a bottle in the dead Chevy), "you'd
think he died."

"Luther!" Matty says and the boys are crying now, too.

"I just meant people talk more after a funeral, and it's not
like this is like that."

"Shut up!" Mama screams. "Shut up! Shut up! Shut up!"
She's half-risen and posed like an animal, her knuckles on
the table. When she sinks back to her chair in the frozen
silence that follows it's like she's got nothing left inside her.
Mama's just an empty raw shell, muttering "the bastard, the
bastard" like Daddy did something mean to her on purpose,
and all she can do is clutch her hair with ragged hands.

It's then I abandon them. I could stay any length of time,
wait till the trees bud out, witness any number of daily humil-
iations and accommodations, but I'm already going away. I
slide my spoon down next to the half-consumed soup (the pot
roast I've reduced to stringy clumps and picked over those

like rags) and I wipe my mouth. I nod to Mia and she gets up, too. We're at the door before anyone reacts.

Dorie! Dorie! It's Matty calling me. Mama is motionless. Anything could happen now—the house catch fire, a tornado blow in from the horizon, Indians gallop up the driveway with flaming arrows, and Mama would sit wild-eyed, her hands abstractedly playing with random curls of hair.

I'm fueled by the disgust in my stomach that feels like a cramp and the Mustang's door opens with a reassuring click and thuds shut even more reassuringly. I'm inside now and the wheels spin out gravel as we churn backward up the drive and Mia's pushing her clipped hair back with a sigh like she's glad that's over with, and it's not till we're past our house, too, that she asks me where we're going.

There's that party tonight. The one at Pankow's that Netley mentioned. It's a weekly thing.

Dorie, you're not serious?

I hit the accelerator. We gather speed and glide. Over rises the wheels hug ground, but the car itself seems to rise into space. Down slopes the car and our bodies settle. We take whole fields at a clip, the brown diarrhea of earth I love and loathe.

Dorie, we can't—

Shut up!

You sound just like your moth—

And I'm flailing at her, the wheel forgotten, the wild scramble. Just let me get to her eyes, pull the skin away from underneath, tissue and cover-up cream for the purply circles curling under my nails like stripped paint. Mia's screaming and she's scrunched her eyes, her whole body shrunk and gone away in terror and I look to see the telephone pole looming, we're riding the ditch and I pull the wheel hard across me and there's the groaning muffled throw of gravel and shredding turf and the sing of the tire mounts turned to their extreme and the pole—I can see every knothole on it, the tar-slathered base, the texture of the grain—seems to take one step sideways and we're past it, one set of tires still off the road and the car anxious to kiss death again, or at least brush shoulders with it.

I set the parking brake, the road dust-clouded behind us, my hands still tight to the wheel as if I were squeezing a rope or had just bent one of the rungs of the water tower catwalk. My breath comes and goes in short, terrified gasps. Mia has a stain down both pant legs.

She pries one hand off the steering wheel, then the other. Just what in hell do you think you're doing? she asks. Here, have some of this. She quiets me with the nipple of the boda, which I suck hungrily. The wine is red and hot and flat. It burns all the way down, my throat feels scalded. I can't get enough.

Mia drinks deep, too. All right, she says, screwing on the cap and tossing the flask on the backseat, we're crazy but we're ready.

10

PANKOW'S IS A MUDDY BACK FIELD on School Road cut with a
double-rutted secondary road that rises into a woods on one
side and on the other side is the Pankow house on Highway
M. School Road is a side road only poachers and teenagers
have call to use. The poachers come for geese and to jack-
light deer. There's a slime-covered pond opposite Pankow's
field that's ideal for October fowl and deer coming up from the
river. The land's low here, a mile from the river, and even in
early June the earth's wet and smells of something heated.
Right now it smells of beer. They've got a couple of kegs up
the rise a little way and cars are parked on both shoulders, so
the road's only one car-width open, each car headed away
from where it came, a chaotic used-car lot, and judging from
the number this is going to be a good one. Twenty cars already and it's early.

"What about my pants?" Mia says.

"It's dark, who's going to see?"

"Only everybody."

"Since when did you worry about everybody?"

Netley's president of the keg. He beams with ownership,
wants to let everyone know these squat aluminum beauties are
his alone. "If they knew at Buss' they'd kill me," he's saying.
"Kill me first and then fire me." He's wearing his shirttails
out and his sleeves rolled up. The cuffs hang loose about his
fish-belly biceps. Even in the dark you can see the greasy
shine of his face, the buttons of pimples as prominent as stop

signs. He grabs my elbow as I'm plucking two plastic cups from the stack.

"You made it," he says. "I knew you would," as if he's personally responsible. "Hey, everyone!" he calls out and my hatred of pustule-ridden Kevin Netley hardens to a solid nut beneath my sternum. "Everyone! Dorie's back, like I told you."

I expect them to line up for a cheer. Everyone so brave and friendly with three beers inside them and the fourth in their hands, twelve-ounce cups they slosh on their tennis shoes and each other's back pockets. I introduce Mia around, she's clearly bored but smiles anyway, practiced as she is, some of the other girls catch that vibe, can tell she's older and resent her, resent me for bringing her, for being here myself after being away. But everyone acts like the annual's just come out when even long hate gets written down as Good Luck, Remember and Best Wishes.

I say, Yeah, Chicago's a blast, a lot and, The lake's beautiful, in the winter it crashes like the ocean, like they've never driven over to Two Rivers or Manitowoc to see Michigan for themselves, and Yeah, everything's fine at home but it's a drag, we just came up for a visit, Mia's leaving tomorrow (smile like you own the whole world, Mia, thank you) and maybe me, too. No, I've got a job, good money, I just answer the phone and tell people Harrison—that's my boss, he's English—is out for the day, can I take a message. It's no big deal but I've got to look good every day, no jeans, you know, yeah, this haircut was a whim, do you like it? I have to figure out a way to get it past Harrison, he's very proper, he's going to freak when he sees these spikes. Maybe I can just sort of tease it over, what do you think? Of sure, everything's expensive, but that's Chicago, right? Of course you can come on down, I'll give you my address later, it's on Michigan Avenue, twenty-third floor with a balcony, beautiful, sure, talk to you later, yeah, nice to see you, let me just get a refill here—

And Mia whispers to me in singsong, "Boring," while we're

having our beer poured for us by one of the old rooftop crew who can't figure out what to say past a stumbling, "Shit, you look good, except for that hair," and the hollow laugh, like he's realized he's just blown his chance at getting me alone later.

"It certainly is," I tell her, "and I don't care. I'm not going to have to think about anything, not my goddamn family or anything."

And I sit on the hood of the car, away from everyone, and Mia ends up sitting inside, disgusted, smoking a joint and sullenly drinking beer, and I wait for them to come to me now, those who want, the boys cruising like sharks, come to admire my leather flight jacket, borrowed from Mia, but really with their noses atwang with the scent of citified meat.

"She's just gonna sit in there?" Bob Baumerhaut says, his wide nose and insolent eyes pressed against the window like Mia's an exotic exhibit at the zoo. Careful, boy, don't put your hand inside or you're likely to lose it.

"She does what she wants," I tell him.

"And I does what I wants," he says, and pulls on the door handle, which he expects to be open since nobody here ever locks theirs unless their car stereo's a good one. "Hey," he says, his fist pounding the window glass. "Open up. I wanna talk with youse."

Mia extends her finger. Bob stares dumbly and then he's got his pants open and his white briefs pulled down and he's shaking himself at her like he possesses an obscene Slinky. "I wanna talk with youse," he says again. "Hey," he says, on his knees now, his chin on the window ledge. "Just talk. Inna woods." Mia blows him a kiss from her middle finger. Bob catches the kiss with his moon and then walks away, tucking everything back into place.

They're bringing me beers now, supplicants with libations. I'm holding court. The one who went away. The one who didn't keep it and went away. She's back. Dorie's back. The girls say it with dismissal, a complaint, touch their own hair in comparison. The boys say it with the optimistic fragile cocksureness of possibility, patting their stomachs to remind themselves they've got tone.

And there's this obviously older, obviously bored dark-haired woman with the milk-white skin with me, she's the one who must've taught me the slightly punked-out look, not yet seen in these parts. That chunky dark one looks like she's really into it, probably has been for some time, does hard drugs, her skin like a milk shake. So that's where Dorie's headed. This is what they tell themselves, full of envy and awe and aloof superiority, even as they come to see the dream up close.

The beer is brackish and cold, the carbonation chewing my tongue, ah! I'm standing on the car's hood now. I think it's time to make a speech. I want to start with, "We're not in Kansas anymore," but they wouldn't catch that. They'd say to themselves, She's drunk, we've never been in Kansas.

It's no fun explaining a joke no one's going to get anyway.

So I don't say anything. Smart girl. Keep your mouth shut and your eyes open. Observe from the pinnacle, feel the heat of the car coming up through your feet. Netley comes by and tugs on my pants. "What are you doing up there?"

"Watching."

He climbs up too. Puts his hands on my shoulders for balance.

"What do you see?"

"Nothing."

He's looking over my shoulder, tries the extra step closer for an embrace, a hug from behind, and over my shoulder I say, "You get any closer, Kevin, and you'll be taking your balls home in a sack."

He waits an extra minute to show what I said isn't connected to what he does. Then he says, "This is stupid," and jumps down.

It's like King of the Mountain. Two or three guys lean against the Mustang in poses of nonchalance, talking loud about cars they're taking apart, or deer they've shot or tracked, or who bench-presses the most, and every so often one climbs on the hood for a pitch. Subtle things. "I've always admired your ass, Dorie, it's too bad you went away before I could tell you." "Bet you're hungry for real meat after all them city fags." "Wimps is more like it," Charlie Moore on the ground says. He's waiting his turn but figures to start the assault early.

Larry Fields wants me in Minneapolis. Mia Zolkauer wants me in Milwaukee. Tweed wants to roll with me among open tubes of paint, the ultimate finger painting. Smeared colors and a blonde all the way through rubbing against his coiled belly hairs—true art. Daddy's got one arm and Mama's got a dead Chevy for long drives to nowhere. Why am I on the hood of a blue Mustang listening to boys with tongues lolling from their mouths?

Because I want to. And I don't want to. I shiver all over and it's not the cold. My hands and shoulders and face are chilled, but I'm hot where it's important. Talk dirty, you bastards. Three more beers—I look at the garland of discarded cups around the car, the litter of attempted courage—three more beers and I'll want to be fucked by every one of you. Want to feel two male arms around me, callused hands cupping my ass. I'll want to be fucked with your fists. Scream into the woods and night sky, and heads will snap back with the knowledge, that's Dorie, can you believe the abandon?

The legend lives on.

Only I want Calvin to see me first. Calvin and Mia, to show them something. If I could I'd gather around everyone who wants me, tell them, Watch this, and ride faceless boy after faceless boy until they got the message: nobody fucks with me, but I can fuck with you. *Capisce?* Calvin for starters, though. Through him I'm tied to this time and place. I could not think about it, but I do. Tough shit, Dorie, you should have used something. Up till then I might have even said, But I loved you, but that would have been desperation and he would have laughed. Hey, I'm sorry, and he was already backing off, Don't shoot, babe, hey, it's nothing, just pop the bun out of the oven. And I did, only I had lots of time to think about that bun in there first. They say you can't think of it like that, but I did. So Calvin has to see me now and know nobody gets away clean. I want his heart to twist to see me now, better than ever, and with this older friend, the mystery woman, and just what is it that we're up to, so apart from everyone, so smug and self-contained. Let him stew in that awhile.

Lois Hasselbean and Tina March come across the road, beers in hand. Girls travel in pairs like this: Lois, stout of body and bland of face, Tina quite pretty, though her makeup's always too thick, you can see the line on her jaw where it stops, and she snaps gum like a cow chews cud. They want two of the sharks. Any two. If they don't ask now, when it gets later there'll be just the grabbing and pushing away. You start early, you can pretend it's been social, too: You have an *understanding* with the boy. You have a true connection. You're not just cheap.

I bend down to Lois, who keeps tabs on everyone, as if she's marked them all with a colored pin to follow their progress (it's what keeps her well liked, her wellspring of information, that and that she's a purse-holder for Tina or whoever has her along, the designated rescuer from the overzealous: "I can't, Tony. Lois is waiting").

"Where's Calvin?" I ask her, not like I really need to know but I'm curious.

"He's liable to be along," she says. Her voice goes to a whisper. I lean in close enough to see the hairs on her upper lip. "He's trying to be responsible."

"Calvin responsible? Why?"

"You'll see when they get here." Lois's bland cruel smile, full of almost-witnessed evil. I want to smack her good-humored face. Let me tell you about evil, I want to tell her. Let me tell you about Doyle and the things I do every day. If I could I'd show you my chest cavity, show you the hollowed-out place where my heart used to be. See? That little bitty cinder there. But them? Who's them, Lois?

"Oh, that's right. You being gone and all." And sure enough, Tina unslings her shoulder bag and hands it to Lois, the waiting second, and after a stop at the keg for fresh-frothed cups Tina and Randy Kreppl go arm-in-arm into the stinking woods, Lois taking it all in.

"So Calvin and who, Lois?"

Lois shifts Tina's purse so it and hers hang together. A runner, a carrier of provisions. I see Lois in the Army after graduation, feeling good in a uniform, directing traffic or becoming a radio operator.

"Who do you think, Dorie?"

Of course. Grade school addition. Subtract Dorie. You can't add Wendy, Wendy's already taken. So add Bonnie, the other girl who used to run around, though not so much as Wendy or Dorie. Or if not Bonnie, then anyone. At any rate, a woman's sexual parts. Someone stupid enough to go for it. And when they show up, holding hands (of course, of course), Calvin in baggy Lee jeans and pointed boots and a plaid sport shirt and Levi's jean jacket, Bonnie in a billowing blue dress and clogs and knee socks and Calvin's letter jacket (football and wrestling until he started smoking sophomore year—he tried giving me the jacket once, but I said, What is this, a joke?). Of course she's monstrously huge, always was big-boned, his jacket actually fits her, but the dress, large as it is, is distended, stretched to the limits of the cotton fabric, canteloupe breasts splayed to either side of her swollen belly, and I think, with frightening envy, with hate, with relief, with longing, with disgust, with every contradictory emotion I can imagine, That could have been me.

I get down to meet them. They're getting married two weeks after graduation. Calvin has work lined up at Buss' Foods in the meat department. Been working there weekends and after school all winter. He's learned responsibility. He's going to do right by Bonnie. Their child should be born about then. Bonnie's only going to have a little beer. "The baby," she says, patting the watermelon, having to reach to get anywhere close to her navel. The good father, Calvin's already on his way to getting quietly smashed. He's all grins, waiting for his chance to say something, anything.

"How's Wendy?" I ask. We'd been something of a group, getting drunk with the boys and laughing as we spilled beer down our chins. Or just the three of us, drinking Mama's Teacher's (or the good stuff, Johnny Walker) out of coffee mugs on the front stoop of an evening while waiting for it to get dark so we could do something else.

"She and Danny McCain split up. But the baby's due any day now. He says anyway he'll pay for it, but everyone knows he's on, what do they call it? Deferred enlistment." She grabs hold of Calvin's arm like she's hugging a pole. "I'm lucky Calvin's not like that. He's been terrific. Aren't you, honey?"

"Yep, sure," Calvin says, throwing back two-thirds of his beer in two long gulps. "Aaah!" he says. "Beer and my baby. Who'd think I'd get so peaceable?"

"Not me, Calvin."

"Oh, Dorie," Bonnie says. "That was like another lifetime to Calvin. Wasn't it, honey?"

They look welded together. They don't know anything, they're ignoring what they do know and they're so happy with that ignorance I want to throw up.

"Say," Calvin says. "I always wanted to tell you." He rubs his nose. "What was it? Shit, I forget." He pulls his arm out of Bonnie's grasp to hold her around the shoulders. I do one of those ass-on-the-car-hood-swing-your-legs-over numbers so there's a car width between us. All that metal.

"Who's your friend?"

"She's from Chicago."

"What is she, locked in there? She doesn't want to party?" He raps the window with his class ring. "Hey, you, you want to party?"

"Oh, Calvin," Bonnie says, her arms around his stomach in a stranglehold. "You want to party with everyone."

"What say you get us a beer," he says. "I could use one."

"He's certainly gallant, isn't he?" Bonnie says.

"Doctor says you can use the exercise." To me, "You know I go with her to the doctor's and everything."

"He does," Bonnie says, crossing the road for the beer. She walks penguin-fashion, as if everything were sheathed in ice.

Calvin leans on the car hood, his eyes very intense in the dark. Or maybe it's beer gloss. He looks serious with his high forehead and his brown hair combed back. I'm leaning on the car hood, too, and between us is Mia inside the car, like she's watching us at a drive-in. "What I was gonna say but didn't because of Bonnie was—well, hey, last summer. I told Bonnie we never did, it was just rumor, all that talk. I mean it's like that, isn't it? You could pretend it was just talk, couldn't you? Bonnie'd go crazy if you told her. It's water under the bridge and I like Bonnie. You won't mess it up, will you, Dorie?"

A little vacuum cleaner goes on inside me. Vvvvrup! All gone inside and yet sometimes I feel the little hands in there clinging.

"You're going already?" Bonnie's back with Calvin's cup, and I'm standing by the driver door, knocking on the window and Mia's reached over to open the door. A sweet hot odor billows out.

"Yeah, Dorie and her friend are hitting the road," Calvin says. "They got places to go, people to see."

"Oh, that's right," Bonnie says. "I heard about your father. I'm so sorry."

"What about her old man?"

"His arm, honey. Cancer." She turns to me. "They took it off, today, right? Sandy Falco works at Appleton Memorial as a candy striper. She told me."

"Oh, say. Tell 'im to hang in there for me."

Someone should tell my legs what to do. Somewhere between sitting and standing they're stuck. My feet try to remember where they've been. First the floppy steel of the hood. Then gravel and clumps of road weeds. A pebble directly under my corn. Tiny hands inside me scratching. Mia's still bent forward and tugs my wrist. Bonnie and Calvin wave, and then they're across the road to join the others. Mia tugs again and I'm back in the car, examining my arms like they're the only things I recognize as me.

Mia says, "You look like your rabbit died."

I'm looking at my knees. Then a rectangle of blue eyes and brown brow and the upper third of my nose in the rearview mirror. I'm made of pieces as separate as leaded glass.

"Ex-boyfriend?"

"Yeah."

"What can I say? Ex-anythings are usually scum."

I feel with my hand for the shift, ball and socket, and we're gone. Dust like a brown mist behind us. I'm shaking. Two and a half miles back on County Trunk Z Mia says, Pull over here. I do. We sit looking at each other. Mia's eyes are black and glassy. Her hand calmly rubs the small bone at the back of my neck. She is patient. She says it was only a stupid party, and I've been to stupid parties before, right? Mia says, Relax, kiddo, I have everything under control. She is all of one piece and touches me gently. All of one piece—blunt-cut hair topping her round moon face, the hairs dying on her nape, the smooth neck flowing into her alabaster thorax and under her open sweater the little strip of buttery stomach marshmallow soft curling over the waistband of her pants, her beaded sweater shrunk so her belly shows. Breast mounds as perfect as my own. Thick creamy thighs, a brief waterfall of legs. Everything connected, seamless. I never realized she was so short. A luscious milk-fleshed fire hydrant.

We spend a long time making up, and all the while it's

going in my head, This can't last, this can't last, and I want to laugh and do and then we're both crying, but for different reasons.

We're in one twin bed, me in flannel, Mia without clothes, cuddled behind me, a spoon. During the night she says, I love you. I am a stone in her arms. What are you thinking? she asks. I say, I'm wondering what Ramona would say. And what would she say? Mia asks. Fuck you, I say. Fuck you is what she'd say. I say it again and roll away crying. Fuck you.

We don't make a fire and in the morning we can see our breath. The grass is crunchy with frost, the morning light orange. After coffee and toast I drive her to the Greyhound station.

"I may be awhile," I tell her.

She says, "Take as long as he needs," and kisses my cheek. "I know you didn't mean it," she says. "I know you just need some time."

Driving home, I watch the sun turn gray, that sad light that colors Sunday mornings in March. There's no one at the house; they must've stayed at Matty's, the beds are unslept in and they won't be back till after church. I make myself a second breakfast, grate potatoes for pancakes, pour juice, heat bacon, take out marmalade and eat with a good appetite. I give Mia and me two years, tops. It's good to have things decided that way. In the meantime we will have the wonderful and the awful in unequal portions. As does everyone.

11

WITH MIA GONE and my head clear I'm able to think or not think in the cold dark of early evening and it's all the same. I find myself doing more around the house—laundry, meals, sweeping—and strangely I don't mind. There is a small explosion for my leaving so abruptly at dinner, but I don't give details, I just say, "I couldn't stand it, I had to get out," and after some exasperation on Mama's and Matty's part the whole incident slides away, excused.

Now Mama walks around like someone drained the blood out of her. Daddy's working hard at passing off his missing limb, as if God had played a little trick on him and He's going to return it directly. The doctor says it's one of the phases amputees go through. Another is disbelief and crying. Belief and disbelief alternate. He says it's important he shows us he can take it—that he can talk about it with a grin. Early on he can't control himself. "It's just an arm," he says. "It's not like they took off, oh, I don't know, my head," and then he bursts into tears again, and Mama holds his remaining hand—even that no longer looks real, it's a plastic prop they've given her to hold—"Here, ma'am, this is a hook for you to remember it by." And Matty cradles him, as if he were a child with measles. Scott had the measles once and one of the sores was right on the head of his penis. Every time he had to go—and Mama kept him pumped full of liquids, ginger ale and 7-Up —he screamed and then whimpered like a dog left out in a blizzard. Matty holds Daddy like Mama held Scott, a sack of tears with no shape; every so often the fabric of his back shudders and a new wave of sobs breaks out of him.

"M-m-m-m-y-my-my a-a-a-ar-ar-a-armmm," he says. He sounds bewildered and weak, as if he's trying to recover from a blow to his groin that he never saw coming.

But after several days he gets better. "Sucking it up," Luther calls it. Acceptance, a doctor quietly tells Matty and Mama. Whatever.

We visit late mornings and evenings, Mama chain-smoking. At the hospital doors Mama puts the cigarette out with impatient stabs. We sit with our thighs on our hands and get comforted by Daddy. "They'll fix me up with a hook, no problem," he says. "Ugly as sin but functional. Tommy and Scott'll have to take up the slack, I suppose." They do. After chores Matty drives them in for the last hour of visiting. Daddy gives them the rundown on what needs doing the next day. It's too soon yet for Frank and Harm and Clete. Scott says, We won't need them anyway, the two of us are plenty. And you, too, Dad, he adds. Uh-huh, Daddy says. Then how come your grandmother has to drive you into town to see me? You're not old enough to drive yourselves. We would, Tommy says, but Matty won't let us. Shit, Scott says, we drive the pickup all day and the tractors, and they're plenty more dangerous than a car. Watch your mouth, Matty says. I sit on the end of the bed with my back to everyone and read Daddy's get-well cards.

It's hard to think of Daddy having any more family than what's right here. But there's lots. The other side, like marriage is an argument—the two sides lining up to throw stones. Some of Daddy's side even come to visit. Not for long and just one visit each, but they do pop in and sit a little while and look at us and try to be cheery and sympathetic, everything hollow, the usual comments and half-hearted embraces. Then they're gone again. Like life is just such a rush, and time away from anything they're supposed to be doing makes them anxious. Like on their way out they should pause

and wash their hands of us. After all, Daddy's gone over to
the other side.

Daddy has two brothers and a sister, all married, all with
kids. The sister's in Kenosha, a high school principal, the two
brothers have factory jobs, one's a millwright for Appleton
Coated, the other one's a forklift driver at the Neenah Foun-
dry. They have names, of course—Aunt Sharon, Uncle Steve
and Uncle Roy. But there's no connection, like everyone's
embarrassed to be related and pretty much put out in making
an effort at good cheer and breeziness, especially on holidays
or hospital visits when it's expected. I call them Daddy's sister, the one and the other one. If put to it, I could remember
the kids' names, but that's like trying to name what you get
every single time a cookie cutter hits rolled-out sugar dough.
Blond sameness.

Daddy's parents are in Florida, all wrinkled and tanned
like old sailors. They moved two years ago—had sold the
farm years ago to Daddy, since he was the only one interested
in staying on. And after fifteen or twenty years of town living,
Grandpa Brown fixing small engines as a way of keeping se-
nility off his street, Daddy had them paid back and they went.
"Our dream since we turned fifty," Grandma Brown would say
on the phone when we called. "And a little something's
always going wrong so your grandfather can fix it." Matty's
called them and they've sent flowers. On the card Grandpa
has dictated to the florist, "I'd tinker with you, Son, but they
don't make humans like they do small engines. Still, my heart
goes out to you."

But it's not that half I'm interested in. I'm not interested in
anyone, but reading the cards beats looking at Daddy, who's
well enough now to have his bed tilted so it looks like he's
tied to a wall. Uncle Fred and Aunt Mary stop in every day or
every other day, and there are cards from the rest—a little
forest of Hallmarks. Mama's brother and sisters, the word
given out by Matty, and so the deluge: a card from Matthew
and Kathy, who live in Maine, and a separate card from each

of their children, done in crayon; one from Isabel, who lives in Rochester, Minnesota, with her husband named Dean. They wish they could come, they will later in the spring. Rose sends a card from college and says she'll be down on the weekend. There'd be two cards more, but one's dead and one's just gone. He took off and nobody talks about him, or if they do I don't know about it.

I don't want to know about any of them (except the one who ran away, Frankie). Who wants to keep score for a game you're not playing, but the cards are all there, a little cemetery of scattered family. I look at each card like it's a dead leaf or a rock, turn it in my hands, even look at the tiny print on the back with the UPC symbol. Matthew and Kathy's is on recycled paper. Isabel's card cost the most—a dollar and a quarter. Fred sent a funny one. I can just about see their faces, but for the people I've not seen recently I don't bother. It's like these cards are those letters they leave on tables in historical homes so you can see how people lived at one time —how they wrote letters, communicated with each other. Artifacts from nobody I know.

"One week more," Daddy's saying. "They got me for one more week and then lots of what they call rehab time, but at least then I'll be home." To Matty he says, "Do you think you and Luther can spell Amanda with driving me back and forth once it gets to that?"

I sit with Mama and everyone those late evenings, nursing a diet cola and watching Mama sneak whiskey. She pours it into a coffee mug herself like it's sugar and adds coffee to that, holds the cup between her two hands, her hands on the table, as though it's the last thing she can possibly hold on to. The undersides of her eyes are puffing as if she spends all her time crying, which she doesn't. Her hair hangs like frayed rope. She bites her fingernails, chews them till they bleed, then puts an uneven layer of watery rose polish on the remnants.

"Aren't you a sight," I tell her.

She bites a nail that hasn't dried yet. She says, Shit, and wipes the goo off her lips and teeth with a tissue. Uses polish remover on that nail, wincing where it burns at the raw chew marks, then reapplies the polish as if anytime soon someone's going to ask her to hand-model cosmetics or jewelry or alcohol.

There's always alcohol. Thursday she's in the beached Chevy again, mid-morning to noon, her Teacher's and Southern Comfort and the Dixie cups lined up like various medicines she has to take, measured doses of each. I watch from the kitchen window until it's time for lunch and then I go out, pulling on the door handle. She has the window rolled down and her elbow on the frame. When the door opens her arm drops to her side, lifeless as a diseased limb.

"Mama, it's time to visit Daddy."

"Go ahead, I'm driving right here."

"You're on the passenger side, Mama."

"Excuse me. I'm riding. Right here. Someone else must be driving." She looks to her left. "Hmm. No one. I'm a passenger with no one. I could've *sworn* I was riding with someone." She looks at me with her sunglasses on, huge oval glasses with thick white rims, a different generation of sunglasses, Marilyn Monroe at the beach with a scarf and sunglasses. Mama's got the look and smile of an insect.

She says, "I wish the radio worked. Or maybe I should get a portable. Or even something that could play George Jones tapes. What do you think?"

"Are you going to be here all day, Mama, or what? You want me to fetch your lunch out here, too?"

"I just can't go to the hospital today, Dorie." She gets out of the car slowly, testing her legs. "After lunch I'll go to town for groceries. We need them, right? I've forgotten?" She pulls her unwashed hair into a tighter ponytail and redoes the rubber band. "A mother can't forget the groceries, can she? What would people think?" She reaches back for two Dixie cups and downs them one after another. "Good for you," she says.

We leave in separate cars after lunch, Mama lurching out in the Impala, thinking I'm on my way to the hospital, but I follow her instead. Once she sees me in the rearview she starts weaving intentionally, shoulder to shoulder—like any minute she's going to lose it completely—and then she straightens out and accelerates with a rattling of the clutch over the radar hill that falls away into the long curve into town. Topping the hill, I remember the nights I was here with Calvin. We parked against the fence, the bunker at our backs, the two towers, one shorter than the other, each with a conical dish (they are actually microwave relay towers, but that was radar to us), winking at us with their red lights.

Mama catches a shoulder on the curve and her wake is dust. Yellow sun and blue sky and brown hanging dust to plunge through. Driving after Mama. All of a sudden she's my age and I can deal with her.

She parks on Main Street in front of Erndt's. Goes in the door next to the store and up the stairs. Flowered wallpaper wilting off the walls and the banister's loose. We meet on the second-floor landing. She has trouble with her keys, keeps shaking them as if the right one's going to drop itself into her open palm. The hallway seems airless and we don't talk, as if we were on a submarine waiting for a chance to breathe. She lets us in, holds the door for me to enter first.

"Hardly worth your trouble," Mama says, but she's proud.

It's as I imagined it. Maybe larger. A scruffy wood floor streaked black with heel marks as if Mama and countless other women had been skidding and sliding to dance records, night after night. A linoleum-top kitchen table with chipped black-enamel legs. Plant cuttings, which die and get replaced, in jelly jars with too little water, new cuttings that never see dirt. A wooden chair and a twin bed with sheets that need changing. A blocky chunk of radio I remember listening to on winter mornings hoping the announcement of school closings would include Augsbury. Patterned sheets resewn as drapes on the two front windows, one of which is missing a shade. Mama's pathetic little room over the butcher shop.

"My secret life," Mama says, lighting a cigarette. "Only everyone knows. Though not your father, of course. Or at least to me he pretends he doesn't. I can never tell with your father how much he really doesn't know and how much he just swallows."

In the bathroom a pair of nylons and a white cocktail dress are hanging on a bar over the tub. The black pumps, one tilted into the other as if it were resting, are nestled next to the toilet.

"And what does everyone say, Mama?"

"What do you think everyone says? They suspect and talk about all the lewdnesses they wish they were guilty of themselves. I was marked as soon as I wanted a room of my own."

Mama sits on her chair. I stand by the window. "I'm everyone's bogeyman, Dorie. I steal children off the streets, lure little boys with candy, take husbands by the hand and lead them astray. I am the woman with the room in town." She turns to me. "Jesus, Dorie, if only."

Leeman's Café is across the street. They probably can see her from there, if she stands where I am and they're looking up.

"So what do you do, Mama?"

"Same as with the Chevy. Drink and dream of elsewhere."

"You could've gotten out."

"Could've gotten out she says! Could have gotten out! So easy for you to say, seventeen with your tits still warm and up high. Look, you think I wanted to marry a farmer? Spend my days washing cow flop out of pant cuffs? He was nice to me, your father. I was twenty, and my looks were already gone, and I was working at the canning company summers and the toy factory winters. I was drinking beer at shift's end until me and Meg Thiesen and Paula Brennan were falling off the bar stools. Did I know my belly was gonna sag two years out of high school? I was the Homecoming Queen, for God's sake. I petted with the captain of the football team, he had his hands between my legs. I had loads of future. I was going to be beautiful forever, and everyone would always want me."

Mama gets two glasses from a cupboard and pours Usher's for each of us. "Oh, and then you children! You really did wonders for my self-esteem. Fucked up my plumbing but good. Wonderful. You should see my veins. You know what we figured on? We figured to hit the Appleton bars, the good ones. We were underage, but they winked at that even then. We were going to marry lawyers from there—from the city of Appleton—hot stuff—or at least some executive from one of the paper companies. We had plans all right. Some nights we escaped clear to Fond du Lac. We didn't know any better. Men—they could run off. That was expected. Run off and maybe take a woman with them. But a girl going off by herself? Ridiculous. My own mother lamenting the boys going off, one after another. I was the oldest. I didn't realize you *could* leave."

Mama does her Usher's in a gulp, pours another. She stands next to the table, strikes a pose probably very much as she did when she had to give a speech in school.

"Then there's the two-to-ten shift, lots of reason there for going home to shower and change and drive to Appleton for maybe an hour of God knows what. I think we thought that after a man fucked us blind he'd offer to make us honest. I don't remember. I remember we kept driving over, though, until we finally got cynical about it—the almost-off-with-the-dress,-but-stop-right-there,-Mister,-I'm-not-that-kind-of-girl routine, though what other kind of girl could we be? And even after a while it was known we were the kind who would almost but then pout and say, *No!* And then one night I just said the hell with it. We were in separate cars and I pulled off onto the shoulder and Meg and Paula did the same, asking what was wrong, and we ended up in Augsbury that night and every night after that. You want a laugh? I didn't sleep with your father for four months, and by then he'd asked me to

marry him." She moves next to me at the window, dropping
her cigarette in the window track and lighting another. "I'm
still careful, Dorie. You think that's funny, don't you? Careful,
that's a laugh. I rent a room and everybody accuses me of
everything. That's ironic, isn't it? Isn't that what they'd call
ironic? That nothing, just nothing, nothing, nothing, ever
happens here?"

She sucks back another mouthful of Usher's. "You want to
know a thrill, an honest-to-God whooppee? Sometimes I take
all my clothes off, the dress and all, leave just the heels on,
and I prance. Sashay nude across the window, I figure *someone's* got to be looking. Let them know I've still got it. Even
strangers appreciate a naked woman. That's the spirit,
Amanda! Shows at two and four, matinees only, I still need
time to cook dinner. You can't feed a farmer TV dinners, can
you, they expect meat and potatoes. Mushroom gravy. Did you
know I've never made a gravy that didn't have lumps in it?
Those fucking flour balls always in there, they wouldn't break
up. Let me tell you something. Never make a dish to pass that
has gravy in it. Somebody sees a lump and you're branded for
life. But I have a life, don't I? I just have to get up the energy
to get out of the Chevy. I put on the nylons and that dress—
it's a nice dress. It shows off what figure I've still got. Can you
imagine me pretty? It takes some effort, doesn't it? You have
to squint a little. Blur me at the edges. Up here, though"—
Mama taps her head—"it's easy. I could have led lives if I
hadn't fallen into this one by default, you know. Default,
mind you, not my fault. Your father's a decent man, he's given
me more than what a lot of men would, Dorie. He's given
compassion, but he's kept me from my lives. And he's a bastard, too, because I don't get the lives except for when I
dream them here. He really is such a nice, nice bastard."

Mama waves her hand, like Daddy's just out the window
and she's gesturing at him, exhibit A. She sits down, sort of
folds herself onto the bed, leans forward and talks into her
glass like it's a microphone. "Bastard," she says. "Hear the

echo? All across America women are talking into their glasses. The great discovery that their husbands, through no fault of their own, through nobody's fault, honest, they just come out that way, are bastards." She puts the glass to her ear. "You can hear them. Little tiny voices saying *bastard* over and over. Like the ocean. Is that why seas are always *shes?*" Mama pours some Usher's in her ear. "I'm listening," she says. "Voice of America, come in." She puts her glass down. "Damn, am I clever. I'm so smart I just don't know what I'll do."

I'm by the window. Mama says, "Isn't it a nice view? An old friend. Like a man and his dog. Good boy. Sit. Dorie, tell the view to roll over. Tell it to fetch the paper. Ha. Tell it to sit up and beg. We're talking hind legs here. Ha. Watch it, it will. Sit up and beg."

It's raining now, one of those March rains that turns everything to gray mud. The buildings look like saggy tea bags, as if they've given up on standing and just want to lie down in the street and get rained on. Mama pulls the top sheet up so it covers the bed and lies down. "Amazing. A well-trained view. A view that's gone to obedience school. I come here and dance by myself to the music on the country radio station. I can prance and twirl, I can take my clothes off if I want, and I'm in a crowd, you see, and I'm the center of attention. When I get tired I just lie down here and close my eyes. Peaceful."

Mama has fish eyes, like when one of the boys pulls a fish from the water and even as it's flapping and struggling, probably wishing for arms to tug with, it knows it's a goner, its eyes wide with calm, not terror. Mama lies on her back with her hands folded on her stomach, her whiskey glass within easy reach on the floor. A goner if ever there was one.

Her breath is the heavy sigh before sleep. "Dorie," she says. "Dorie dreary quite contrary. Smarty pants and dancing ants." She giggles, then stops. "Let me tell you something, Dorie, it's easier than you think to give in. You keep that in mind, Doris Ann, that's one to ink your palm with." She turns on her side and drains her glass, avid, as if she were parched in a desert. Then she collapses back. "I'm going to sleep now," she says and closes her eyes. In minutes her jaw's slack and her mouth's open, not the way people sleep in ads, or the way children sleep, innocently as if waiting for God to take them. Mama sleeps ugly. She'll wake up with red blanket marks and creases in her cheeks. Her breath will be bad, her eyes water-heavy with a cracked red glaze, like badly fired pottery.

She used to be beautiful. I've seen pictures from before she entered high hagdom. A face longer than mine, her whole body generally longer—the kind of prettiness you see in the "Young Mrs." section of a Sears catalog. The kind of prettiness that gets severe as it ages, and when it gets puffy it gets grotesque. I think of what it's going to be like for her when things are back to normal, whatever normal means anymore. I think of Daddy touching her. Can she bear to have her flanks stroked, her breasts fondled, with his praying mantis hand? I think of parallel steel framing my own nipple. Her husband's hand as machine. Made love to by a machine—a thought that thrills and sickens me. And the other men? Surely there have been, or surely there will be, other men? I'm sure she's done more than she'll ever admit to, times from before Daddy, maybe even after, that she treasures in this room alone. Past and future. In the present she snores, mumbles, "No." She's lying, because how could she not about something like that? I have a cigarette, watching her. Maybe she really hasn't but knows already that she will. Mama is discreet. She could pluck them like dead blossoms, men from out of town with two strong arms who'll cease to exist for her once they leave this room. Her other life. Her mistaken belief in the life I don't have, either. And then there'll be more talk, but deflected. After all, her husband's only got the one arm. Yes, but still—

I'm going to have to call Doyle. I hate him so much I had

Mia call him Monday to tell him I had a family emergency and would be back by week's end. I pour myself a good amount of Mama's Usher's and leave her there sleeping. Mama's getaway. I'd laugh, but she's my mother. Until they took Daddy's arm away I wouldn't have thought that would be reason enough for not laughing, but now I know better.

I'm stopped by Clayton Jones at the pay phone in front of the bowling alley. "Yo, punk," he says and gets out of his car. He looks like a Roman emperor with a garland of orange hair. Or a bald Ralph Cramden. The Pillsbury Dough Boy in a khaki and forest-green cop suit. "What you got there?" He takes the jelly jar away from me. He sniffs and has a sip, rolls it over his tongue like a connoisseur.

"Open liquor's against the law," he says. He takes out his book and in the midst of writing me up takes two good looks at me. The first time down the way men take you in, discarding clothing as needed, the second time with recognition. "You're Leotis and Amanda Brown's kid, aren't you? I heard about your father." He puts the book away. "Bad business. Dorothy, isn't it? Doris? The eldest? I didn't recognize you with your hair cut short. You look like one of those city punks with the lawn mower haircuts. You actually like to wear your hair ugly like that?" I shrug. Best not to give Clayton lip directly. "Look, I'm gonna do you a favor on account of your dad." He pours the liquor over a bush. "Don't let me catch you like that again."

We're both getting wet in the rain, only Clayton has his little hat on so he's immune to the elements. He tousles my head. "And comb that mess. You used to be pretty." He's very pleased with himself. For five minutes he's become my uncle. He's gotten to play the hard-ass and the understanding cop all in one shot. If he touches me again I'll knee him like I did Doyle.

Getting into his car, Jones becomes the community leader. He frowns. "Sorry about your dad," he says and then his wipers start.

My shoulders are soaked and cold. I call the hotel collect, person to person to Doyle and he says, Uh, yeah, okay, I'll accept the charges, and when I come on he says, This is coming off your check, so you better explain yourself in a hurry.

"I'm going to be another week or two, Doyle."

"Fine, fine, dearest Dorie, but I can't guarantee your job when you get back. We've been busy, but it's not like we can't get along without you."

"Yeah, well, they just took off my father's arm so tell me about it, asshole."

"His whole fucking arm? Really? Hey, I'm truly very sor—" but I've already hung up on him. There's a third of a bottle of Usher's and Mama's still asleep and I take that with me and drive home stinking wet, getting warmer with each slug straight from the bottle.

Only I don't go directly home. I show up at Matty's wet and drunk and she says, "What, have you been raising hell in broad daylight? Just because you're old enough you think it's all right?" I shake my head and look about to lose it and she says, "You take a warm shower and then we'll talk."

I've got the bottle still in my hands. She takes it from me and starts toweling off my head. I wrench away. "What do you know about anything, Granny? You're just a bewildered old fart."

Her hand comes out of nowhere and then she's picking me off the floor. "A lot more than you think," she says gently. "You've got a head screwed onto that body, Dorie. Don't forget that." She gets me sitting in a chair and pulls back my shirt to rub my neck and shoulders and forehead with a warm washcloth. She scrubs and talks and scrubs. "This won't do for a real shower. When you get home I want you to take one. I'll follow you in my car to make sure you get home. You're in a world of hurt, young lady, and you don't even know it yet. Your father's going to be fine, and that's not just me saying so. There'll be adjustments, sure, but God watches after his own and if there's anyone God's going to look after it's Leotis."

She goes on like that, well meaning, while I look around her kitchen. The kitchen of someone who expects to be someplace a long time. Broken in, the lunch dishes washed already, a pot roast simmering on the gas stove, three kinds of tea in glass jars alongside the toaster, potted plants hanging from window baskets and arranged around the sink. Not just cuttings but real plants—plants that have flowered and been trimmed and repotted as needed and had the dead leaves pulled off and been sprayed or washed when insects threatened. All this greenery and I don't know any names. Matty can probably tell stories about each plant as if it deserved its own history. I hate the comfort she takes in her life. Oh, sure, when I was thirteen her husband, Ben, died, that was cancer, too, but she keeps talking, then and now, as if God's got this neat plan and even the grotesque fits in one way or another. It's how she can slap me and then pick me up and smug me off with a damp washcloth as if I were still thirteen. I cried a lot then, cried till my cheeks were streaked red, and I didn't even know quite what I was crying over. Grandpa Ben had seemed very much like Mama, bitter and a drinker, only the tiniest bit pleasant at odd times, and yet I was crying horribly, crying as I am now, and I don't even know why I should be, but my head's back and the sobs are rushing out and Matty's going, "Cry, Dorie, let it all out," as if I had something in me pushing the salt. It feels good crying and I don't want to stop, but eventually my energy for it lapses or something inside peters away, and she takes me to the living room couch and has me lie down and says, "When you're better we'll drive home, okay?" and she leaves me alone.

I hear her moving around the kitchen, hear the teakettle whistling, hear the rain still drumming at the window glass, hear it soaking through the trees just outside, I can even hear Matty sing-mumbling to herself a song one of my uncles taught us. It was called "The Dutchman" and it's about this old man who goes blind and how his wife, Margaret, still loves him and together they remember when they were young. I always liked the song, it's pretty. At Ben's funeral my aunt Isabel got everyone to sing it. Matty especially liked it, her eyes were shiny bright when she sang the chorus: "Let us go to the banks of the ocean, where the walls rise above the Zuider Zee. Long ago I used to be a young man, and dear Margaret remembers that for me." It was always her song, and I fall asleep hearing Matty hum it.

I want to wake up finding everything different, but it's only later in the day. Matty comes in with tea and says, "It's probably best you don't visit your father tonight. I'll tell him you're not feeling well," and I say, "Yes, please tell him," and I realize I don't particularly care to visit him in the hospital or anywhere else ever again.

I sip tea with my legs folded on the couch until Matty says, "We should be going."

She sees me into the drive and honks, heading toward Appleton. No one's home yet, and in Mama and Daddy's room, the only one with a shower and a full mirror by the wardrobe, I strip just to remind myself of what I look like. My clothes are still damp and I hang everything from hooks Daddy fixed to the wall, just like in the mudroom. In the silver I'm all there, shoulders narrowing into waist, the packed tiny swell of belly, I touch myself, the blond pubic wedge, the athletic legs (why not those long and perfectly fleshed creations in the swimsuit ads? I wonder, why did I have to come out sculpted short, sort of pretty but of insufficient length?). I shower and towel off in front of the mirror again, my wet spikes of hair looking surprised but menacing. I think of Wendy and Bonnie, the dull lank hair of their motherhood, their bellies distended as if someone had played a cruel joke on them while they slept, but upon waking, they smiled and accepted this trick, too. I towel myself with vigorous abruptness.

Sitting on Mama and Daddy's bed to dress, the pulled-back

sheets not quite smooth on my ass (maybe I lodged in Mama's belly starting here—the long road of darkness—what, maybe four inches? two? Or was it elsewhere—a parked car, or deliciously over a kitchen table, or on earth and leaves under stars—too bad parents never tell you that sort of thing), I see the door's been cracked while I showered and two wide eyes, piled vertically, with matching half-mouths half-open, gasp silent awe. I stand up slowly, let them drink me in. I can imagine what they'll say and do when they're alone and it'll drive them crazy with guilt knowing it was their sister, and then the tennis shoe on the bed that I was about to put on smacks into the door, and when I yank it open they've already fallen all over themselves and clattered down the hall and pell-melled it outside, their chests choking with triumph and terror.

If only everyone else were so easy.

A week goes by. Mia calls every evening and I give her my half of the week's monotony: I sleep late for no reason, wake as if these March days were fixed on me with midsummer heat, and then lie in bed contemplating the ritual of each day—the shower, the breakfast that's more nearly lunch, lolling about afternoons (Mama in her Chevy or in her rented room, a bottle moved from one shelf to another), my late-afternoon drive in the Mustang, shooting over country roads that rise and drop and go straight out as if they were themselves alive, finally turning for home and supper. And then a committee of us, Scott and Tommy and Mama and myself, Matty, too, in some combination based on who can stomach the visit again and whose guilt over not having gone the day before is strongest. Matty always goes, shows up in her own car bearing gifts—Louis L'Amour paperback Westerns, a fresh pajama top, oranges. I remember when Matty's son Rupert and husband, Ben, were dying—Grandpa Ben, of cancer, and Rupert, of God-knows-what—it was said she couldn't find it in herself to visit them much, that instead she was out and about with Porter Atwood. I wonder if her attention to Daddy this time is atonement.

And after the visit and some beer or wine or whiskey or whatever I drink by myself in the bunkhouse (Mama has the day shift, I have the night), I just lie down and wait for that call. Long distance. Outside and away, like a baseball pitch you watch the whole time it's coming at you. I wait for that. Tommy knocks and announces, "It's Milwaukee," as if the whole city is calling me. After my dull repetition of the day it's like her calling *is* the whole city. I find myself hungry and nodding, listening to her as she tells me about real days and nights, events—classes, intrigue, men, men calling—Larry, of course, but also that guy from Chicago, and the professor, and Doyle and she goes on and on, her litany making me breathless, and she finishes with, Come home soon, Dorie, as if I belonged with her in that one-bedroom apartment with my futon on the floor next to the row of albums with the unwashed windows right above them and the brown and gray warehouses outside and beyond that steel and glass and milling people. And I want to say, Oh, yes, but I hold back because I should be here, should stay with Daddy till the trees break out like popcorn.

I tell Mia, "The only time I feel good is when I'm driving the Mustang. The speed of it slaps me; I could drive forever." I close my eyes and see the fields: watery brown, waiting, pockets of snow in the shadows of woods, trees skinny as young boys, branches getting thicker like tested muscles. I could love this place if I stayed in the car all day long, skimming over the road like a hurtled stone.

"I know what you mean," she tells me. "I felt that in the car with you, too." Her voice heavy with connection and meaning. You and I, she's saying, you and I. Larry, too: you and I in Minneapolis, he tells me—you and I away from here. And Doyle: you and I right here, have I got a deal for you. And Tweed: I will paint you and you will take your clothes off for me. You and I, the goose-pimpled subject and her painter. As if I were sucked whole into them, something fleshy that becomes workable metal, ratcheted into place, a part of an engine, a component in the machinery of their lives. And here, too—we want you with us, Dorie, to live with us and be our Dorie.

Oh, Mia, I'm so tired of being desired, I say into the vacant phone line. Only Mia's already said good night and hung up, and I'm still holding this buzzing thing in my hand like only now is when it's good to talk, when no one's listening.

But then I'm outside and it's cold and the sky is a clear deep black, the black you get after long, lingering rainstorms that clear out after dusk, so black you can see the Milky Way dust, a white powdery hazed band across stars and stars. The house lights are off and there's only the bluish purple glow of the mercury lamps on our drive and up the road at the neighbors'. It's cold and it's like I'm on an empty planet. Naked trees like bayonets against a sixteenth-moon. I shiver. I've got on a boy's hood jacket and my favorite Levi's and not a stitch more except for scuffed tennies. The cold freely seeps into me, immediate and sharp. I feel like I'm all husk, like people could—have—pulled at the sheath and there's nothing under there, nothing but the nibs of something not yet formed. But even incomplete, even pulled at, the husk is perfect. The cold has got me awake. There is dew on me mornings. I glisten in the sun and everyone wants the harvest, hungry. I hunger for their hunger, I'm hollow without it. I desire desire. Everything is awful and wonderful. My body is pricked luscious with goose pimples. I'm all husk and cold. If I could I'd touch myself everywhere, revel in the silky flesh, the sheen and depth of it. I throw my head back, delicious arc of feeling. Even the tips of my hair are chilled. The blood moves within me and I start running, not ready for elsewhere but damned if I'll stay here.

12

AND SO I CUT OUT before the pinned-sleeve business with my father. Take up temporary residence in Milwaukee and miss his schooling; Daddy trying to plow with one arm, first with the spring-tooth, and then with the disc. The daily humiliating awkwardness of one hand for everything—pulling on the wrench, setting cotter pins, hammering nails, greasing the power take-off, setting posts, moving bales, hauling cattle feed and mixing milk replacer. And, and, and, all with one arm. Reaching over with his right arm to handle the gears, the throttle being okay, on his right side, but he's always looking for where things are, as if with the arm a piece of memory has gone, too. He's uncomfortable on a tractor for the first time in his life, as if it's a foreign car. I don't want to watch him relearn everything, which he does, patiently, slowly, uneasily, like one sadly affected by alcohol, determined and grim and clumsy.

Oh, sure, he has the hook, but after a short time he stops wearing it. The harness chafes him terribly and even after he develops calluses he says he can still feel the old arm inside the mechanical new one, as if it's being crushed, held prisoner and shot through with workings and wirings. So he buys a package of extra-large safety pins and upon dressing each morning he pins his sleeve as neatly and painstakingly as he combs his hair.

• • •

Tommy tells me all this over the phone. I don't want to go back to find out anything, but Tommy calls on a regular basis, says somebody should keep me in the family even if I don't want to be. And as years change, he keeps track of me. Every few months or once a year he calls and runs down gossip or whatever, like I need to know all this. "Who gives a rat's ass, Tommy," I tell him, or when he tells me how he had to hold one end of the wire stretcher for Daddy so Daddy could work the spring half, the half that does the work, I say, "He's just a one-armed dolt," and Tommy goes silent for a while and then he says quietly, "Okay, fine. I'll try you later." And he does.

Through Matty he finds out the most, Matty hearing from others what's going on in her daughter's family almost before the family itself knows, the boys especially. Tommy gets pretty perceptive, though. And serious. He enrolls in the two-year extension and transfers to the U in River Falls, getting a regular four-year degree in agri-science. Scott gets a milk route and takes classes at the extension, too. "So the two of us, more or less, are college-educated," he says proudly. "We're nobody's fools." And all the while still working with Daddy, even keeping Harm and Clete and Frank because Tommy buys the Kelleher beef farm when Kelleher has a stroke (he put up our place for collateral) and converts the whole operation to dairy, too. "Only way to make money," Tommy says. "Stay with dairy and keep old equipment. None of that ostentatious blue Harvestore shit that looks pretty, state of the art, but busts you paying for it."

"And how's Daddy?" I ask and Tommy says, "The one-armed dolt?" and he tells me about Mama instead, whether to torture me or because he senses that's what I want to hear, I don't know. He tells me how after Daddy came back and had to go through all those adjustments, Mama said she'd understand. Of course she would. Only she won't let him touch her. Once from behind their door he heard Mama shout, "Steel!" as if the very thought revolted her. "And after he put the harness aside it wasn't any better," Tommy says, whispering.

He says he heard the stories, too, told by lots of people in hushed tones but with a certain sideways grin, as if heaped shame was a taste the tellers relished. Totally out of hand, was how Augsbury said Mama had gotten. Over the line. Clacking teeth saying how after a long time of not letting Daddy touch her, others did. Men were seen going in the doorway next to Erndt's and coming out. Mama with the sheets pulled close as if she had privacy. Of course it was going to come to that. Everyone said so. And the ensuing discovery, as expected as a dog barking at a car's wheels. Daddy finds out. Not that he does anything, but he finally can't close his ears to all the talk, can't not hear the names whispered, the litany of Mama's lovers, true or not, the names or occupations crop up and up like weeds—truckers stopping at the café across the street, the foreman from the canning company on his lunch break, a farmer from out of town, Burton Schwendt, and that Wandtke character who years ago had had a bastard from an Indian woman. And our own Indians, supposedly. Mama going down there evenings with fresh towels and linens and not coming back for over an hour. Harmon, probably. "Girlie, girlie," I hear in my head. "We throw you back." Tommy says Daddy doesn't do anything, he just walks around all day slump-shouldered like somebody let some air out of him. Tommy says Daddy tried to bring it up once and Mama just stared him down, daring him to actually say it.

And Porter Atwood, auctioneer and real estate agent. He was talking big. "He always talks big," I tell Tommy.

"Yeah, but you don't have to hear it," Tommy says.

"So what's he saying?"

"Like mother like daughter."

That story I'd heard when I was fourteen or so, how right around when Grandpa Ben died, Matty and Porter Atwood had— Well, that was the story, and Porter was in his fifties now, too, so it was particularly sordid for that cross-generational thing, and Porter shooting his mouth off, probably making public comparisons. "Now Matty, she had more spunk," he'd be saying. "But Amanda—Lord, how she howls." My stomach turns hearing that, or not even hearing it, but knowing it could be said, said like that, with the attendant grins and smirks and winks. Everybody knowing and, even if it is a lie, it becomes the truth with repetition, as real as if it'd happened right out in broad daylight on a platform. I want to find Porter Atwood at the café sometime and say to him, How 'bout going 'round with the granddaughter, the daughter of the daughter, three generations of us, how about that? and work a knife up his stomach just as he's coming, but I find out a long time afterward what the stories were, when it hardly matters, like putting down sandbags after the river's in your kitchen. Besides, maybe it's true; being away, I could see Mama better, there seemed less reason to loathe her—to hate her with my special kind of fury.

And Mama is right about the talk. Those are people who want something real in their lives, too, and have settled for way less, have settled for sideline-watching and gossiping about anybody who does stuff.

I can see Mama on one of her Chevy mornings. August, maybe. The sun slanting hot and yellow over the black dashboard, the windshield a rain- and dust-patted gray, the car heating up. Windows down and the air tastes like wet cornflowers. Her eyes go from closed to half-open to closed. Everywhere the heavy green smell of things growing. She can even smell herself, the musty odor of whiskeyed desire baking up from her thighs, and the sweat from her neck and thorax, the gone-sour tartness from under her arms. A fly buzzes at her ear. Crickets from the field's edge. She sees her husband, and in her mind he has become one gigantic stub of crinkled tattered flesh, raw and purple and white and cracked like the knuckles of his remaining hand. Her husband is a long way off in the fields with her sons and she should be in the house with her forearms dusted white with flour, but what's the point, really? They'd eat anything she put in front of them, snatch it up like dogs, they seem like that, sometimes—dogs who eye what she feeds them, looking up at her to confirm that that's all there really is, spaghetti with ketchup, and they'll eat it anyway.

Time ticks away. Sweat beads her temples and on her upper lip, runs past her eyes and down the corners of her mouth. She licks the beaded sweat and tiny hairs of her upper lip as if grooming herself with a thickened tongue. Even breathing seems hard. The whole summer like this and the rest of her life and her husband, Jesus, she can't stand it with his shirt off.

And after another smidgen of whiskey scrapes her teeth and burns cleanly across her tongue, she feels she's ready. Something's going to happen and after enough thinking in place, it does. The drive to Augsbury, rising over Radar Hill, is strangely liberating, the dizzying speed of damnation. She can feel it. She's forty-something and it's like breaking free of the coffin, tearing the cloth wadding free of her mouth so she can breathe. Cotton sheets dangling off her like streamers. All her clothes are off and she's in the window, beckoning. Or maybe she's pulled back, hunched over a coffee and bored, she's gotten away, but now there's the long dead wait at Leeman's Café for someone, anyone (she'd like to think she's particular but she's not) to sit opposite her. And with almost no preamble she comes out with, "I've got a room." And then she blooms, brilliant as thistle.

Mama always admonished, "Don't get caught," but she's in a place where nothing but that can happen. Or maybe being there is being caught in the first place.

But that's a situation I can only guess at, and while it's cutting its teeth, irritating itself into being, I have my own troubles. The first time back at the hotel, and it's business as usual. In his office back behind the kitchen Doyle says, "Let's see what we can do for hours" and he closes the door, begins pushing back the tongue of his belt, and I say, "Bull-shit, Doyle," and he shrugs. Like because I let some men pay for access while I feign interest, no options for now, but I'll rent out the mystery, waiting on hope for something better, and in the meantime this available disinterest—then that's supposed to be me. That known slice. He gets to see me that way once and now it's the secret of the universe. "This is business," he says, his hands still loosening his belt, and I spit on him. He belts me once on the mouth, hot blood from cheek crushing on teeth, and then my nails come across him, same as razors, and I'm trying to figure out how to catch him again, fake with the hand and then knee him again and again until he has no air at all, just a complete hollowed center of pain where his balls used to be, but instead Doyle opens the door and steps back. A draw. "Purely business," he says. "I can live with that." And I don't even say anything. I just walk away, sucking blood.

After that he keeps his distance, is almost diffident, so in that we continue. I meet him from time to time as I'm coming out of the service elevator or cutting through the kitchen on my way back to the bar (there's a sandwich menu, too, meat piled high on whole wheat or rye and a dill wedge and rad-ishes for $5.95, something else to absorb the alcohol and keep them drinking). Doyle makes a small informal bow to me and then, eyes bright with anticipation and his hand out, asks, "And how'd you do?" like I'm just back from a day at school and he wants to see my papers. His bills go in a black-and-gold clip in his jacket's inner breast pocket and then the bow again, more formal, like he's practicing for Japan. The hair on his head is thinning. When he bows like that I can see where he combs it over. With a magenta-pol-ished fingernail I want to poke through the combed and slicked hairs straight through the thin spot, stick my finger in like it's a pie or a baby's soft spot, and waggle my finger in his brains like he's filled with eggs. "Like them scrambled, Doyle? I'll give you scrambled." But I just bow back, equally formal, and then smack my tongue loudly over an eyetooth, which is the kind of lower-class thing he hates. He knows to keep his distance. His balls whisper him reminders.

Mia, though, is like the sophomore geometry problem: if you keep halving the distance between yourself and what you desire, do you ever possess it or are you stranded in the infinity of approximation? I laugh, using words like that: infinity of approximation. You hang around people enough you pick up their tics, even if the people are pretty forgettable. Tweed with his wonderment at my "alternating passivity and desire." While he's painting me he reaches to touch. True awe. He says things like, "Texture. There's a humidity to your stomach I want to capture," while his fingers trace the runnels of my belly, though he'll say, "the parallel indented curves of your abdomen, good God," as if he is solemnly in contact with Art itself. I have to smack him when he gets grabby, only he loves that, too. "Fire!" he cries, like he's the one holding the match.

But that's the running battle, and with Mia I am more interested in an unholy peace. I learn compromise. Acquiescence without surrender.

Mia goes into her Christmas eyes when she comes home late that Friday night/Saturday morning and there I am, back, smoking cigarettes in the kitchen with the stereo going and all the lights off except the one over the sink. "Just let me wash myself," she says. "I thought it was going to be ages. I was with what's his face, Jeff. He's a total jerk, but when he's on he makes me feel like I'm the only woman on earth—like his wife or anyone never existed. I keep saying I don't want to see him and he keeps saying I can't do that to him and then I get the I'll-leave-my-wife bit as if he thought I'd believe it, which from sheer repetition I sometimes, awfully, catch myself doing. Though, really, in his own way he can be wonderful. I like to see him just to keep in practice, though practice for what I don't know." She giggles and talks with her skirt pulled down in the bathroom doorway. "How's home?" she asks.

"You want some wine? I've got a red, Jeff gave me three identical bottles and there's still one left." She washes her face and reapplies mascara, looking at me from the mirror. I've followed her to the bathroom doorway and she is bent over the sink, her skirt exuberantly kicked into a corner so she's wearing just a sweater and her panties, the soft bulges from where her behind and thighs meet gone now, stretched into unbroken white, though when she straightens up they'll be back. From inside the mirror she says, "Only eyes for you, Dorie. What do you say?"

And I say, "I'm not going to be your lover, Mia. I'm not going to be anybody's lover."

"Oh, bullshit, Dorie. Of course you are."

"Take lovers, maybe."

"You're not pulling some born-again shit, are you? The trip home didn't give you religion, did it?"

"I just want some distance from everyone."

"Distance," Mia repeats. "Fine. I can deal with distance. Put on this lipstick and we'll go dancing. We can dance with distance. It's still early." She looks at her watch. "Only twelve-thirty. See?" She holds her arm out.

"I don't want to go dancing."

"So we drink the wine here at home and cuddle and you can tell me about your week." She moves past me into the bedroom, drops her skirt on the heap in the closet and takes a pair of black jeans from the shelf. They have narrow ankles and a tight ass and after sitting on the bed to work her feet through she takes a short hop to get them the rest of the way on. Then she lies back on the bed to pull up the zipper. A little bit of doughy belly shows when her sweater rides up.

"Damn pants," she says. "Who in hell decided these were in fashion?"

"We're not cuddling, either."

She lifts up her butt to pull the sweater back into place. She's still on her back. "Oh, that's right," she says. "Distance," giving each letter a nasal emphasis like little kids do, mocking me. "Well, fuck you, Dorie. Jeff stuffs all this good blow up my nose and even gives me some outright and I hurry home to enjoy and, even better, you're back, and you say something perfectly stupid about 'distance,' which just ruins the whole evening."

"So find a party. Someone else can stuff you with blow. And other things besides."

"Holy, holy, holy," Mia says, getting up violently and rummaging with exaggerated clatterings in a kitchen drawer for a corkscrew. "Like you never let loose in your life."

"I stayed up to see you, and now I want to go to sleep."

Mia keeps her attention on opening the bottle. She makes it a struggle—the foil, positioning the corkscrew, working it in and then back out, like she's never done it before. "And no company?" she asks me. "Never ever? Not even when we're feeling especially affectionate or drunk?" She pulls up her sweater to reveal her belly again, the few black hairs that curl up to her navel like a very young boy's attempted mustache.

She forces me to smile. "Sometimes," I say. "Maybe."

"Dearest Dorie," she says, pouring wine into short glasses, handing me one and taking my chin in her free hand, "we'll have to work out a schedule."

13

AND THEN THE SUMMER. We wash the windows and discover the fire escape outside Mia's bedroom window. In the winter it'd seemed useless, another rusting wrought-iron sculpture. But I think now it reminds Mia of the open-air thrill of the water tower, though she only mentions this once, accidentally. "Let's climb up," she says, when she means "Let's climb out." To me we have a see-through parlor, and it's nice to breathe fresh air on hot nights, air that seems cleaner for being off the street. When it rains we sit with an umbrella and watch the lightning flashes go off like strobes. Warehouses back-lit, the sky gone blue-green and black. I am mesmerized by the raw geometry of shadow and light, the buildings brilliant with each flash and then the switch-off to hulking monsters. Mia intoning, "It was a dark and stormy night," and then giggling. We move the speakers into Mia's room so the sound dances at our shoulders.

It's a street of little traffic, so on sunny days Mia sits outside in just sunglasses, a V-neck sleeveless tan cable-knit sweater and her panties, black stubble dotting her calves and upper thighs like newly seeded grass, rubbing herself with oil till she glistens. If men walking across the street look up and shout something, she lifts the sweater and sways her breasts back and forth. Then she yells, "Now bite yourself, pig!" and goes back to reading. I never read. I sit with my eyes narrowed to slits and the music going, the bass a lazy thrill inside me, and every shift of my eyes is a new postcard.

Industrial water towers, khaki brick warehouses like the trousers of a fat man, boarded windows for the zipper, broken stoops like crumbled cuffs. Fat men with no torsos. Four stories max and scattered trees like belly fuzz.

"Hell of a neighborhood," Mia says.

Our parlor. The rain coming down and we sit on worn-out velveteen cushions, a bottle of wine growing out of Mia's crossed legs. My legs are crossed, too, and we sit with a hand behind each other's ass for balance. We like it when it rains best. Water on all sides and the iron cage and we can climb up or down, or sit on the stairs, smoke cigarettes and giggle. Mostly we talk. A very rainy, talky summer. And lightning so the sky seems important and immense, which it is.

I tell her I'm going to get Tweed to teach me design.

"Designing what?" she wants to know.

I don't know myself. "Clothes, buildings, it doesn't matter," I tell her. "Just so I have a pencil and I'm drawing. I think I'd be good at that."

"What does he say?"

"I'll have to ask him. I doubt he'll be too keen on it."

And the next time it's raining, warm and muggy, the street steaming, the air like shredded wool, and I'm lying with my head in her lap and she's stroking my hair, especially the tendrils that have started growing back around my ears. I'm in shorts and my legs are wet, my toenails deep red like a truck fading away in the dark. I can feel the plantar's wart like a deep weight.

"He said he couldn't teach me anything. He had me do some drawings—simple things like a coffee cup and the radiator in his studio. He had me draw his face. And then I drew my own feet. 'If you can draw feet you can draw anything,' he said. And when I was done he didn't say anything about it. He said I should take off my clothes and we should start the regular session. 'But what about my drawings?' I asked him. He wiped a brush on his shirt and said I shouldn't worry about that. 'I wouldn't encourage you, Dorie. You haven't got the talent. Not for that. Oh, sure, you could take courses and squeak by, if it was me or the right person, but you really don't have it. Look here,' he said and turned a picture toward me. 'This is a foot? It's a *cartoon*. It could be a hand if you looked long enough.' He put down his brushes. 'You just don't have it, Dorie. You're a great model but a lousy artist. What you do have a talent for is this—the inner workings of your thigh, the lilt of your shoulders, perfect—' And he took my shoulders and arranged me how he wanted and when I turned my face so he couldn't see the tears he patted my crotch and said, 'This is magic, you know. You should be very proud,' and he squeezed my thigh as if that confirmed everything."

And I'm not sure anymore if I'm wet from my own crying or from the rain, but it seems I'm wet all over and I'm sweating besides. Mia keeps pouring wine into me and when I wake up the next morning in my own bed my clothes are still damp and Mia is in the easy chair, where she must have been the whole night after pulling me inside. She's watching me wake up. She has coffee and aspirin ready, and while I shower and come back to myself, she pokes her head past the curtain and says, "You know, you're a very weepy drunk." And I want to cry thinking about it, but Mia says, "Fuck him, he's an asshole."

I rinse my head and say, "So you think I should go into design?"

And she says, "No, I saw the drawings you left on the table. But he was wrong about everything else."

And over breakfast she says, "Forget him, Dorie. He'll say anything just to keep you naked in his studio. I bet he uses the brush on himself once you've gone. Paints himself to orgasm in front of your picture."

"But that's what he was saying."

"Because he's afraid."

She's right. I double my price for him not to touch me with my clothes off and the addict keeps his wallet open like it's a faucet running money.

And over beers we talk about Larry Fields and Mia's Jeff. Larry wanting to take me to Minneapolis. "Summer's the best time," he says. "Trees, lakes, parks. Water everywhere. It's incredible." So I agree. For his sake. To show him how wrong he is and to puncture his hope gently. We stay in the Best Western by the bus station. He says he's sure he can find work—maybe in this very hotel, but better still, in one of the classier places, the Marquette or the Northstar—and we should really think about moving here.

"It's cleaner than Milwaukee," he says. "Look at the lakes." Larry's big on lakes.

"And what's Michigan?" I say. "Somebody's farm pond?"

"Seriously, it'd be better for us." He sounds desperate, like he has to convince me of this. Only we've just checked in, too soon for passionate pleas. I want aspirin and a drink.

"I bet you could get into one of those modeling agencies. All the blond models in New York come from Minnesota— Jessica Lange."

"She's an actress."

"See?" Larry says. "It's better than I thought." I give him a look and he says, "Just give it a chance."

We're at the hotel pool, an indoor trapezoid ringed with screaming children and two fat girls my age or a little older. Their fathers, I bet, are in the bar drooling over the cocktail waitresses, who at least get to wear black slacks and long-sleeved white blouses with black tuxedo studs and bow ties. A family establishment. That afternoon, while Larry's buying drinks in plastic cups to take into the pool area, I say to one in sympathy, "I'm a waitress, too."

"Big deal," she says, as if I've been bragging.

"So where are the lakes?" I say to Larry. "Minneapolis— City of Lakes. It says so on their trucks. And here we are at a hotel pool with chlorine that's going to ruin this suit."

"Okay," he says. "We'll go for a spin."

I pull on jeans even though there'll be a wet spot and let an oversize T-shirt fall down my trunk. I tie a knot to the left of my navel and parade past the front desk, just for a reminder to myself. The clerk eats me up. In the flashed reflection of the glass door opening I can see him chewing his mustache. I feel better even though it's cloudy and windy.

"I can't believe it," I tell Larry as I get in. "A fucking indoor pool in June."

"I thought it'd remind you of the Y. I just wanted you all to myself."

"I thought we were going to see the lakes. That's what's so special, right? We'll see them all."

"There's too many." He shows me.

"Well, just the ones that count. This chain of them here for starters."

Larry drives us through Kenwood Parkway and then around Lake of the Isles, and we ooh and aah at the mansions as if they're fireworks. After completing the loop we cruise Lake Calhoun, which seems to be the thing to do. On the south end of Calhoun I say, Here, and Larry pulls into the parking lot.

Only I don't like it. We're lying on Larry's Woodstock blanket, that yellow bird with the punked-out haircut in Peanuts ("Just like yours," Larry says, tousling my hair), with the sailboarders skimming in front of us and the bodies going past. We're talking flesh like there's a fire sale, and I turn to Larry with the sun finally coming out so he's squinting, his sunglasses left on the dash. "You know Minnesota is nothing but blondes? Healthy, lean, tall, well-tanned and well-fed blondes?"

"What about that one?" he says, pointing to a chunky brunette with pasty breasts spilling out of her halter. She's reading *The Brothers Karamazov.*

"Exactly." I gather up our things, pulling the towel out from under Larry. "Come on," I tell him. "Let's go."

"But we've been here all of twenty minutes."

"There're other lakes, Larry."

In two days we cover Lake Harriet, Lake Nokomis and Lake Como. Everywhere the same. No matter which beach on

which side of the lake. Different crowds, perhaps. High
schoolers on one beach doing the Frisbee and strut, late
twenties/early thirties achievers at another, Windham Hill
tapes on their Aiwa boom boxes, scattered family groups at
another, still another for gays and one for blacks, but mostly
the same. Clean blondes with rounded faces and big teeth.

I only feel comfortable two places: Hidden Beach on Cedar
Lake, an illegal tongue of sand that pokes out of the willows
and pines across from the official beach, which we find out
about from somebody who asked me to dance at an uptown
club. And on a dirty spit of sand and wood under the Franklin
Avenue Bridge, on the Mississippi, which looks too dirty to
swim in, though people are swimming anyway. At both places
some girls go topless, and if anyone looks with more than
casual interest you can stare them into cinders. Larry feels
very proud. Under the Franklin Avenue Bridge it's mostly
graduate or foreign students with or without their girlfriends
and wives. Iranians and Afghans and Italians and Koreans
and Greeks. Also three American Indians, two men and a
woman, sharing a bottle. When we settle down, the husbands
roll their eyes up into their heads with visions of a blond and
bare-breasted America, even though my bra stays in place,
just the strings undone, like I'm faintly shy on this particular
U.N. of a beach. Still, the exposed parts, the public-view
places, bake a shimmery red that by evening has the gloss of
copper. Cheap victory, I think, peeling back the bikini bottom's elastic to see how far the tan has seeped into the short
hairs. I'd have baked the rest of me brown, too, except I think
a seamless tan looks like cheating, and ultimately boring,
everything brown, like a uniform. There's something about
having some parts of you brown and other parts red and finally the parts that are pure fish-belly white that's terribly
erotic, like having cardboard cutouts of your private parts
available for close inspection. Only written requests consid-
ered, thank you. See the manager to arrange a viewing. Only
it'll cost you, and even then management reserves the right to

say, Fuck off, Charlie, who are you kidding?

Larry has the right idea. Even in our hotel room he treats me like a gift I've reluctantly agreed to give him and can ask for back at any time. He touches me like the untanned areas could burn him. He moves slowly and carefully, cupping me with awe until he can't stand it. He's moved nearly to tears every time he's inside me. After we're finished he puts his glasses back on "just so I can see you in perfect focus. I want to remember exactly how you look," he says. And touching me like his fingertips are cameras. Like he knows it will soon be just him and the photo album. Credit Larry with sensitivity of vision. In bed he is attuned to the ultimate wrongness of things, and the need for small salvagings.

I bet his wife taught him that, though she probably didn't mean to.

But outside of bed he's still going for the big picture. On the drive home he talks about the city like it's the promised land, like we had a much better time than we actually did, like the mere fact of going means he's won something. Like we're really going to move there in, say, September, a couple months to find the right apartment and get fresh new jobs.

"Forget it, Larry," I tell him. "It's like California with snow."

He drives a long time trying to figure out an answer. He changes stations as if the right one is there, he knows it, he just has to get the bead and simultaneously he'll know what to say. I'm looking out the window and smoking a cigarette.

What he comes up with is, "So what about living together?"

My body's slouched up to the door like it's my date, my shoulders and head tilted away from him. With my head still back I take the cigarette out of my mouth and look at him like he's just said the stupidest thing in the world, which he has.

"Larry, I'm not even eighteen yet."

"So?"

He stares at me and stares, glancing only occasionally at I-94, like it's an imposition on him to keep us on the road.

"Come on, Larry, you know I'm not going to live with you. I'm not going to live with anyone."

He pulls off at the first exit, roaring up it like he expected the car to take flight at the top. "Is this supposed to be it then? I mean, we take our little trip and you toss me over, that's it? Is *that* the point?" He goes louder and louder, then stops and catches his breath. Much quieter he asks, "So are we finished or what?"

He waits. A fly comes in and buzzes against the back window. You can see Larry's struggling for something inside, some sort of calm. He shakes and goes still like a deck of cards has been shuffled inside him, a double shuffle, prrrrit! down and ththrrrit! back up. And now rearranged, internally different, but calm.

"Okay," he says, putting the car back in gear and crossing over to the down ramp. I haven't said anything. He accelerates smoothly, deliberately, breathes in and out through his nose like an exercise. "Okay," he says again. "I mean, it's not like I loved you or anything."

And then an hour later he tries the small salvagings, as if we were in bed, talking. "We can still see each other, Dorie, can't we?" We're on Highway 16, the route before the interstate, with the shoulders crumbling and only one lane each way but it's pretty, the green and lack of traffic. "We're not cold turkey, Dorie, are we?" I reach to tap my cigarette ash and regard how much I've got left.

"Say something, Dorie."

"Don't be childish, Larry."

His right hand comes out of nowhere. It's on the wheel and then it's crossing my face. I can feel the blood pop out of my nose.

"Childish, huh? I'll give you childish." And he swerves the car back and forth, in our lane and then flat out in the opposite lane. We go a long way until there's oncoming traffic, but even then Larry won't swerve until finally he does and the other cars, half in the ditch, ride past honking like hyperventilated geese. He does it again with another car coming, turns right into its path and I scream. And once I scream he straightens out and drives along as if nothing had happened.

"Childish," he says. "Like you know all about it."

He hands me a tissue for the blood coming out of my nose.

I turn the rearview to check myself. A ribbon of dried blood under one nostril. I spit on the tissue and wipe myself clean. The lucky bastard, I think to myself, he's going to recover. In two years he won't even remember I was the cure.

14

MILWAUKEE RISES in the dusk ahead of us, a scab of poured concrete and I beams and glass boxes. I like it because it looks like it's waited a long time to get finished, only somebody forgot to get around to it, so it's still waiting. Even the lake as it nudges the city's eastern edge seems to say, You're going to rust. A city half-finished and getting old. Larry wants to stay with me, says he's sorry about everything and that he'll make it up to me. I tell him my nose still hurts.

The next morning he's knocking on the door at six and when I groggily get up and open the door halfway he thrusts in a bag of doughnuts and tissue-wrapped flowers, which he must've gotten the previous night since they're already wilting. I let him inside and he also has a quart of orange juice. We eat on the futon, junk breakfast in bed, and then take a nap. He's curled around me like we've been sewn together. At eight he kisses my forehead and leaves. And every day after that, flowers. He doesn't say anything but when he gives them to me I rub my nose and he smiles. Our little joke.

Only I don't rub my nose for the laugh.

The next rainstorm Mia has hot wine for us and we're wearing cotton sweaters. "It must be a drag," she says, "having him dote on you like that. Or is it wonderful?" giving lots of exaggerated emotion to *wonderful.*

"I don't know," I say. "It's weird—I think he sees a lot more in me than I see in me."

Mia says, "Or a lot less."

The next day it's raining again and colder. We're drinking Leinenkugel's from long-necked bottles and we feel like lumberjacks. Plaid shirts and thick white wool socks. The air so cold with the rain you can almost see your breath, one of those late June days that has you convinced it's April. "Larry's a lot healthier now," I say, as if I were both introducing the topic and concluding it. I think of healthy and see my father on a rooftop opposite, plowing tar into ribboned black snakes. He looks lopsided and weak, even with the bulk of his shoulders. If the breeze were to hit him hard on that side, he'd topple over backward, drop back on top of his own plow.

And Larry with his weights, getting healthy. I hold out my own arm and close and open and close my fist. Healthy. Not what I meant.

Mia's fingers travel up my extended forearm. "You've really taken him seriously about that window weight, haven't you?"

"Yeah, we're regular Schwarzeneggers."

Mia opens another beer. She likes being the tender, likes watching for when I'm ready for the next one. She keeps my glass full, keeps her eyes on me. She's like Larry.

"So what do you want for your birthday—a Nautilus?"

"What does any woman want?"

"You got me," she says and laughs.

"It's not so funny. What would you want?"

"It's your birthday, kiddo."

"Yeah, but what do you want?"

"Who knows? To tell Jeff to fuck off, I suppose, only I can't or don't when he's right there with me."

"You want me to tell him for you?"

"But that still leaves me with what to get you for your birthday."

"How about the pearls he just gave you? They're freshwa-

ter, I've already heard you say you don't like them. It would
save you buying something."

"My thank-God-you-had-your-period pearls? I don't think
so. I treasure them just so much."

"So why don't you just tell him?"

"So easy," Mia says. "And you just telling Larry. And we
all live happily ever after."

"I actually like Larry."

"Oh." For a long time just the rain and Mia lifting the
bottle from her lap to her lips and back again. She looks at
me. "Don't you find that rather sad?"

"Not terribly."

Mia runs her hands over the base of the umbrella stand we
had Larry make us so we didn't have to hold the thing each
time we came out here. She and I chipped in to buy a huge
umbrella, military green. Mia says, "I wish we had more
room. I'd put those plastic wire chairs with stuffed cushions
out here and a table with a Cinzano umbrella covering everything. Like we were in Greece. Wealthy or poor, it wouldn't
matter. Even poor we'd have a great time in Greece, don't you
think? We'd really have something."

Only it's never anything. We pretend we have a little café
society of two, but it's really just two white chicks on a fire
escape, which lasts until October, when it gets too cold even
for pretending. We even throw parties out there—Mia's
friends mostly, eight or ten people who latch on to me quickly
like they're remoras and I'm the big fish cruising without effort. Mia pouts, me in their midst like a princess, everyone
wanting to touch. Mia's friend. I wonder what she tells them.
Everyone so smirky with liberal knowledge—Mia's "friend"
—I feel like I should announce at every gathering, Hey, I
fuck men, too. But not just an announcement, proof. I have to
wean Mia of me, her friends watching.

I start with Geoffrey Ghest, latch on to him at a party and
don't let go. Geoffrey looks like a mannequin. He's terribly

small, maybe five-six, and has the fine tight waxy look of
someone not real. "Cole Porter slumming," someone says.
Geoffrey wears white linen pleated trousers and an open-
throat white cotton shirt that's never quite ironed, the French
cuffs rolled back, and he holds his martini glass as if he
expects someone to come by and refill it from a chilled
pitcher as soon as he's sipped it sufficiently for the servants to
notice. He plucks his eyebrows and slicks his thinning black
hair Fred Astaire–style, has it razor-trimmed, and you can
catch the fragrance of men's cologne from his neck and wrists.
His skin the creamy white you often find on female models.
Vaguely Chinese, as if his almond eyes and round flat face—
a face always smiling to itself—have something to do with his
father being in Asia after the war, though he never told me
enough about his mother for me to know. "I only knew my
stepmothers anyway, dear, and I'd really not care to talk about
them. Classic Grimm's. Too depressing for words," he says,
and his fine thin lips disappear, pulled into his mouth, an
inverted purse.

But that's several conversations into our knowing each
other. What he first says when Mia introduces us at one of
our/her July cocktails-among-the-warehouses, fire-escape-
attire parties is, "Lord, I'm so pleased to make your acquaintance. Mia has told me you're a harlot, and I never thought I'd
get to meet one." And he holds his hand out as ladies used to,
palm flat, the fingers dipping as if he's divining water, as if I
should take it and kiss the fingernails.

"A harlot, Geoff? What makes you think that?" I run my
hand under my shirt collar and down the front buttons, pulling the blue oxford open slightly, so he can see the cream and
no bra, and he doesn't even blink.

I like him immediately. He is not Larry.

"Mia has stories," he says, "about you and Harris Vandersol, what do you call him, Tweed? How you pose and have
just swept him away. How you sweep everyone away." His
hand flicking, the unspoken shoo, shoo, as if that is what I

do. He leans close, smelling of washed neck and men's perfume. In heels I am as tall as he is.

"Incidentally," he says, "it's Geoffrey, not Geoff or Geo or anything else. Geoffrey."

So of course I use Geoff and Geoffrey interchangeably.

He always arrives and leaves with someone named Mark, one of those balding linebacker types who tend to squire tall gaunt men or five-two pixie women. But once early in July Mark is talking to a different young man, taller and pastier than Geoffrey, a man who touches the silk scarf at his neck and who from time to time inspects his own impeccably groomed nails and then, satisfied, reaches for his glass. A man with lightly rouged cheeks and hair combed back and held in place with a gold barrette, a man in black stirrup pants and ballet slippers and a gray cardigan, and after much talking and laughing, Mark and the other man leave together. And Geoff watching, doing a slow burn, like Mia does when she imagines me with Tweed or Larry or anyone not like Geoffrey.

And once they're gone he turns to me and says, "He's such a slut." Geoffrey lights a cigarette and watches them cross the street and get into Mark's Civic. "One argument and he's carrying on in public like I'm supposed to be tormented." The car pulls a U-turn and Geoffrey shouts at it, "Well, I'm not, you bitch!"

People seem arrested in mid-sentence. Yellow slants through the buildings. You can see the dust from Mark's car still hanging in the air like a furrow. I shrug and say, "You always hurt the one you love," and people start talking again, fresh animation.

Geoff lifts a hand, waving me off, his eyes glistening. "Oh, love, Dorie. Love has nothing to do with it. But thank you anyway."

"So let's go somewhere," I tell him. "Mark'll come back later and you won't be here."

"That would be nice. Quite suddenly, and no offense, but I

find your apartment a dreary little place."

"None taken. I often find it dreary myself." And Mia and the others listening. I can imagine the scene with Mia later, when we'll both be drunk, Geoffrey having seen me home and Mia still there, sitting among her party's garbage, the half-filled and untouched glasses, the ashes and butts, the spills and roaches, the mirror and razor, the bottles and scattered albums, maybe a towel. She'll look at me blurry and say, "But he's gay!"

Exactly.

"Dorie, you are *such* a dear," Geoffrey says as he follows me down the stairs. And I can see Mia and Larry, both of them kneeling and strangely pleading. And I shrug and say, Half-answered prayers are better than none, and Geoffrey says, "What, I didn't hear you?" and I tell him, "Oh, it's just I'm not what anybody hopes I am."

And Geoffrey says, "It's like that with everyone."

"Maybe, but I haven't the foggiest even for myself."

"Who does?" Geoffrey says.

My new confidant. We go to Hooligan's and we sit with our hands in our laps, our hands straying from there only to snatch at our drinks or our cigarettes. Only Geoffrey doesn't smoke, and his drink has no alcohol in it. "I've had my martini," he says. "More and I'm not a very happy person." His hands play with my cigarette. "I like holding them," he says. "So," he says, "do you playact at one thing more than another?"

"I coast a lot, Geoffrey." I take my cigarette back. "And, frankly, I'm getting tired of it. There's Mia, of course, and Larry, my human holding pattern."

"But you're rather fond of Larry, aren't you?"

"Do you ever sleep with women, Geoffrey?"

"Good Lord, not in years, but you didn't answer my question."

"How old are you?"

"Thirty-two. I'm about to begin my public life," he says

and laughs. He coughs into his hand and then runs a finger over one eyebrow, then the other. "And in my public life I will be stoned to death by a rabidly homophobic crowd on the Nicollet Mall in Minneapolis, no doubt in front of my father's office."

"What's your father do?"

"He's an accountant, a good profession if it weren't so boring."

"I like you, Geoffrey."

"And Larry, too."

"Of course Larry. He's getting to be like an older brother."

"And isn't that him now? You can tell him."

And Larry is in the doorway, and I can see the sequence leading to this: Larry coming by right after we'd left and Mia telling him I was with someone. And he knew to come here, since this was where he and I came often enough after my day shifts, and it was probably this that I wanted anyway, for him to show up and see me with someone. Ha, ha, Larry, and I don't even have to say anything, he can paint his own picture. And even better, it's the right wrong picture.

I can't keep the smile off after Larry's gone again. Guilty relief. I want to laugh out loud, it's ludicrous and perfect.

Geoffrey pokes at his lime. "I take it I've served a purpose."

"Accidentally."

"Accidental use. I'm not sure I buy that."

"You want to go back home?"

"Our separate homes?"

"Mine."

"A late show for Mia or are you actually trying to see this through?"

"I just want to go home."

"Tuckered out, love? Devastating poor Larry is tiresome, isn't it? What with Mark earlier, I actually sympathize with Larry. Poor man. First Mia, and now me."

"It's not funny."

"Oh, but it is. Even with liking him, it's funny. You think so yourself, don't you? A tiny bit funny? There, of course you do." He kisses my hand and stands up. "Come, love, I think we've had quite enough for one night. We'll have other nights and other nasty things we can do for each other, I'm sure."

With my key out at the front door he says, "Incidentally, I really do like you, you know. For a woman you're almost attractive."

15

ONCE A WEEK or sometimes twice Geoff comes to the apartment and we sit on the couch, two humans talking. Incredible. I make coffee. Geoffrey sits with his stockinged feet behind the small of my back and gives me back rubs with his toes. I sigh and arch my back a little. Geoffrey, bemused, asks, "What? You look like you just swallowed an entire chocolate rum torte."

I say, "You know you're the first man I've ever been able just to talk to, just to sit with, without the follow-up touchy-feely?"

"What's this?" Geoffrey asks, his big toe digging into my hip.

"That." I laugh. "From you that doesn't mean anything."

"Oh, yes, it does," Geoffrey says. "It means I like you."

I seize his toe and massage the ball of his foot. I don't have to say anything.

"Thanks," he says, scrunching farther down into the couch. "I needed that."

Mia is in the kitchen, drawing and pretending not to listen. Larry is outside, throwing pebbles at the window. Tack! Tack! Like I should shimmy down the drainpipe and we'll run off together. He can't see in, but I get up and pull the blind just so he sees me in the window.

"You know you're going to have to have a talk with the boy," Geoff says.

"But it's going to be months and months, Geoffrey." I can

see Larry from the window. I can see the immediate future.
How I'll keep seeing him even though I'm not now. The two
mornings I work I have to go to the safe and make my deposit,
and he'll stand beside me while I fill out the slip. He has to
initial it and our hands will touch and I'll look at him and
he'll look at me, and it's going to continue to continue like
that and I know I'll go back to him and we'll have the ago-
nized confusions of false endings and startings like this was a
bad high school romance. And in closing the shade on Larry's
tack! tack! I am overcome with longing and sorrow. I even
shrug for his benefit. In my head a gun goes off, like we're on
the gun lap and inside my legs are stretching out, responding,
pin spikes clawing cinder, and Larry is running to keep up,
only he's on a different track, in a different race. I'm sprinting
and Larry is a long-distance runner and I want to laugh. I can
see myself saying to Larry, We're in different events, Larry,
and he'll just look at me. What are you talking about? And I'll
try to explain. And he'll say, Bullshit, over and over, and he'll
be right, but I don't know of any other way of telling him
except in parables—that word from Sunday school—like
you're supposed to see how the mustard seed relates to life or
something. And here I am with Larry, and liking him too
much to just cleanly tell him ta-ta and please don't keep in
touch.

In the meantime there's money and Geoffrey's friendship.
Geoffrey likes to talk about money since he seems to have a
good deal of it, only he doesn't sound like the men at the
Blaisdell who have money and talk about it. He doesn't need
to impress me, he just likes talking about money the way
some people talk about books or the weather or corn silage.

For a regular job he buys electronics for a department store
chain, but his money, I quickly gather, comes from what he
calls outside interests. He says he learned stocks and property from his father. "The only reason he doesn't out and out
hate me," Geoffrey says, "is that I did learn about money. I
didn't learn much, but enough for my own little nest egg."

"So how do I learn?"

"Ah, the age-old question."

"And what's the age-old answer?"

"Who knows?" Geoffrey plays with me. "A penny saved. . . . Them that haves. . . . The lack of money is the root of all?"

I think of a time with Nancy and Pauline. Nancy complaining she never had money, but Ramona always did. Nancy said Ramona could sniff out money. "She used to steal tips from my drawers."

Pauline was getting ready to meet her regular slime, who usually picked her up after work. Pauline said, "That's what you get for keeping money in your undies."

Nancy said, "Ha, ha."

"Do you?" I asked.

Nancy said, "I keep it in my bureau if you want to look. Second drawer down. With my underwear, yes."

Pauline was piling up her hair. She talked with bobby pins in her mouth. "You see? You don't have any money because you keep it in the first place people will look. Ramona certainly did."

"So where do you keep your money?" Nancy asked.

"If I told you then I wouldn't have any money, either."

I still have a wad rolled up in my socks. Available cash. With Geoffrey I feel like I don't know the first thing. He says, "It's complicated. You learn a little here, a little there. It adds up."

He takes me to Chicago. A field trip, he says. We watch the Commodities Exchange. "Ants with money," he tells me. "Crazy, isn't it? The screaming and waving of arms and running bits of paper back and forth. But it's a serious business." He sighs. "Next time we come I'll explain what they're doing in detail. But not now. I just wanted you to see. Now I'll show you something else."

He drives me to a vacant lot near the river on Halsted. Broken glass, some loose sheets of newspaper, metal posts roped together with chain. "*Land*," Geoffrey says. "Except for Holland, where it's a full-time business, and Florida, where they dump concrete into swamps, they've stopped making this. Now this doesn't look like much, but if you own it and it's in the right place, people will pay you ridiculous sums to get it from you."

"So big deal. First you have to have the money to buy it."

"In a manner of speaking, but not necessarily."

And then he ticks off all the things you can own, the list going by so fast it seems like it's on one of those rolling screens—the words going up and disappearing before I can take them all in. Town houses, he says, shopping centers, warehouse conversions, apartment buildings, office complexes, pieds-à-terre, suburban strips, boondocks hideaways, foreclosed farms, abandoned schoolhouses, renovated row houses, urban bungalows, mobile home parks, inner city parking ramps, vacant lots and condos.

"Everything from A to zed," Geoffrey says, mock-British accent. "You can own it, or a piece of it, for a fraction of its actual cost, then sell again to someone else, pocket the difference or use it to invest in something else."

"Quite," I say. Like I know what he's talking about. He's going to explain later. I'm getting the overview. His word. "Overview. Over hill and dale. So you can see the forest *and* the trees," he says.

Geoffrey brings over maps and photographs and newspaper articles about planned developments. "You see what they've done?" he says. "A run-down hotel and presto, sold to someone and they've made it an old-age care facility, funded by the government, and the developer nets a bundle. Adults playing Monopoly. It's obscene." Then he breathes in my ear. "And we can play it, too," he says.

I don't understand. We?

"Sure," Geoffrey says. "Sort of like partners."

But it isn't just money. With Geoffrey comes movies, visits to the Pabst Museum with their miniature doll collection, gal-

leries, dinners at the Pfister, drinks amid sandbags and
bunkers and bamboo at the Safehouse, plays, concerts, the
Mitchell Park Conservatory, even the ballet. Geoffrey in a
tuxedo, looking like he existed only to have my hand on his
arm. Milwaukee as an oyster. Geoffrey says even in a blue-
collar city there are pearls. "Cultured pearls," he says.

But it isn't just the la-de-dah of traipsing through Milwaukee's social and cultural landscape, with Al Jarreau's "Milwaukee" as the recurring soundtrack. I invite him over for a
Saturday lunch of tuna fish sandwiches and tomato soup, and
he brings chilled white wine and diet Pepsi—Your choice, he
says. It's as if we've separately decided to be nice to each
other. To treat each other carefully. "I'm a fragile being," he
tells me. "Oscar performances to the contrary."

Some nights we just hold each other, or drink tea and
laugh. "I'm not so hot as I usually think I am," I tell him.

"I know," he says. "Watching you is my favorite channel."

Then he calls me at work and asks if I'd like to go out after
for coffee and dessert. "A treat," he says. "We owe ourselves."

Larry calls and I tell him I'll be out with Geoffrey till late.
The next day when I'm making my drop Larry just flat out
asks me, "Are you sleeping with him?"

"Not hardly," I say, writing in the final amount on the envelope and stapling the cashier's receipt on top.

"Good," Larry says.

"Look," I say, "why don't you just start seeing other people?"

"Maybe I will," Larry says. "Maybe as of tonight."

"Good," I say. "Then you won't follow me home then, either."

"I don't do that."

"Constantly," I tell him.

"Okay, I won't then."

"Good."

"I'll wait and we'll go home together."

"I'm meeting Geoffrey after work. He has tickets to Jean-Luc Ponty, and then we're having dinner."

"How about Saturday then? We'll lift at the Y. I bet you and Geoffrey don't do that together, at least."

"How do you know he doesn't?"

"He's just plain too small."

I'm walking away to punch out when he calls across the lobby, "Look, I'm gonna take in a movie tonight. See you later?"

"Larry, you always see me later."

"Ciao," he says, like we're old friends.

I want to turn back to him, to tell him, If only we can keep it like this, Larry, if only you wouldn't be such a puppy sometimes.

How do mothers stand it? The long weaning?

16

THE PROBLEM WITH LARRY is I actually want to see him from time to time, to see how he's doing. My first investment as a human.

I bike home, after changing into shorts and a halter, the wind rippling my hair and tunneling down my chest, good, the sun warm on my back and thighs. I'm going up Memorial Drive, past the big houses, and I'm thinking, I am turning lovers into friends, an absurd business, like trying to recycle socks. What's the point? I want to say to each of them, Go away. Socks don't make good quilts or scarves or anything. When they go threadbare, you throw them away.

The problem with Larry: the problem with Larry is he is not a holey-toed sock. And Mia: by accident we have found ourselves in a single pair of pantyhose.

Somebody should tell these people.

17

THAT IS WHAT I TELL MYSELF: Somebody should tell them I
am not particularly safe or good to be with. Somebody should.
Not me. I'm too busy wanting everyone to want me, but on my
own terms. Geoffrey is perfect because he makes no demands. He doesn't muck up our relationship with all sorts of
expectations, which suits me fine. I have laws of constant
motion. No one can absorb my energy. I bounce off people as
if life is a slam-dance contest. On your feet. Spin. Waggle
your finger in the air and go.

I am eighteen. For my birthday Mia throws a party.

Mia says to me, "We're going to have problems, you know,
each of us with a Jeff."

"Jeff and Geoffrey. Like we're not going to be able to tell
them apart?"

It's Mia's crowd. Tweed shows up with flowers, wants to get
me off to himself in Mia's room. Larry comes with flowers,
too. But he sees Geoffrey and goes into his balloon-wheezed-
of-its-air routine. I take him by the elbow and introduce
them. "Larry, my friend Geoffrey. Geoffrey, Larry."

"Delighted," Geoffrey says, his plucked eyebrows bobbing
and hard black eyes shining.

Larry mumbles something and takes Geoffrey's hand
weakly. I want to lean into Larry's stricken, pouting face and
say, "He's gay," but Larry would shoot back a wounded,
"You'll convert him," as if that's what I am to people—priest-
ess of sex and healer. Besides, I want someone to like me just

for me. I want that to be possible. I want it to be like that with
Larry. So I take him off in a corner and hiss in his face,
"Geoffrey's a *friend*, Larry. We don't share sheets or anything.
Friends, understand? It's possible to do that, you know, be
friends."

"Like with me," Larry says. Exactly, I say, exasperated. I
walk past him into Mia's bedroom, away from the crush of
people. For dance room we pulled the futon away and pushed
the kitchen table up against the wall. People are starting their
gyrations now, knees up and legs splayed. Those two rooms
are rolling with bass notes, the floorboards throbbing. Mia's
crowd. We're talking someplace between a Frederick's catalog
and Halloween. Girls wearing men's black knit socks and
miniskirts with brown oxford shoes. Blue-and-black-striped
scoop necks with white collarbones showing. Anemic skin
and flaunting anorexia. Boys in tousled hair, or men trying to
be boys, all of them with hair slightly longer than the girls'
they're with. Baggy pants and misshapen sweaters with T-
shirts visible from where the collar's stretched. Others are
fashion plates, lots of silk and makeup. The men in solid
colors and slightly rumpled. The fashionably trimmed four-
day beard, as if they remembered to forget. Pretentious assholes, all of them. Primping for themselves. A
twenty-seven-way tie for best dressed. Like we were doing a
film and this is the section that calls for a crowd shot. Cue the
extras. Chatter chatter chatter.

And I'm trying to tell Larry, who won't believe that this is
what we've come down to, the boy-meets-girl business, the
essential No, Larry, I won't ever marry you. Because that's
what he wants—to be married. His perfect state of being is
being married. Like everything else is illusion, not quite real.
There's being married and everything else. And everything
else has been too much for him ever since his wife left.

How did she leave? I asked him once. Plane, he said. She
said she had a cousin in Pittsburgh. She was going there to
get away from me.

I believe you, I had wanted to say, not wanting to hear any more, having gotten the essential and awful facts.

Larry said, She probably did have a cousin, but anyway she met a dentist in Pittsburgh and had an affair. She's married to him now. She's his receptionist.

A dentist?

It's up the scale from desk clerk, Larry had said.

I suppose, I said. To myself—she left Larry for a dentist? Good Lord, to have been left for a man who looks in people's mouths.

But anyway, we are trying to have this conversation. Only Larry doesn't know it's actually coming. But it is, it's here. You want me forever, Larry, and I no can do. I want to reduce it to clichés so it'll seem easier, only I like Larry and that's a complication.

Why can't you be more like Geoffrey? I want to ask him. Why do you have to want me so much? I feel awful. I've allowed this to happen. In a way I've worked at it, goaded Larry's desire into running away with him.

In Mia's bedroom it's like we're the only people, just us and the disinherited summer jackets piled on her bed. I take out the sign Mia uses for such occasions, the one that says BUSY, and hang it on the outside doorknob and then close the door.

"Can't you see, Larry, that we met at the wrong time? You're all hung up on this rejection thing and for me just to say no, it's like I'm personally responsible if your life stalls. That's not fair."

"I just want to be able to see you."

"You do, all the time."

Larry pushes the jackets to one side and lies on the bed. He holds his arms out. "Just for a minute," he says.

It's good, lying next to him. With my head on his chest and his chin nestled in my hair, I can see silly possible futures, all of them turning out badly despite the niceness now.

My hand plays with a button on his shirt. I undo it and slide my hand on his stomach, along the ridge separating chest from stomach. He's done a number on himself since we met. He's worked that stomach, the muscles along his rib cage, his pecs and biceps. Solid. I undo another button and whisper into the wisps of hair curling between his nipples, "I'm not ever going to be your wife, Larry."

"Yes, my wife," he says, springing up to stand by the window, looking outside as if she were standing on the fire escape herself. She's standing next to her dentist, filling out a patient's card, the patient in the recliner with the napkin and his mouth all mapped out. Everyone's smiling, except the patient, who looks like he's frozen in mid-howl. I see this very clearly, as if I were right inside Larry's head.

There's a hard thudding on the door and then it swings open. Mia says, "It's getting stuffy. People want to get outside."

"Show them through," Larry says. "It's not like we were fucking or anything."

"Oh, Larry."

"Shut up," Larry says and redoes his buttons. People come in, bright summer clothes and whites, ice in their glasses rattling. "'Scuse us," they say and dip out the window. A small parade. One of them says, "How quaint, an upstairs dungeon." Me sitting up on the bed now, Larry holding the sash up like he's the doorman. When the last one's through he slams the window down like he's locking them out there.

"No," he says, "it's not like we were doing anything at all."

Larry. A wounded desk clerk. It's no big deal, right? I mean, he's got the sophistication of a northern pike. And he's gone now and I'm in the bathroom touching up my cheekbones red and the rest white, paler than untanned skin, and my lips bright enough to stop a fire truck. I manage to drink too much and dance like a tribal shaman. At some point I do a crotch grind on Geoffrey's knee, much oohing and aahing, more from Geoffrey being with a woman than from anything I'm doing. And while I'm tossing my head back, eyes half-closed as if I'm getting off, I see Larry leave, see him as if he weren't already gone, which he is. A replay, Larry with his poplin jacket and no good-byes, just going out and me trailing and at the door the little box he handed me. "For your birthday," he said. "Enjoy." And it was a sapphire ring with two empty mountings and a note that said, "The diamonds are coming." But he's already on the street and then I'm dancing with anyone or no one. For a while I dance without a partner, part of the hub of bodies working up a sweat, the windows open and cool evening city air mingling with the heat, and then everyone takes off for a club, even Geoffrey. Like they had synchronized watches beforehand.

"Got a date, love," Geoffrey says, kissing my cheek, and I find myself with Mia and Jeff, whom Mia has been with most of the night, only we've not yet met. I mean, all those quickies with Mia he was here and gone like he was in a shuttle race or a scavenger hunt—number 16, cheat on wife, number 17, go home to same and kiddies. But here he is, woozy as both of us, in the flesh, his thick glasses and large lips making him look like a bewildered fish peering out from his bowl.

"I'm gon' havta go home," he says. He's got his arm around Mia's waist. She's small enough so his hand goes all the way over and his hand's on her right breast. "Or mebbe no," he says.

"You've never stayed over," Mia says. "Not once."

"Never?" He turns this over in his head. You can practically hear remembered leave-takings tumbling into place.

"Perhaps you should call your wife and tell her you'll be late," I say. "Tell her it was somebody's birthday."

"Ha, ha, ha!" Jeff says and pulls Mia back, her eyes up in flames and her one fist raised.

And when Jeff's in the bathroom, Mia says, "You almost blew it."

"Who needs him?"

Water runs behind us, we can hear him singing a little tune, one of those dabadabadees people sing when they're about to be treated and they know it. Mia pulls the futon out from the other side of her bed and drags it into the living room.

"Just tell him to get lost."

"It's not fair," Mia says, yanking the futon when it seems it's stuck in her doorway. "You get everything you want, and I'm the one shorthanded."

"So what's-his-face is what you want?" I clean an area of plastic cups and wipe the floor quickly with a wet towel and then a dry one. "I can't believe it. You with him and it's my birthday and it's not even two and everyone's gone."

Mia gets the futon free and stands with her hands on her hips. "It's not like I didn't offer, kiddo."

"So kick him out."

"The one time he's buffaloed enough to stay?" She yanks the mattress to where it usually goes and gives it a kick. "There," she says. About a minute goes by with the two of us looking the other straight in the eye. Then the toilet flushes and Mia looks over her shoulder like that's the cue. "We'll make it up tomorrow, Dorie," she says. "We'll talk." And the door settles with a click that sounds like something's fallen into place.

I pick up cups and telescope them together, dumping contents from one to another until the top cup's brimming and then dumping that into the sink and tossing the stack into a green plastic garbage bag. I mop up spilled-on patches of floor and wipe countertops of ashes and peeled beer labels and cigarettes nervously crumbled to death. I empty ashtrays. Mia and somebody's husband. I shake my head and, almost laughing, make myself coffee and call Larry. It rings and rings, and when he answers he speaks in a hushed voice like he's made his apartment into a museum or a golf course.

"You can come over now, Larry. I've cleaned up and our futon's back on the floor."

"I can't," he whispers.

"Can't? Come on, Larry, it's my birthday."

"I'm with someone."

The phone stays right by my ear. Larry explaining how he met her, like I'd be interested in his technique, but it's not that, he's telling me like he's apologizing. But I don't hear any of it and then he's going with my name, Dorie? Dorie? And I think of the woman lying next to him, hearing him plaintively speak my name, and both of us are losing this round—that woman and me, and Larry, too, since he's got her next to him and he's going to have to come up with a different fumbled excuse for her. And then I'm attracted by the buzz of space, the silence. Larry not saying anything or me either. A car outside accelerates, changes gears, rumbles off. Absolute black out the window except for the white and purple street-lights.

"Dorie?"

I put the phone on its back so it looks like a cradle. Larry's voice is thin and far away. "Dorie? Dorie?" I turn the door to Mia's room. Click. Like static from an AM station signing off at dusk. "Dorie?" The lucky bastard. And Mia on her back with her nightgown open, one breast clutched by Jeff, like he was holding a favorite softball, mashed and slightly lopsided from use. Both of them out, comatose. Jeff sleeps on his stomach, his mouth misshapen, his round face an ellipse, his glasses upside down on the bureau. I take the glasses and push the window open. In one hand I hold my coffee and in the other his glasses. I lean over the railing of the fire escape. His glasses clack and at least one lens shatters. Nobody parks on our street except for a rusting Chrysler parked near the fire hydrant. No clouds or stars. I stay out there with my hands cupped around the steaming coffee mug, which makes my hands, at least, feel warm and good and somewhat larger than they are.

Mia and Larry. I want them both and neither.

18

THE DAY AFTER MY BIRTHDAY Mia comes home late in the afternoon, her eyes all blurry and rimmed red and purple and brown and her mascara's run, as if she's washed but hasn't used a washcloth to wipe her eyes clean.

"Hysterical," she says. "I met his wife. She's pretty and pregnant with his fourth child. They're moving to California." She sits down with one side of her face pressed in her hand. "It's so funny I can't stand it."

I clean her up with a bowl of warm water and a washcloth. She lies on the couch, her head scrunched against the upholstered armrest like she is trying out a too-small coffin just for the fit. I start running water in the tub. "Forget him," I say. "Just soak and keep your eyes closed."

"Oh, right," she goes. "Like everything that ever happened to you you just sloughed off, old leaves and dead scales. Right, right, right," she goes. "You bitch, Dorie. He's an absolute bitch."

I start undoing her blouse so she can lie in the tub, but she sits up, snapping, "Don't touch me."

Then she lies down again with her two hands folded and gripping mine hard until she goes to sleep, not waking up till the room goes very dark and I turn on the light over the bookcase. "Well," she says, one eye still closed and the other testing the light, "haven't I been the perfect all-purpose fool?"

"We take turns."

"Don't try to make me feel better, Dorie. I'm feeling particularly bad right now and I'd like to stay feeling that way for a little while at least." She shakes her head. "Now be a dear and heat up some soup. My stomach feels empty and awful."

I can feel us going away. Like a ball made up of two different strands of yarn and we're separating the colors, like we had an allotted piece of being roped together and now we're into the slow, steady unraveling.

It takes her maybe three weeks to start seeing Rhuebal Newton, a painting student like herself, and I can feel myself third-wheeling it. Rhuebal seems legitimate, his eyes and brows are dark, his hair is shiny black, his body average-size but tight, finely honed, and he's not currently married to anyone. "Oh, when I was like twenty-one," he says, and his hand flicks off the memory as if it were a mosquito.

I can see where this is going. Rhuebal, nearly thirty, wants to live among us. He rents the first-floor apartment, actually pays for the space, and our back stairway becomes a night highway, the conduit of comings and goings. Rhuebal as Larry II. I can see the two of them getting to be buddy-buddy, doing the "our girls" bit when they talk about us, the four of us, the double couples—neat and bound as any chemical compound —our evenings and weekends engaged in couples stuff, everything rounded off, complete, whole and wholesome, suitable for framing. We will smile out of pictures, *cheese*, getting strangers to take our photo so we can all be together, always always.

I can't get through a full evening with anybody. Larry, Geoffrey, Mia, it makes no difference. Everyone seems like a damaged magnet, spinning attraction and repulsion. Even the occasional magic of Mia when she isn't with Rhuebal ends up empty after the initial delight, like we're waiting for a train that never shows up, terminally off schedule.

Just to make the raveling a break I almost move in with Nancy. I'm all set to tell Nancy that I'll take the extra bedroom, Pauline having moved out a couple weeks before—

something about missing tip money and Pauline's son—but then the Ramona story clicks in. I can see the big circle swinging round. "Dorie—just like Ramona," as if I could be like anybody and so I sidestep that one, even though I need a place.

For a brief while I am back among the want ads. I have a couple of dinners with a woman named Martha, older, thirty-eight or so, before I even see her place. Martha has an egg-shape face and wide-apart dull eyes that, without the makeup, look almost invisible under her washed-out straw-color eyebrows.

She obviously likes me. I wonder if she's figured out how women often travel in pairs, the beautiful woman and the plain-looking friend, the arrived and the not-quite-ever-going-to-get-there. Or maybe it's the yogurt-complexioned women who seek us out, calculated self-torture in a bid for vicarious beauty and attention. Anyway, her house. We're talking one of those huge brick houses on Memorial Drive, 1920s huge. Room after room of missing furniture, rectangles of original color from where pictures were taken down, even the air smells like someone else has been using it. The downstairs guest bathroom will be mine, she says. It smells like pink powder, like someone comes in every day and sprinkles scented talcum over everything. When we're in the living room again, sitting on the floor side by side, admiring the size of the room, Martha touches the inside of my thigh, smiles as if we have agreed to something. I can't get out of there fast enough.

"Well," she says.

"Strike two," I tell her. I think of Tommy or Scott wanting me to catch for them. They want to make the baseball team. Not that they could play, Daddy needing them too often in the spring, but just to make the team so they have that in their pockets for later. Trying the finesse pitches when the only thing you need in high school is a good speedball. But they're working with their fingers, strange grips, permutations of their throwing motion. Nothing but curves. Martha hoping to blow one past me.

"I thought we had something going," Martha says.

"A 'Twilight Zone' episode maybe." I'm out the door, shaking the car keys, the apartment keys, the bar keys in my hand. My head's going, Consider, for your approval. . . . And the sky's that yellowy gauzed black that makes you think there's been one of those chemical-plant disasters, an explosion or something, and you're the only one they haven't told.

Thank God for Geoffrey. Geoffrey's got his own pitch, but it's one of those underhand softball lobs that top out coming down at twelve feet and it's so comical it has its own charm, arcs and drops plop! so you don't even know that was supposed to be the pitch until he's holding it out in front of him again like it's a grapefruit, tossing it straight up three inches and catching it again on his fingertips. Over on the side there's wine and smelly cheese and delicate crackers. Geoffrey's version of hardball. He's pitching Minneapolis at me like it's the last upscale frontier.

"Dey's white-collar money there, Miz Dorie, nuthin' but white folk wit' money they don' know whut to do wit'."

And I'm like, "Oh, come on, Geoffrey—"

And he's like, "No, ser-i-ous-ly," like each syllable is another argument, and I'm like, "So what am I going to do in Minneapolis," and he says, "Be beautiful," and I say to him, "I'm doing that here," and he says, "So who notices?"

"Everyone, it seems."

"Not hardly," he says. "Look, Dorie, you're not that pretty. I don't want to sleep with you, so I can tell you this straight, if you'll excuse the phrase. You're really not that pretty. But— and this is the *but* that launched a thousand wet dreams—*you* believe you're beautiful. You believe it, you exude the belief, and that's all that matters. So why waste it here? This is a low-profile town. Strictly blue-collar. *No* aspirations."

"What, and I'll be taller in Minnesota? The air is cleaner?"

"Life," Geoffrey says. "High profile, in focus, sharp. Exciting." He touches my face. "Really," he says. "All that cold air and your cheeks'll be pink and you'll be awake all the time."

"And what do I do really?"

"Nothing. Pretend we're married."

"Pretend?"

"Mostly on account of my father. Dada thinks I'm suspect. Thirty-two, lots of 'friends.' Make that thirty-two with a beautiful young wife and I'm fast-track, stable. Earnest. Safe. Not only Dada but people in general will give you money if you're stable." Geoffrey lights me a cigarette and pours more wine for each of us. His eyebrows dance. I try imagining him in a baseball cap tilted slightly askew but with the brim absolutely uncreased. How gauche, as Geoffrey would say.

"It's a town ready to happen, dearest. I've checked. Downtown's been down for twenty years. Now they're rebuilding, all that urban renewal stuff, the vibrant city, et cetera. They're knocking down landmark buildings like dominoes. It's awful, but somebody's going to make a lot of money buying up what's left and sitting on it. Dada'll front me the cash. There're warehouses on the north side to gobble, old grain and mill buildings on the river that will be very chichi in a few years, and other things—apartment buildings, old row houses, even vacant space itself."

"Haven't lots of other people already figured this out? Maybe there'll be nothing left."

"There's always something, darling. It's like a gold rush." He licks the rim of his glass, delicately, like it was a lover's body or broken glass. "Sure, we won't get everything, Dorie, but even just a couple, a couple . . ." He's leaning forward, his short and slight fingers pressing my knee.

"We don't actually get married?"

"Heavens, no. But you do get to wear the ring, darling. Like playing grown-up. You'll look divine in diamonds."

Geoffrey's nose is even with the top of his glass. I can't see his mouth, but just looking at his eyes, I know he's smiling.

"So what do you say? You know if just thinking about heterosexuality didn't give me the heebie-jeebies I'd be tempted to be like everyone you're already tired of?"

"What a lovely thought, Geoff."

He claps his hands. "It'll be fun, Door. Think what we'll have to laugh about each and every day. What do you say? You want to go to Minneapolis and make like Fred and Ginger?" He sees my blank look and says, "Dancers. Glamorous dancers. You never heard of them? They're so good they danced on ceilings, on walls. Light on their toes and fast, dearest. Fred and Ginger, Geoffrey and Dorie—what do you say?"

It doesn't look any better than with Larry, but Geoffrey talks it up better. Like we can run across fields just for the exhilaration, not that Geoffrey would want to run anywhere, but he'll indulge me. Geoffrey promises me my own money. We understand each other. He doesn't want me in the usual sense.

I try telling Mia this. Only there's no time. Only it's not the real reason, not the complete reason. All my things are in a little pile in the middle of the living room. The futon's rolled and bound with rope. Mia's watching me from the window seat. I have to tell her something. "Look," I tell her, "to me it makes sense, what with Rhuebal wanting to move in. He's here all the time anyway. I give you two years and you'll be married to him."

"I don't see what the deal is," Mia says. "Married? Give me a break."

"I can feel it coming, Mia. It just makes sense, me moving out so you can have the space."

"Yeah," Mia says, "everything you do makes sense."

What I don't tell Mia: I want to feel clean. It's like she has vines, lovely, spiraling tendrils wound all around my body, and how am I supposed to extricate myself? I can't unless I go with Geoffrey. We're going to shift into a different gear. I'm walking around the room revving up, inside me the motor humming, my skin translucent, bones vibrating anticipation. I want to go and I can't tell her that.

I can see things coming, the loss. Mia marrying Rhuebal Newton. Worse, there's Larry. Without thinking, I've had Larry pegged as fading with time, a snapshot left in the sun. Larry is supposed to be a dead letter. But with Mia and Rhuebal, and once you see them together you believe in the *and*, I have found myself at Larry's more and more, or calling him to come over. We sleep long hours, clinging to each other or not, like old marrieds. It hardly seems a question of sex. Infrequent abandon. We continue to continue, and I find that I like it. The whole vague idea—just Larry and not fade away. Larry with his two good arms and kind face and glasses that steam when he kisses me until he takes them off (he always said he'd get contacts). It becomes a little game, breathing hard through our noses till his glasses do steam. "Wow!" Larry says. "Passion!" And then we both laugh and my hand undoes the two buttons on his shirt and dips in, my middle finger on his nipple like I'm taking his pulse or pushing a button to get things started. True comfort with a man. Amazing.

And then Larry says, "Let's get married." And the whole vague notion, the little lies and dreams you comfort yourself with, wham! the ridiculousness thrown into full relief. What's it going to be with Larry? Larry Fields from Plover, Wisconsin, the land of sandy potatoes. Insurance? Larry calling on friends and neighbors in the evening, telling them about fixed term and variable rates? I can see us back there, a three-room bungalow two miles from the Ore-Ida potato factory. For entertainment we'd go what—bowling? The Saturday night whoop-and-a-holler out at a bar after an early movie at the Plover Mall Tri-plex while our teenage baby-sitter gets felt up by her boyfriend on our couch while the inevitable baby screams and eats the phone wire?

Thanks, no.

Even if he doesn't want to return to Plover, I mean, what does he have for options? So instead of Plover it's a three-room bungalow in a working-class suburb, everybody with curlers in their hair and snot-nosed kids and a mortgage that reads *tilt*. Fun.

Only Larry won't let go. Credit to Larry.

"You going to end up with him?" Larry asks. The morning of the getting out. Mia's called him. Like they're going to block the door or something, the two of them. Drama.

"End up? What does that mean, end up?"

"You know what it means."

"What do you think, Larry?"

So he follows us. All the way. I never see him after the last trip down the stairs, Geoffrey trying to wrestle the futon into one of those U-Haul tow-alongs until Larry helps him, flipping it in like it's a hay bale, but I'm sure of it. He stops where we stop, eats at the fast-food places across the highway from us.

For a while I think it's just something I cook up in my head, Larry following me. The romantic bulldog. I even have this vision as Geoffrey and I are moving into our apartment, a vision of Larry standing across the street, his hands in his pockets. Just standing there. I have to go across the street and I start by saying, "Larry—" But then what do I say to him, him standing there, his face patiently waiting for the blow, the slight flaring of his nostrils, like a steer that knows the bullet's coming? So is that the scene, me taking a gun to the man for following me?

I tuck away the small comfort of Larry being in the city with me, even if it isn't true. There will always be Larry—ha, ha, like Paris. Then I assume he isn't until I actually meet him, a couple of months later.

He really has followed me to Minnesota. He has an identical desk clerk job at the Curtis Hotel, one of those dreary family hotels not long for this world. I'm coming up Lagoon after finishing a grocery shop, heading for the Mr. Donut for coffee and there he is, sitting among the fashion punkers at the McDonald's across the street. All these McPunks with the shaved hair and the stiff colored remnants and the leather and the studs and chains. And Larry. I take a table outside and once he sees me he crosses the street like he's wading a river, exaggerated motions, like this is a real effort. We stand there looking at each other. Larry coughs into his hand and says, "Well." I touch the broadening of his cheek near his ear and say, "Yes. Well."

And he says, "So how's it going?"

"Not badly."

"Not goodly, either?"

"So-so."

"Are you angry?"

"Good grief, Larry. I'm flattered."

"I thought you'd be angry," he says.

"Christ, Larry, it's been weird."

"What?"

"Everything."

"You're telling me," he says.

He tells me how he's in a newer city but an older hotel, real underbelly, he says, and I tell him I hardly see Geoffrey, he's out so often with a new friend, Michael, and Larry says, "No conversion, eh?" Even the bad jokes make it seem like we can still be friends or something. But even without saying anything directly there's this edge in his voice, there, and there, Larry pushing for more more more, like he'll never be happy till we merge. Siamese twins. Stuck together hip and thigh. Going through life side by side, the ultimate movie fade-out. He asks if we can exchange numbers, and I do but caution him about calling me, how I don't want him doing that all the time and he says, "Oh, I expect you to call me," and he laughs, a little worried, like we both know he's been caught lying. But I do call him, and we do the affable bit. But Larry always with that edge, that, "We should be together, you and I," in his voice, so that seeing him is dangerous.

I can tell him things, though. We meet for coffee or lunch, and I provide him with a new installment. Larry listens, keeps our cups full, scoops them up as necessary for refills. He replaces the shredded napkins, asks for more cream. A waiter in every sense. After we sit down and sort of look at each other for a minute, reacquainting ourselves with the territory of emotion, he leans forward, his elbows on the table, folded like bookends, his shoulders hunched, his glasses flecked with dandruff, his smile crooked, like a pie slice gone awry, and with practiced ambivalence he says, "So how goes the saga?"

I tell him how we're not making the bundle Geoffrey promised. How we pretend we do, but really we're living on Geoffrey's dwindling savings and on his father's good graces, which would be fine except I'm tired of feeling like I owe people and I want something resembling control—something I can say I did, something I can own. Larry just nods, silent. I don't go into details with Larry. That would have him swaying with hope. Details: how it seems some days that Geoffrey couldn't care less about anything we ever agreed to since he met Michael at that Walker opening. Geoffrey apologizes to me for his inattention by saying that he's very caught up in "the love latitudes."

"I have a shallow heart," he tells me. "Near to the surface and easily scraped. You understand, don't you? I have to be careful."

But he's not. Geoffrey in love is nervous and talkative. He walks quickly through the apartment, bounds the stairs, his hands always in motion. He's self-pleased but anxious, positive both that he can keep things with Michael light and airy and that he's already a goner and it's not going to work out. He says he's sailing through and straight out of the love latitudes, but he carries a blue glass ashtray about with an array of lit and unsmoked cigarettes—he recently took up smoking—as if he wants to show people an assortment of chalk sticks.

"You don't look like you're sailing to me, Geoffrey. You look like you're becalmed. The doldrums of love, Geoffrey. Not pretty or fun, is it?"

He says he's not in love, his hands fluttering like birds. "It's just a fling, Door. A summer romance."

"It's March, Geoffrey, not even close to summer."

"Yes, yes, yes," he says. "But when it's summer in your heart—"

Michael is tall and thin and lithe and very, very droll. At our apartment he takes his shirt off as well as his jacket and arranges himself on the couch like a casual meal, his long arms stretched out, one leg bent under the other thigh, his head tilted back, the whole effect that of being listlessly sprawled and waiting to be taken. "Come and get it," he calls to Geoffrey upstairs. When I come in he says, "Well, for you just a snack," and waggles his toes at me. His complexion is naturally dark and he rubs the long tan hardness of his stomach as if when he opens his mouth to laugh, he could conjure out of himself a genie. His eyes always seem to be lit inside with candles, as if he were a gypsy at least. Geoffrey is hypnotized but recovers once Michael puts on his shirt.

"Off to slay the peasantry," Michael says. "Don't wait up."

When Geoffrey comes in much later his lips and the skin all around them are swollen and blotched reddish purple, as if he'd been drawn facefirst into a plumber's helper. I tell him this and he laughs and touches himself gingerly, as if his mouth were still smoking.

"Yes," he says, "temporary passion can be like that."

"Not love, Geoffrey?"

"Love, infatuation, insanity—I don't know," Geoffrey says. "Michael and I are in a realm of our own—starry-eyed double solipsism." He sighs. "Dangerous but fun."

I just look at him, my cigarette at a critical angle.

"I know, I know . . ." he says. "We should be cuddling with Dada. But I just can't right now, Door. It's . . . I don't know. It's—" He gets the grins and places one delicate hand on his stomach, the fingers spread, and holds the other hand up as if to let the room examine the back of his hand. He starts waltzing.

"Have you ever heard that Screamin' Jay Hawkins song, 'I Put a Spell on You'? It's a terrific song," Geoff says, and cues it up on the stereo. He's waltzing again, but also throwing in a little bit of a polka hop and step to go along with the wheeze of the music.

He stops. "Dorie, Dorie, Dorie," he says. "We will use Dada as a resource and become independently wealthy, but just not right now, okay? Okay?" He gets me to nod assent and then he's off again, twirling in his white cotton socks and black pumps, his lips larger than they should be, looking like Gene Kelly, whom I know about because after Fred and Ginger he sat me down in front of the Betamax with a stack of videocassettes of old dance movies, and he's so exuberant he's growling along with Hawkins about putting a spell on—me? Michael? It doesn't matter.

So I start paying attention during dinners with Geoffrey's father. Geoffrey's father starts taking us to dinner once we've "settled in," which is to say it's been long enough that we look like a real couple. During most dinners Geoffrey is very good on form: holding my hand, making cooing noises along my cheek, even giving my neck a one-hand massage during dessert to show his father how intimate we are. But his heart's not in it. He's thinking about Michael. Even the pads of his fingers against my neck bone confirm this. It feels odd, a man who wants to be touching another man touching me.

And sometimes he barely hears his father. I have to cover, squeezing hard on Geoffrey's hand and saying, "Isn't that right, dear?" so Geoffrey can back into the conversation. But he's still distracted, and I'm left with the odious task of seeming eager to please, since it is ultimately Geoffrey's father who controls the purse strings.

Mr. Ghest isn't just an accountant. He owns company after

company—all with different names but with the same Minneapolis address. And each company controls a different property—apartments in Atlanta and St. Petersburg, Florida, mobile homes in Crescent City, California, whole trailer parks in Arizona, a motel in Biloxi, Mississippi, and another one on the 494 strip near the Minneapolis/St. Paul airport.

Mr. Ghest moves major amounts of money around as if playing some kind of elaborate shell game; and after getting me to hunger after what's under the right shell, Geoffrey's interest has surged elsewhere: to hearth and home and Michael, the tall dark angel. Geoffrey has become less ambitious for us. He seems content to be his father's elegant, immaculate, perfectly oiled gofer.

Geoffrey's gone a lot during the day. Doing the Dada runaround, he says—title research, looking at property, talking numbers with owners, but never with bankers, or with other investors, or with potential buyers. It's as if Mr. Ghest buys a steak, eats half, then tosses it to Geoffrey, who gnaws it clean, and by the time it reaches me it's dry and gray and ready to be buried.

And night after night Geoffrey's out with Michael—visiting the Jockey Club after hours, or at the Nineties, or anywhere Michael and Geoffrey mutually agree is chichi. Even with Geoff's anxiety over Michael's fidelity—Michael is sometimes late or shows up drunk or even cancels a date at the last minute—he's essentially happy. Meanwhile I sit home like the good little woman, content merely to paddle in Geoffrey's and his father's wakes. In the evenings I curl up in the living room with black coffee and I sift through the once organized files of Geoffrey's and his father's dealings, which Geoff now piles in sliding heaps on his desk rather than keeping them upright. I try to make sense of the changes as they occur—how such and such numbers on this sheet compare with these other numbers and figures, and how do you know if X at twelve percent is better than Y at eleven and a quarter? It's no good without a guide. I feel like I'm studying notes for a class I never attended. I know it's all important, but what does it *mean?*

Finally I can't take it and I say, "So what about me, Geoffrey? You're off with Michael all the time or tense and stable with 'Dada,' and I'm left with the Mrs. Geoffrey Jackshit smile on my face and nothing to do—"

And shit, I think to myself, I'm sounding like the bitchy wife.

But I can't stop myself. "I want something to *do*," I say, and Christ, that sounds pathetic.

"Do?" he says. "Hey, Door, come on. We can hang on to Dada's coattails indefinitely. We needn't *do* anything. I mean, the salary's not great, but he can't cut me off. I'm being his good little boy and if I keep that up we're fine."

"But Geoffrey—"

"I know, I know. But I can't think right now, Door. Not objectively, anyway. When I can it'll be like—"

"Fred and Ginger."

"You see? You understand. Allow me my time with Michael, and I'll be happier and I'll make it up to you. Michaels don't come along every day, you know. Marks are much more frequent. Meantime," he says, "why don't you teach one of those aerobic dance classes? Yours is a body people naturally lust after, Dorie, men and women both. Dada certainly does. And people are willing to pay big money if they think they can have what you have. Why don't you try that for now, Door? Until I'm ready again to take up the reins of capitalism and fight the good fight? To boldly hang on to coattails where no man has hung before?"

"But Geoffrey," I say, "aerobics? What did you do—pull that out of your ass? Do I look even remotely like a leotard lady?"

"Of course," he says. He has one hand around my waist and the other upraised, holding my hand, and he guides me backward across the living room whispering "cha-cha-cha" as if everything is fine now, everything is delightful. And for Geoffrey maybe so, but even dancing with him, I feel like he's oblivious to me. He could be carrying a flower or a vase, dancing with a broom or twirling a favorite dog about on its hind legs, he's so happy for himself. Absentmindedly he's tossed me aerobics—gnaw on this, Dorie, it's good for you.

When he leaves for the evening, I sit down and have a cigarette and think out my options. Aerobics? Larry? I look at my fingernails. They look abused. I chew on the cuticle and around the sides of the nails. What options? I think. Who am I trying to kid?

So for nearly a year I do that anyway. Go out to the Edina Body Electric five days a week, Tuesdays through Saturdays, and teach aerobic dance. Geoffrey's father thinks it's wonderful, me telling stupid women with money who are eager to look like Jane Fonda that they have to lift and kick and roll their hips and all the way down and point your toes and arch your back and yes, that's it, Good! And stretch and reach and three and four and sweat like a pig and yes and two and three and four and reach again and all the way down and this and that. And during my breaks I'm doing cigarettes like they're the last thing on earth I can still enjoy. I have to keep telling myself, Don't blame Geoffrey for this. Don't put him on the spot for something you decided yourself. And then I stretch and feel the muscle under my arm get tight. I'm looking at my hand and wondering what the hell it's doing off to my side, out in space like that, like a sculpture of a hand, like a waxed fruit. And what am I doing selling these women on the grail of "... And two and three and kick and reach. And ready? Again."

And how did I let Geoffrey con me into thinking we had it made?

Sometimes Mr. Ghest drives out during the lunch hour and takes me to Perkins or the Lincoln Deli. He wants me to feel like I'm "in the family," such as it is. Mr. Ghest smiles and wipes his mouth with his napkin and says he should stop eating so much and enroll in a course like mine. He grabs his stomach with both hands as if to offer up what it is he wants to lose. "I don't suppose you could help me with this? Run my butt off or something?"

"There's a course just for men," I tell him.

"Ha," he says. "I'd never go through with it. Only way for me to lose weight is to sweat it off one on one." And he gives me one of those fat-eyelidded winks, like now we're officially accomplices—like now he's going to lose twenty pounds and in private we'll sweat together in all sorts of ways. He says something about he needs to be "dripping with sweat" and it comes out of his mouth with the same slippery lewdness as "dripping with sex." Even Geoffrey doesn't deserve this father.

At the house I work out by myself. I do the weight exercises I learned from Larry. I spend the afternoon and evening getting angry at Geoffrey and his father, repeating the lifts until I'm all sweat and seething anger, and when Geoffrey gets home he just looks at me and starts right up with his defense.

"Hey," he says, "don't think this has turned out like I thought, either. I didn't *plan* on Michael, you know. I thought it'd just be me and you, too. And it's not like I didn't get us this"— sweeping his arm, meaning the apartment we share, the three bedrooms, one for each of us and an office for Geoffrey, on the seventeenth floor of a grain elevator conversion, one of Geoff's father's projects. On the sixteenth floor our living room, kitchen, dining room and bath, windows added and enlarged for views of Lake Calhoun—the sailboarders out there and the sailboats—the oval rooms connected with short straight hallways like yoked eggs waiting to fall. Geoffrey's Mama complex, I say to myself. His father bought it for us. Geoffrey's idea, his father's money. The agreed-upon pattern.

At first he tries to pass it off as his, his money, as if once I believe that, he can, too. "Some deals worked out," he says to me.

I don't believe him. He doesn't even talk like it's true. The couple of small things he gets on his own—a parking lot near where they say a domed stadium is going up, close to Chicago Avenue and Sixth Street, and another lot under the Washington Avenue Bridge off 35-W—he likes to talk about these places, ones he arranged separate from his father.

"People used to live there," he says. "Poles and Czechs and Lithuanians when they first immigrated, but now it's parking for a freight company and a paint factory. Imagine."

"I know all about it," I say. "My Daddy's land and my grandmother's lover's land are surrounded by little bitty houses where there used to be fields and fields."

"They should get the right price and sell," he says, as if he knows exactly what to do. Geoffrey's face, his father talking. It's scary when he sounds like his father. As if once you grovel, it's easy to think like the one who makes you grovel.

But he doesn't talk that way about this huge set of grain elevators—three of them connected, a trio of concrete penises steel-banded together—completely renovated, wood floors put in, larger windows, elevators, new walls and insulation, fresh whitewash, so you feel like you're living in a windmill in France or something. Geoffrey talks about them like they're borrowed. Like he's whistling in his father's closet. Like he knows the curtain's been pulled back and I can see him, the Wiz of Oz without the thunder, but he's yanking desperately on the levers anyway.

"I did get us this, didn't I?" he says.

"Geoffrey, you didn't 'get' us anything."

"Yes, but if I hadn't agreed—"

"Yes, okay. You agreed. You agreed and I agreed. And for agreeing, your father gives us a present. Big deal." I light a cigarette and lift it out of my mouth with two fingers like a forklift. Geoffrey pretends to be straight and I pretend to be his soon-to-be darling wife and Mr. Ghest pretends to believe in everything we tell him. Mr. Ghest beams every time he sees me. Even if we aren't married yet, we're planning to be, right? And all that homo stuff is done with now, right? The straight and narrow, eh? Mr. Ghest has hairless, lizard eyes. He blinks behind his glasses, his tongue flits out, lewdly. Oh, it's great to have Geoffrey in the business, sorting things out with his dad, a real son again.

We get the same rap every time. Mr. Ghest isn't buying word one from us, but the apartment must be a cheap price for making Geoffrey squirm and do tricks. And while Mr. Ghest talks he won't quite let go of my hand.

"It's good to be married," Mr. Ghest says. "I've always been married, it seems. When I fall in love with a woman I have to marry her." His palms are cool, it feels like his fingers are trying to read my wrist, as if my skin is in Braille. He smiles, cool and dry as his hands, little square teeth showing like he wants to gnaw on me, but he's too polite to start without an invitation. "Once I find the right woman I'm sure I'll marry her. But these days— I'm so glad Geoffrey's found someone as lovely as you." And the whole time he's been going up my forearms with his hands, like the best thing for me is this preliminary touchy-feely. He's allowed, of course. My future father-in-law.

"God, he's tiresome," I say to Geoffrey afterward. We're in the bathroom. Geoffrey's put on a bow tie for a date with Michael and he keeps licking his index finger and running it over his eyebrows so the hairs are all perfectly aligned.

"He's always been tiresome. Do you know what they need? They need to invent a little grooming brush for your eyebrows. Toothbrushes are all right but then you have eyebrow hairs among the bristles when you want to brush your teeth." He shows me his toothbrush and flicks the bristles. "Gross," he says.

I still have Mr. Ghest's pimple-scarred face stuck in my head. The knowing, amiable grin. Geoffrey is satisfied with himself in the mirror and sits down on the toilet, crossing one leg over the other so it dangles, his foot swaying in space. He lights a cigarette.

"What you need, dearest darling Door, is a Michael of your own. To take your mind off Dada."

"But isn't dearest darling Dada why I'm here? So he can think his little Geoffrey with the smooth, smooth complexion and wet-look eyebrows is balling me every night? That's what we agreed, right? Fine, Geoffrey, no problem. Only he knows, Geoffrey. He wants to fuck me himself. You got me here so your father can fuck me!"

I'm screaming. It comes out of me so fast I didn't realize it was there in the first place. Like I had life lined up in the crosshairs and somebody blows me away from behind, so I don't even see it coming.

"You think that? I never—not for a minute—" Geoffrey jabs out his cigarette and takes hold of my shoulders. "No, Dorie, I never intended for a minute—I can't believe you—" He steps away from me and into the bedroom, pacing. "No, of course. We're here, I'm with Michael, my father is his usual weasel self—of course you would." He comes back to me and again holds me by my arms. "I'm sorry, Door, you were placed in a position to even think that. But you shouldn't. Believe me on this—I would never, never do anything like that to you. I simply couldn't."

Geoffrey lights a fresh cigarette and moves about like an impatient salesman. He starts to laugh. He sits on the leather love seat in his room and laughs. He's French inhaling and popping smoke rings in between sentences. "It's funny, though, my father wanting you. I can see him, all beady-eyed like a rabbit, all curled up in his chair waiting for his chance to jump you. But you can't let him bother you, Door. You don't have to play house with him. So he wants you? So who's he? Nobody. Be shocked. 'Daddy! I'm almost your daughter-in-law! I'm *family!*' Knee him a good one if he gets too close. You're allowed." Geoffrey elaborately blows a large ring and then propels a smaller, thicker one inside it. He chuckles. "Incest, after all, is a terrible thing."

I'm in the doorway to the bathroom with my arms folded.

Passive and motionless. Geoffrey gets up and strokes my cheek. "Dorie, I'm sorry it's gotten away from us. But we can recover—we could really get married! Wouldn't that be a screamer? Michael as our best man? What do you say? Small stuff, a little ceremony for my several mothers and for my father's pals. His buddies. They'll be obliged to throw us tips. You know what kind of cash goodies you get for a wedding? Everyone's going to like us. I'm back in the fold. And it's nothing major for you—I mean years from now you could marry somebody else and still be a virgin, correct?"

I start laughing with him. Geoffrey takes me by the hand and sits me on the toilet seat. He gets down on one knee, his official suitor pose. "Oh, please, Door," he says. "Marry me. Oh, please please please say yes."

I kiss the knuckles of his interlocked fingers. They're pressed together, red and white. "All right, Geoffrey, you be a hubbie and I'm wifey, but this is going to be a modern marriage, *shared everything*—understand?" Geoffrey says fine.

We do the paperwork, the Sunday section, Miss Doris Keillor is engaged to Mr. Geoffrey Hamilton Ghest blah blah blah, I even get the photograph, the first picture of me since Larry snapped one of me sitting up in bed with my fingers laced around a coffee cup, I was wearing a T-shirt and panties. But for the newspaper we're talking an off-white demurely revealing trifle, something Geoffrey thinks his father will want to see. "Not hardly," I tell him. "Your father doesn't want me in grainy black and white. He wants to see me glossy and airbrushed, the full-color girl-next-door whore."

I let him put the moves on me and I just keep smiling. I have an idea. It has to do with, if not Geoffrey, then me. I am used to being the bartered-for one, the hungered-after one, the how-much-is-that-lady-in-the-window one. Bought and sold. If not all of me then at least a piece, some aspect taken and gone, which I have to replace or fake for the next one and the next one and the next. And sweet Jesus, how I hated that, the repetition of use. Geoffrey, thank God, hasn't, but then

right now he has no interest in me at all. Some days he barely
remembers I'm a friend. I am an acquaintance of the opposite
sex with whom he shares an apartment. Michael is all, and
the only good thing about that besides Geoffrey's sometimes
tortured happiness is that I have entire empty evenings in
which I do nothing but drink coffee and think.

And what I think about is Geoffrey's father. The thrill for
Mr. Ghest is the proximity to beauty and seduction. He
doesn't ever do more than touch my elbow, but his eyes shine
and his cheeks flush purple. Future knowledge. A middle-
aged Kevin Netley. A Tweed with much money. A man with
hope and hot shorts. If Geoffrey can't get money out of him,
maybe I can. And maybe maybe maybe with one more promise of granted knowledge I can be done with it once and for
all. I see, perhaps, a way to go. I meet Mr. Ghest for a late
dinner and I tell him I want to surprise Geoffrey by making
my own money, just a little.

"And you are," he says. "I think these classes you teach
are simply capital." Now I know where Geoffrey learned the
mock-British accent. His father wants to be a lord for Henry
VIII. Or Henry himself.

I tell him capital is my problem—I have none and I need
some to get started.

"To get started on what?" he asks me.

"St. Paul," I say.

"You're going to start on a whole city," he says. "I like
that."

"No, just a small area that I think could be renovated."

"Renovated," Mr. Ghest sniffs. "St. Paul is a lost city unless you're in government."

I lean toward him, my arms folded, my breasts bunched
and swollen forward—I'm in a white evening gown with spaghetti straps and I hate myself, but it's automatic, this promised exchange. You can look if I can touch your wallet, peeks
for cash, futures leased but not sold outright. Mr. Ghest turns
his face sideways so he can pretend to look elsewhere while

one eye gawks. I expect him to reach, to run his finger between flesh and fabric—just testing—but he's content with pretending not to look. This last time, I tell myself, it's this and then you can own yourself. You say maybe, and he says yes. And then no more partnerships, no more rentals, no promissory notes, no options to lease, rent or purchase. Free and clean self-ownership. Burn the mortgages, first second and third, and don't let anybody—yourself included—sell you again.

"What if I told you, Mr. Ghest, that I think I could buy a number of beautiful houses for almost nothing and with a little work could resell or rent them for a nice profit?" My hand is on his arm. My smile is a complete promise. "Wouldn't you be pleased? Wouldn't you be happy your son's not marrying a dunderhead?"

Christ, I hate myself. Hate myself for acting on what I know, and yet what else is there?

I go to St. Paul. For three or four blocks on either side of Summit Avenue, the old money street—stone mansion after stone mansion, overarching elms, huge lawns, carriage houses, refugee gardeners—there are literally hundreds of three-story wood-frame houses for sale. Big houses cut up into flats, cut into rooms so tiny even children would feel cramped. I get my own checking account and a loan from Geoffrey's father. I lie about my age to get a title. I lie about everything. To the bank I'm a face-lifted divorcée from California who's moving back to Minnesota with more money in alimony checks than I know what to do with. With the first house bought and partially rented, I have the equity to buy a second. And a third. And so on. For nearly a year it isn't my money and then it is.

And all this time Geoffrey and me playing house. Geoffrey and me supposedly planning our wedding. "My only son," Mr. Ghest says. "If he doesn't have children by you, I suppose I'll be forced to impregnate you just to keep the name going, eh?" The eyes and lips closed to slits, supposedly a joke, but he's looking at me like it's only a matter of time. Better if it happens after Geoffrey and I are married. More sordid, a bigger thrill. Or Mr. Ghest can be Sonny from *The Godfather*, page twenty-seven of the paperback version, and just before the ceremony I'll ride his pole. After all, I owe him just so much, him getting me started.

Only it's not really Mr. Ghest at all. Oh sure, he dreams his little dream, maybe fondles himself under his desk while drinking his mid-morning coffee, then checks on how fast I'm repaying his initial loan—our little secret—his fingers moving back and forth while he hopes I default and he can call the shots on a renegotiation, "Dorie, daughter-in-law, let's talk. Please step out of your shorts." But really I'm moving as I am with no one's help but Geoffrey's. The help of absence. The fuel of withdrawn promises.

Unintentional. I know this. Geoffrey's in love. He's visibly torn. We had an agreement and he cares, but he's in thrall elsewhere. "I'm so sorry," he keeps saying and running off for a new fix of Michael. Michael like a drug, thin with deep-set eyes and the permanent flicker of a smile about his lips, creases that aren't quite dimples lighting his face.

At first I blame the two of them, then each individually. But I like Geoffrey in spite of my hating him. And Michael— less nervously energetic than Geoffrey—absorbs Geoffrey's excesses each night, and grinning like we amiably share a secret, delivers him back to me each morning exhausted and happy. I envy the shit out of them. Geoffrey has only enough desire during the day to keep his father off his back. He is happy with his apartment and his salary and his occasional commission and his Michael. Over and over I hear, "Everyone should have a Michael," as if there were a factory somewhere putting out a limited edition of the man.

What I have instead is the hope-on-hold of something better than Augsbury, than Milwaukee—than anyplace I've ever been. I'm putting in dry walls and stripping floors myself. My shoulders and back ache. I come home sometimes still wearing my belt with the rule and hammer and nail pouch attached. Geoffrey, so taken with Michael we only talk as he's going out the door, another apology tossed over his shoulder like salt, thinks small-time carpentry has replaced aerobics in the scheme of things. He has left me to my own devices. I take to sleeping in the houses I'm working on, feeling the distance of me from anything. It's pleasant. Just working and the smell of stripped wood and my own sweat and the smell of humans working around me is good. And even though I'm disappointed that Geoffrey has less time for me, still we get along, Geoffrey and I. I can come home when I want and Geoffrey is there or he isn't and we make no demands and we're very comfortable with each other, moving about like roommates.

And then I come home one Tuesday night and find my clothes crowded with somebody else's, my shoes shoved into a bag in the closet, my jewelry boxed and put away, my toiletries and cosmetics in a shopping bag under the bathroom sink, as if I'd been away a long time and was not soon planning to come back.

"Geoffrey, what's going on?"

"I'm sorry, it just sort of happened," Geoffrey says. He's buttering toast for himself and I can hear Michael singing in the shower. Michael has a deep voice, and he's frequently breaking into snatches from *The Marriage of Figaro* or "Don't Cry for Me, Argentina" or something like that. From the bathroom he calls, "Don't forget the Grand Marnier," and Geoffrey shrugs his shoulders and says, "It seemed the likely thing to do."

"Geoffrey, I live here, too."

Geoffrey's having trouble with the toast. It jumps in his hand and dances above his fingers. He coughs. Places the toast and a jar of preserves and another of orange marmalade and twin shot glasses and the half-gone bottle of Grand Marnier and another of Wild Turkey all on a bamboo tray and heads for his bedroom. He's wearing boxer shorts and socks with garters. His legs are nearly hairless. I follow. Michael comes out of the shower, reedy-looking without clothes, wipes his face with a towel and then holds it at his side, like David does with his slingshot in that statue. He leans in the doorway, waiting for Geoffrey to notice him, posed. Then he sees me. "Forgot something," he says and the bathroom door closes.

Geoffrey sheepishly pours us each a Wild Turkey. He offers one to me but I shake him off. He smiles and tosses his jigger back, then follows it with mine.

"I'm bad when I'm on this," he says. "Very, very bad. Michael just sips at his Marnier, but I like the Wild Turkey and I have to have whole drinks of it, gulps." Geoffrey pours himself another. "Michael loves me sloshed. I get so out of control and everything is wonderfully chaotic." He lies back on the bed and folds his hands behind his head. "Drunken repose," he says. "A new series of paintings." He calls toward the bathroom, "Come out, come out, wherever you are!" Then to me, "I believe we're embarking on a new relationship, princess. I don't believe I can explain it without it hurting both of us, but with Michael I believe I can actually tell Dada I'm flaming and it wouldn't matter what he'd say back." He looks at the wall and his cheeks clot. It looks like someone slapped him. His hair looks strangely thinner and there are circles under his eyes.

"Then again," he says, "perhaps not."

"And what about me, Geoffrey? I thought we were friends. I trusted you."

"We *are* friends, Dorie. It's just—well, there are friends and there are friends. Close friends and . . . the other kind of friends. You know, the euphemistic 'friend.'"

Geoffrey's eyes look very glassy. He rolls over so he's facing the wall. He taps it gently with the underside of his fist. Over and over, as if he were counting cadence.

The water in the bathroom comes on with a hissing rush and then goes thunderous. I'm waiting for the steam to roll out from under the door.

"I'm terribly sorry, Dorie."

"Geoffrey!"

"I'll lose him if we don't live together, Door. I know it."

"Look," I say. I run back to my room and come back with my accordion files. I dump everything on Geoffrey's bed. All the papers that show what I own and what I owe and how the former is finally eclipsing the latter.

"I've done all this for us, Geoffrey. I've been waiting all this time for you, and in the meantime I started on this. One house here, another there. You know me, Geoffrey, the frugal housewife."

Geoffrey looks at the numbers. His eyes are lined with mascara and seem watery and poisoned.

"I am really and truly sorry, Dorie. If you asked me to say how we happened to come to this, I really couldn't tell you."

"I *trusted* you."

"All's fair," Geoffrey says, his voice full of sorrow and resignation. "Love conquers all. Hell hath no fury. . ." He tries to smile, but he's close to crying. He keeps rolling back and forth from me to the wall. It's as if he were trying to rock himself to sleep. One of his socks has come clean of its garter and is wrinkled sadly about his hairless ankle. I think of the first time I kissed Larry. I was sort of in control then, master of my destiny for those five seconds. Now nobody is.

Geoffrey sits up, his boxers flaring out stiffly around his legs.

"I trusted you, Geoffrey. I put myself in your hands, just like you asked. You asked *me*, remember?"

"Dorie, really. Without me, you'll find your own Michael."

"I don't *want* my own Michael, you idiot! I wanted you and me as friends without any bullshit. Who's going to play Michael for me anyway, huh? Your father? I'm the ultimate Door prize? Or some prick in a bar? What, if I get fucked I'm supposed to be happy? 'Here's my body, let's get married'? Come *on*, Geoffrey! I trusted you—" What I'm supposed to say next or do is beyond me. I'm on the verge of those big chest-heaving sobs that make you look silly and weak.

"I'm not perfect," Geoffrey says. "I never said I was perfect. And really, Door, I thought you'd understand. I thought you of all people—" He touches my sweater, the creamy white one with the pearl buttons, the one of Mia's I'd liked so much. Mia gave me the sweater a long time ago. Everything was clean. Even coasting, we had no complications. Geoffrey's touching me. My shoulders, my collarbones. Like he's trying to make sure I'm still here, and even I'm not sure about that. Then he starts crying.

"Geoffrey!" I cry and then I can feel myself slide over the edge. "Geoffrey, you were supposed to be *safe!*" And then I'm crying, too.

Geoffrey lets go of me and sits down. We're both of us wiping our eyes and sniffling. We regard each other sadly, like everything now is aftermath.

"I am safe," Geoffrey says. "It's everyone else who's not."

He's not yet calm enough to light a cigarette. He tries several times and ends up with an unlit cigarette in his mouth and a ruined match in one hand and the matchbook in the other. The water goes off and Michael, with the towel wrapped around his waist, comes in and lights cigarettes for himself and for Geoffrey and then one for me. He sits next to Geoffrey and pats his head. There, there, he seems to be saying. There, there.

Looking at them together, I no longer feel helpless. Or I do, but I know I'm not going to for very long. Composure. Breathe in composure like it's contained inside the cigarette paper. Look at Michael calming Geoffrey. It's not the same as control but it's a damn sight better than hysteria. I have Larry's number on a slip of paper inside my desk.

I call Larry.

"Come get me," I tell him.

19

I STAY WITH LARRY until he can't take it, either.

"This is only temporary," I keep telling him and he nods and I can tell he doesn't believe me.

"Let's go to Augsbury," he says. "Incognito. We won't tell anyone."

"Give me a break, Larry. I don't want to go back there."

But he keeps saying he's always wanted to see the place, to see what it was like, to really see the awfulness firsthand. "It's not awful if you just visit," I tell him. "You have to live there."

"So we'll just visit. For you it won't be so awful. Think of it as an adventure. You'll be putting something over on the whole town. Right in their midst and they'll never know."

"Not even as a joke, Larry."

"Please."

"Someone will find out. Everyone will."

"So what? You're already away."

"Larry. . . ." But it's like I don't have the will to say no right now. After Geoffrey, I'm just along for the ride. Larry beams. He knows he's got me.

He signs us in as Mr. and Mrs. Fields. The woman who waits on us in the hotel bar is the younger sister of someone from my class. But I'm wearing sunglasses and my hair is high up in a ponytail, and she's too busy checking out my red pegged pants and the three earrings to recognize me.

Mostly we stay in the hotel—the Auger Inn, a place that

was probably nice in the twenties, the Milwaukee Road railroad track running just behind it down to the Kafka Feed and Seed and then to the Everfresh Canning Company warehouses. Lot of business then, people coming and going, but now the hotel's rooms are used by those who get too drunk at the bar to go home and can cough up the $23.50 for a room, though usually they drive home anyway, drunk enough to kill somebody and also drunk enough to walk away unscathed. There are also the woozy lovers out for a quickie, too drunk or bored to care that the folks in the main room are witnesses. Public infidelities. Tongues wag. The legend grows. "My husband was not!" "He was so, I saw the key in his hand."

"Like where I work," Larry says, "only everybody here knows each other."

"Exactly. Everybody knows each other."

"And this is the only hotel in town?"

"It's not even that. It's a bar with rooms upstairs." We've already checked in, thrown our suitcases on the bed and then gone downstairs to drink. "Drinking's what we do in Augsbury," I say. "In the summer we drink and play softball. In the winter, drink and snowmobile. It's October. We just drink."

In a clumsy desire to stay up to date the Auger Inn has modernized in the worst way possible—both downstairs and up white acoustical-tile drop ceiling covers the original tin, and water streaks stain through like brown piss marks. Dark plastic wallboard for that fake paneled look. In our room the radiator creaks and hisses and there's a spiderweb of frost inside the windows because being up to date stops at modern heating.

"Aren't you going to call somebody and tell them you're here?"

"It's late October. People are busy."

"But your family? I mean, we will see your folks, right?"

"I promised to show you the town, Larry. We agreed I didn't have to show you the people."

"How about your house?"

"Don't make me laugh. Maybe I'll call Matty. She'd keep her mouth shut about seeing me."

We're sitting at an uneven-legged table I get to balance by placing the ashtray from the next table under one of our table legs. They look at us like we've just swooped in from Mars. I'm waiting for them to say something and the whole time I expect Mama to come in. Waltz in with some sheepish man in tow, gesture to him as to where the money should go, sweep a key into her palm and, nodding to one and all, head up the stairs on the far side of the bar. But I remember her room very distinctly, right across from Leeman's, and I suppose it's a matter of location, that maybe if we were in a bar on Main Street, instead of this one on Roosevelt, we'd catch Mama's act. Only for Mama it's not an act at all, and damn her anyway for making it public. Usually it's the men without discretion. When we were little we'd hear about them when Mama was on the phone. She'd speak in a hush, like we wouldn't know what she said if she said it quietly. "He did? She should pinch them off with a pliers." Pinch off what? I'd wanted to know. But it always sounded like women were the long-sufferers. I'd gotten that early. Leave it to Mama to go against the grain there, too.

So we lie low, the outlaw daughter and her lover or companion or whatever he is, and after two days I call Matty and she says, "I was wondering when you'd get around to ringing up someone." I ask her how soon she'd known and she says, "Oh, probably the morning after the first night. Marge Peterson was at the Auger with her husband for a perch dinner and said how she thought it was you but she wasn't sure, and I said of course it wasn't, and she shrugged and that was the end of it. But I knew she'd seen you even if she didn't and I also knew it would only be time before you got around to seeing at least one of us. And that's me, is that right?"

"I don't want to see Mama or Daddy."

"Ashamed of the man?"

"No, it's just—"

"That hotel is an awful place. You should come here."

That evening we drink sherry with Matty after Luther goes to bed and eventually Larry nods off, too, his hands folded on his stomach and his chin on his chest, just like he's going to look in his old age. You can see this nap is practice.

"He seems to be a nice man," Matty says.

"Oh, very nice."

"Is that what you don't like about him, that he's nice?"

"When I was ten maybe, you know I thought he or someone like him would be the kind of guy I'd marry. I even imagined then that I would go away and come home with this guy and the boys would size him up, chuck him on the shoulder just to see what he would do. To see if he could take it. But you know he probably wouldn't get past the boys. He's not really tall or really strong or really blond or really anything."

We look at Larry, with his face sort of flat except for his long sharp nose and his deep-set eyes with the single brow above them.

"He looks like an earnest young man," Matty says. "Intense, like he's waiting to go somewhere."

Waiting for someone to take him, I think to myself. But Matty's taken with him. She thinks he's nice.

"You're afraid to bring him home because we'll all like him. We'll keep saying, 'That nice Larry Fields' until you can't stand him, and so you don't like him in advance just so we get the message, right? Drink some more sherry, you'll agree with me."

"You say *nice* like Mia would say it, like I haven't caught the joke. Oh yes, *nice* Larry Fields. Like nice is what you get when they've run out of all the interesting flavors. We've got some *nice* men left, the vendor says. Want to try one of those? You're supposed to fall back laughing, Matty. Nice men seem like they've been palmed off on you. Second-rate goods. Like a man getting a fat woman on a blind date. Like vegetables. Nice men are the Brussels sprouts of humanity, you know that? Is this guy for real? you ask yourself when you're with him." I take a long breath, follow it with some sherry and then another long breath. "He wants me all, Grandma. He wants me forever."

"And there's something wrong with that?"

"I've got other things going for me. It's hard to explain. Did you want to settle down when you were my age?"

"When I was your age I had two children. One of them was your mother."

"Well, it's not like it was then now."

"It's not for your mother, either. She married a nice man and look what she's done to him."

"That's just it, Grandma. You scratch away at the guy to see what's beneath. Out of boredom, really. Everything's just too damn nice and you find out he's mostly nice all the way through and that's when you pitch him—yucko."

Matty just looks at me. She doesn't have a clue.

I continue. "Nice men can't damage you the way you've learned you could be, and after you've had it proven often enough you get to thinking that's that. Everybody has horror stories, men damaging women and vice versa. That's why we're human, right, because we can't connect with anybody we might actually like?"

Matty sets her glass down next to her tea and folds her hands so it almost looks like she's doing a Larry Fields impression, only she's awake. "I'd be the last person to say who to marry or who looks good. Luther in there"—and she swings her head to indicate the back bedroom, from where we can hear the deep snoring of Luther Kraike—"Luther's no prize all the time, and after Ben I wasn't up for another marriage to a difficult man. But that hasn't meant we haven't been together and had more or less a good time of it. It does mean you have to be determined to get what you want. And when you get older—I can talk like this on the grounds of too much sherry, and you have to listen, too, because this is my house —you only get your kids and grandkids and your husband

and yourself, and a lot of times you don't get that. People. That's what you get for your old age if you've been smart. You're a smart girl, Dorie, and Larry seems like a nice man. Those aren't requisites, mind you, but it's something to think about if you're leaning in that direction."

"I'm not."

"Then I think we should go to bed. Larry can find his way over to the couch if he wakes up, I'll put a blanket out for him, and you can have the room that used to be your mother's."

"I'll take the couch, thanks."

Matty gets up and flexes her fingers. "It gets to a point where you can't get them to do what you want them to." She gathers the glasses in one hand and balances the cups and saucers with the other. "We get up about six-thirty. You want us to wake you or do you want to get up on your own?"

"Call us at nine from the town hall. We should be up by then, but you never know."

Matty sets the dishes in the sink and runs some water on them and then comes out as I'm arranging the blanket, fluffing it out over the couch so it spreads right. She touches my cheek with a leathery finger.

"You're a smart girl, Dorie. Just don't be so smart you get stupid."

"You'd laugh if you saw what all I had."

"I think not. And don't look away just because I'm telling you the truth. Your mama is pleased as punch in a hateful sort of way that you've gone and got successful, judging from the money you send her. That's all she talks about is that money. She flies down to Chicago and says she sees you and, from what she says about you, I'd say she's lying about everything except the amount of money that allows her to leave here from time to time."

Matty has on this flannel housecoat and she pulls it a little tighter around her chest. She's a small woman with flat reddish brown hair and freckles turning gray and old-style wire glasses and a mouth caught somewhere between grim and grin. Small-bodied but strong. Like she would tape her breasts down if she needed to and put up her fists. Larry has a softer snore than Luther, so in the distance between the two they sound about the same. Matty inhales sharply and looks from one to the other.

"No wonder we end up with separate lives," she says. "They're always asleep when it's time to talk."

Two things happen the next day: First, Larry and I wake up in the yellow light of a heavy fog, common in late October, and realize things are pretty much over, like it's taken that long to really dawn on us. Matty, before she left, had opened all the shades and drapes so the diffused light comes in, but not harsh enough to wake us. When we do there's this yellow light and twin feelings of empty. The second thing is that Mama calls.

"You little bitch," Mama says first thing. I'm still pushing hair out of my eyes and trying to get a cigarette lit with wooden matches that keep snapping off when I strike them.

"Hello, Mama. I didn't think Matty would tell you."

"She didn't. Luther told Leotis when they were talking this morning trying to figure out whose overdue corn to get in first."

"So who's corn is getting in first, Daddy's or Luther's?"

"Just shut up, would you. You think sneaking into town with some Joe like the Lone Ranger and Tonto is supposed to be funny?"

"I made a mistake. Larry wanted to see the place and I said okay, figuring nobody'd know it was me."

"That's a laugh."

"So what do you want, Mama? More money? You want me to show off Larry for you?" Larry comes into the room with coffee for both of us. He has his underwear and socks on and

a T-shirt gone gray from sleeping in it. I stick the phone out
at Larry. "Here, Larry, talk to Mama."

"Hello? Mrs. Keillor?"

He has to hold the phone away and I can hear her voice,
very tiny but magnified, like she's talking in a metal room.
"Mrs. Keillor? Mrs. Keillor? It's Amanda Brown, you asshole,
doesn't she tell you anything? Haven't you had the laughs
already over who I am? I'll tell you who I am, Mr.-Fuck-My-
Daughter—"

I snatch the phone back. "It's me, Mama, piss off," and the
phone goes down ringing.

Larry shakes his head. "She doesn't like me."

"They don't know you to like you or not. That's just
Mama."

"But they know we're here. They know I'm with you."

"That's not anything, Larry. Christ, once they meet you
they'll love you. You're practically normal. Matty's ready to
eat you up."

Larry sits down. "I am normal," he says. "That's why you
don't want to have anything to do with me."

"Don't let's start, Larry. We're here because you wanted to
be. You wanted this trip like this was practice for some big
event later on. But there's no big event coming, Larry. You
know that as well as me. I'll live with you if you like, but you
won't be able to take it."

Larry looks out the window, his eyes pinched from trying to
see. His finger taps on the telephone receiver. He starts
punching buttons, absentmindedly, like the touch tone is a
calculator and without really caring about the total, he's add-
ing things up. I put my hands on his shoulders from behind,
coming up from under his arms. A backward hug. I clasp him
to me, hard, for all I'm worth.

Larry says, "I'll get the car."

20

ALL MEN are either victims or perpetrators. I read that somewhere, and for a while after getting my own place, that is what
I truly believe—that men either get what they can get or get
trampled by those who do.

I am in my knocking-around years. I have a place in St.
Paul. I have money but live without furniture except for a
drop-leaf wooden kitchen table painted white, two matching
white chairs, the futon, a lamp, a boom box and a shoebox of
cassettes. Talking to people, I've found almost everyone has
years like this—two or three or four that you really can't
account for even if you wanted to. "A bad time," you say, as if
you are a recovering alcoholic. I've found that if you tack the
better part of a decade onto anybody's life, there are going to
be complete chunks of time that disappear. In the telescoping
of random events into that thicket of what you remember,
some things low to the ground simply drop out of sight. Once
when Tweed was doing photographic studies of me he let me
look through his camera, a 200-millimeter zoom lens attached. We were on the roof of his studio across from the
Blaisdell. Downtown. Space collapsed in that lens. Buildings
blocks apart crammed into the viewfinder, hungry to be seen.
Lake Michigan reared on its hind legs like a series of show
dogs performing tricks. It's amazing, that compression of
things right on top of you. Littler buildings just vanish, slide
together into nothing. My early twenties have been like that,
my mid-twenties, too.

I live in the second-floor flat of a house I own. I never dusted, never cleaned from the previous tenant. Pennies are still on the floor, dropped quarters. Lint balls roll in the corners and along baseboards like miniature hay rows being turned. You can still see where the furniture had been, outlined dust. The living room radiators hiss like teakettles. It's winter, and the corners of the window glass are done up in arcs of frost, the rest of the panes dotted with random snowflake frost, like I had cut them out of paper, sat with scissors and infinite patience and then hung them with string from the empty curtain rods.

I have time for such intricacies. I possess this little empire of St. Paul real estate, and I am filled with a boredom that is truly monumental and with an eternally clawing and bone-dry desire.

In the one room I keep completely empty I sometimes sit for hours, tapping my cigarette ashes into a coffee can and hugging my knees close to my chest. I spend part of an afternoon thinking about the men. Try that counting game like men do, the names and the correct order, each face swimming out of memory, ghosts, like worn-out flash cards. After four or five they become as regular and anonymous as waves. Sorting one from the other is as worthwhile as remembering the difference between that particular wave there and that other one over there. No tics or idiosyncrasies worth noting. No distinctions. So much water, wasted and gone. As if the beach cared.

I see men without becoming even slightly attached, and they, recognizing a kindred spirit or something, accept this. Some are actually nice. Not Larry Fields nice but nice in their own way. Distant and undemanding. Some are good lovers but are too much like me, too aware of their own bodies to make anything but superficial physical connections. As if we make love to ourselves and not each other. Gratifying and lonely. One man while he was fingering my breast said to me, "Don't you just hate yourself sometimes?" We were in my flat lying on my futon, and I told him it was time he should leave rather than telling him the truth, which was, "Almost all the time." I see now that it would have been all right being with Larry Fields—as all right as it would have been impossible.

That other people desire me doesn't help at all. I think, Mama, Mama, Mama and consider the nearness of having been that myself. I look down at my belly, at what would have swelled if I'd let it. My belly stretching like a helium balloon. Mama having gone through that not once, but three times. Daddy bewildered, embarrassed and proud. And Mama all alone, even me inside pushing to get out not counting. When I was like that myself for even just a little while it was like an isolation chamber had formed around me. I could see other people but had no traffic with them, no connection. Just me and the stranger. It's almost like that now. Me, and the stranger that's me, the used and the user.

I wonder if Mama thinks of her pregnancies—do they ever come over her in her rented room, how then as now she's waiting for something to happen?

And me in my room with no furniture, not even drapes, the walls a vaguely bluish white, womb color. I feel tiny. There's no one to pace off distance or space against. The room changes dimensions at random. Sometimes smaller, like I can sit on bare wood in the middle of the floor and touch all four walls. Other times larger and larger, till it's like I'm on a raft in a limitless ocean, the horizon receding and no landfalls. None at all.

I spend a lot of time thinking about land. Land as opposed to ocean. Land with and without houses. Rolling land. Open land. Land dotted with trees and animals and fences and split by creeks and limestone ravines and culverts and ditches, but healing itself, healed even of its highway seams. Dark shadows of clouds moving ghostly over the green and the green. The green of all of it. Land. Land that's solid when you touch it, that doesn't move when you lie on it, land connected to itself and unbroken for as far as you can see. Working on the houses reminds me of working with my father. How you forget about yourself completely, there's only the task at hand, the feel of it, the sweat and the ruined palm, and the sight of all that land whenever you look up. And by forgetting yourself completely, you're connected completely.

Then there are the old connections that nearly get away from you while you're thinking only about yourself. And everyone else is somehow supposed to fit around you.

Mia gets married and I don't go.

I dream of myself in Greece the afternoon of her wedding. From what she tells me later it was a small back-of-the-church affair, twelve people to a side, pleasant perhaps, but certainly not joyous. I find myself in the habit of staying up till seven or eight in the morning, and then sleeping off the afternoon like I've been on a bender, or have dropsy. In my dream Mia and I are in Greece, have moved there lock, stock and barrel. Our skins have gotten coppery, her hair has gotten brilliantly black and mine has turned inner-lemon white. Hers is short and mine is longer. We wear oversize T-shirts every day and bikini bottoms. We spend our mornings drinking coffee and fixing each other's hair. In the afternoons the T-shirts come off and we bask in skies so pale blue and a sun so hard and white it seems our skin, the whole line of our bodies, just dissolves into the walled limestone patio that separates our house from the sea cliff. Every day the sun, and our bodies dissolving. We can see each other only because our perspiration shines. We become our own mirrors. And men are just things we talk about, like we haven't seen one in a long time and we can identify them only as distant and more or less remnant memories. "All the men," I say to Mia and we both start crying, our acknowledged necessary evil, what we try to hide from each other. We are hugging each other crying, our breasts touching. My nipples get hard. When I wake up I'm in a hot sweat, squeezing my left breast with one hand, my other hand moving back and forth between pressed-together thighs, everything tightening up, rising, without conclusion. And damn her, I will never get so passive as to weep like this again.

But I will, I will weep. Everyone is far away and I have put them there.

The only men I see regularly are Larry and Geoffrey. Larry I don't see so much as keep tabs on. As if we were old high school classmates and continually curious about each other. If I didn't hate and love myself so much—who knows?

I know. That's the hard part—yearning combined with knowledge. I'm getting better at knowing the why of things but I'm still without connection. I know how men look at me and I'm tired of it. I can give them their half of the conversation before they start. With the exceptions of Geoffrey, who wants to make up with me, and Larry, who's going, going, gone, like old close friends who've fallen out of the habit of being friends, seeing anyone is like reading from a Chinese menu. Everything is numbered, everything is already in place. I know everyone else better than me.

But slowly I'm getting better.

Geoffrey I meet for drinks and how-are-you chitchat. It's strained at first because he keeps trying to apologize and I won't let him. I'd rather we just get on with it, accepting ourselves for what we are. You lose a lot and you get back some.

"Make up for what?" I want to know.

"Michael," he starts and I say, "Look, for a while I don't want to hear anything about Michael. I know you think you need to apologize but it seems a little silly. We've been friends, Geoff, and I don't think we've really stopped, have we? I have an idea of what I want now, and everything before that seems rather distant and small. And we've come out about even, Geoff, haven't we?"

"I've been a bit rotten over this whole Michael thing, Door, more than a bit. I mean, I never handled it very well, did I? I still haven't told my father. I've been practicing the 'This is the real me' speeches for ages, but I can't quite bring myself to."

"Do you even need to tell him? He knows, Geoff. He's always known."

"Yes, but he likes to pretend and I've gone along with that. I'd like to take even the pretense away from him."

"Just show up some evening for dinner with Michael in tow and tell him you're married."

Geoff claps his hands. "That would be a scream. I could never—but my, just to think of it—"

"So is that settled, Geoff? We haven't stopped being friends and so we are?"

"Delightful," he says.

"Okay then. I'd like for you to help me with something. Not because of business ambitions or anything like that, but because this is what I want and I need your help."

"Because we're friends," Geoffrey says.

"Exactly," I say.

I tell him I want him to buy up Wisconsin farmland. I give him addresses and names to contact. I give him a map with the counties I want land in circled.

"You must be joking." We have the map spread out between us, the paper buckling from the glasses and plates and silverware we've crowded to the table's edge.

"This is where I'm from, Geoffrey. I want to own it."

"And you can't do that yourself?"

"I don't ever want to go there."

Geoffrey leans forward on folded elbows. "Well, we'll have to get overalls, Miz Dorie. And I wouldn't dream of being rural without my bonnet."

"Thank you, Geoffrey."

Geoffrey sits up straight and looks at the map. The area around Augsbury circled in red.

"And where will you be?"

"I think Greece. All the pictures show it as a place where you don't have to be anybody."

21

THE MAIL COMES once every few days and, even though it's
been two or three or so years, a telegram is what I expect from
Larry. Something about how he's tracked me down and now
he's coming. Across oceans, through narrow straights and
high seas. Larry's coming! I have to laugh. I haven't opened it
yet, but I'm sure it's Larry, since just the day before I got a
telegram from Geoff. I never got close to anybody else.

Geoffrey sends telegrams every week or so. A property and
its price. What's included—tractors, silos, barns, herd,
acreage listed as to tillable and untillable, age of house and
assorted outbuildings. Also the accumulated debts, outstand-
ing mortgage (and second mortgages—farm families usually
go in debt up to the grandchildren), and anything else that
strikes Geoffrey's eye. Things like 2 VELVET JESUS LIVING
ROOM, SACRED HEART LIGHT SWITCH KITCHEN, DRIED PALM
CROSS HALLWAY STOP LATE 60S PLAYBOYS BARN STOP IS IT
SAFE TO BUY THE LAND OF HYPOCRITES STOP YOUR SERVANT
PANT PANT GEOFFREY.

He finds it amusing. Moving the money around from the
houses and apartment buildings in St. Paul to acquire Dorie's
Dairyland, as he calls it. In a regular letter he can be news-
ier. In one he writes that he has told his father I've left him
for good—that I've taken up with a Greek shipping tycoon
like Jackie and that he's now in mourning. He thinks that will
buy him some time, but it backfires. His father arranges for
women to help get him over me. "Can you believe it?" he

writes. "Me with paid women from Dada? I wonder if afterward they have to report to him; just in case, I'm thinking of giving them some extra money to say we did more than just drink ourselves silly." In another he says he's bought the farm next to my father's and now we're neighbors. I can't understand myself why I want it. Why I want anything. In still another letter he says he keeps in his office various maps of Wisconsin, county by county, of the area he's buying, all my acquisitions colored in like a child's fill-in book. MARGINAL FARMS ONLY, I wire. AND RENT THEM BACK.

The county map of Outagamie he's colored most. Augsbury is on the southwestern edge of that county, with Appleton and Neenah and Menasha the largest cities. I have become Porter Atwood's chief competition for the available land around them. Porter has grown fat with buying farms and cutting them piecemeal and selling the pieces to city people who want to go rural. I buy the farms and keep them that way. Drives Porter nuts. I have yet to see anything I've purchased. The beneficent absentee landlord. They hate me only slightly less than Porter. I own their farms. But I don't show my face so they can pretend it's still theirs. It must eat at them. Matty for years telling them what their taxes were and then taking up with Luther Kraike, and worse, being with him all these years and not married or even thinking about it and she's seventy. Mama making a mockery of marriage, too, her own and other people's, and now Amanda's daughter grabbing their farms, the land baron who had an abortion.

But it's not me they're talking about these days, or Matty. Mama has them talking like never before. "Amanda's gone crazy, they're saying." This in a letter from Tommy. "They say Mama's gone around the bend," he writes. "The Chevy or her room in town. Everyone knows about the room in town." Of course they do. Mama's only happiness is that the town keeps talking her alive.

I've nursed until yesterday, my breasts feel nibbled raw, and even with most of the weight gone and the mirror telling me it's only time till the lines and curves are what they're supposed to be, I still feel droopy-bottomed and my legs know they're never going to be the same. I check myself daily and wish things higher again, tighter. My body has lost its lilt. It's not fair what happens. All these physical distortions. All I wanted was a baby. I have to laugh—all. Like I'm eighteen again and just learning about consequences.

With Mia I have kept up a periodic intimacy. We don't write often, and when we do it's like we're one missed connection. And then there are the lapses when we figure why bother and nobody writes and then, not often but often enough to keep us at it, bingo and we're connected. Mia's better at this. When she feels truly awful she adopts this breezy tone and her letters sail and sail, little boats of words, and it's like early on, when we didn't have to work at anything.

When they bring the telegram and Geoff's letter and set them next to my coffee and figs I decide to open the letter first. A telegram from Larry I want to savor. It's a choice between two good things and I'm going to have them both, first one and then the other. I'll write Geoff and tell him something intimate about Woolie, like how they treat you when you're an American in a Greek hospital having what everyone knows is a Greek baby. Like you're a star. It doesn't matter that they hate America. They think it's wonderful you're having a Greek baby. So I quickly read Geoff's letter—it's one of those "life is so chaotic, I just adore it" newsy letters—and later tonight I'll answer it and then I'll read Larry's telegram and answer that. I'm connected, it seems, to almost everyone.

But not to Mia.

The first evening we talked about the size of her children, Doris and Alexander, what they eat and don't eat, the words they know and shouldn't know, and how it is traveling with children. Rhuebal listed the countries they'd already been to and the museums like they were now part of a stock portfolio, ticking them off on his fingers. Today he's painting on the

open patio outside their rooms and the children are playing on
the patio around him.

"He wants another one," Mia says. "The first two are eating me alive—I love them and I'm trying to do this right,
Dorie, but you know how exhausting it is with one. Double
that and you can imagine—and now Rhuebal thinks three is
a nice round number, a harmonious figure, he says. For all
the thought he gives it, it's like he's contemplating a summer
garden and he wants another row of carrots. I don't know if I
should burst out laughing or sit down with the man and patiently explain to him exactly what he's asking of me."

"Why don't you?"

"Because he won't listen, Dorie. He thinks he's some sort
of ideal person because he has a studio at home and he lets
Alexander and Doris play with his watercolors while he 'su-
pervises.' Last week Doris ate purple, orange and light brown.
My daughter has a multicolor mouth and he's oblivious to
everything except filling these stupid canvases that don't
quite sell. It'd be better if he just painted houses. Oh, he's
good and everything—his agent keeps saying things will turn
around—but frankly Rhuebal isn't any more talented than
me, and I realized a while back I wasn't quite good enough,
though I pretend otherwise. And doing interior design for
Harnek and Marks pays nicely, thank you. But I'm not an
'artist' like Rhuebal, so what do I know about anything? I
know I'm out of the house a lot and Rhuebal's letting the
children eat paint right under his sniffling artistic nose, which
I'd like to bop a good one.

"And for him I should get preggers again. Dorie, I'm
thirty-two. Maybe that's not that old, but some days I feel an
absolute wreck and I know I won't snap back anymore. Alexander was pretty easy, I shed the weight just boop, but Doris
really took a toll on me. It's been two years and I'm still
carrying an extra ten pounds. Like they hollowed my insides
and implanted lead just above my hips, all the way around.

Some mornings my hands feel puffy, like rolls." Mia holds her hands up. "Look at them, will you? Peeling, ugly, red"—she waves off my disagreement—"I use Nivea, Jergens, everything and anything. I tell you a child's piss will strip the skin right off you. Look what it does to their behinds." She reaches for the carafe and pours liberally for each of us, the wine boiling over in my glass because she's reaching, and then she launches herself again, sitting back in her chair and then propelling herself forward.

"But that isn't the half of it. I knew he was seeing a student while I was carrying Doris—he gives these classes—and it's like Tweed all over again. Remember Tweed? For a long time I was horribly jealous. It seems funny now. Jealous of Tweed. Jealous of you with everyone and their eyes. I'd wanted to leap in front of you, my arms spread out, and shout at everyone who would listen or came near, 'She's mine! She's mine, so back off!' "

Mia's eyes are shining. She wants me to recognize this past connection, and all I can do is finger the stem of my glass.

Mia lights a cigarette. "But anyway, about Rhuebal and his little harem of small-breasted artist types. I confronted him and he said that was nonsense. And I held up the underwear one of them had left, obviously too small to be mine—when I found them I kept thinking, That bastard! In my own house and with his son gurgling to himself in the next room!—and we had one of those long intimate talks that are supposed to make everybody feel better. And he did, and I felt worse. I think this new child is supposed to placate me and keep me busy while he takes another long drink from the trough of the nubile and amoral. This Vicki—that's her name—is still calling the house, all innocent and sweet, like I'm the shrew for failing to understand my husband's need for freedom. 'Is Rhuebal there? This is Vicki. Tell him I called and it's really important.' "

"Why don't you get back at him?"

Mia leans closer, her shoulders twitching and her eyes tingling with intimacy. "Let me tell you something. I would get back at him, only I don't have the energy. I keep telling myself, When the kids are in school. When the kids are in school—can you see it? That's a laugh." She collapses back howling.

Rhuebal calls down to us, "Are you all right?" His neck cranes over his painting. Up periscope.

"Peachy-keen, dearest. We're just sharing a laugh."

"You sounded like you'd cut yourself or something."

"Milwaukee, remember?"

"What?"

"Milwaukee!"

"Oh, right." Rhuebal allows himself an uncomprehending smile and sits back down.

"Leave him."

"Leave. Laugh number two, right? Divorce him, maybe, Dorie. Simply leave, no."

"So divorce him."

"You have every answer, don't you? You've just done everything, and it's all so clear for you, Dorie, isn't it? Do this, do that. Don't do this. 'I've gotta go, Mia. Bye-bye. Bye-bye.' For some of us it's not so easy, kiddo."

"I never said it was easy."

"Like you want to hear any of this," Mia says. She jerks her chin back, defiant. "What do you want? You want I should tell you about Connecticut? It's beautiful and boring, boring, boring. Everyone so cheerfully, so smugly pleasant I want to throw up. No one pays taxes. Money, it seems, can at least buy smugness. What else do you want to know?" Mia says, pouring herself more wine. "What can I tell you that's safe? Oh, I know, we're the bourgeois bohemians on the block. We're treated like quaint eccentrics—every neighborhood should have one, as long as we keep the yard clean."

"You didn't arrange a trip to Greece to tell me about your yard, Mia."

"No, no, I'm just rattling on. Next thing you know I'll get

all weepy. The Mad Housewife. In a couple of years I'll have one of those meaningless affairs and throw the body right in Rhuebal's face. If I get lucky, it'll be a meaningful affair."

"Does it matter—meaningful or not?"

Mia stands and leans way over the table. "Does it matter? You of all people, Dorie. You were the one who told me everything touches everything. You do remember that time, don't you? You remember—I was always the one who let things pass, who let things wash over me and then they were gone. You were the one who took everything to heart. But after Alexander I tore the page out of your book and started lining things up, getting things in order because it seemed important. I wanted things to matter. And it seems to me when we were there in Milwaukee it mattered. We were pretty important for each other."

Mia takes a deep breath and lets it out. "Oh, fuck it. I'm just telling you now to see if you remember."

"I remember."

"You don't act like it." Mia tips her glass side to side and the wine swamps and swells. She laughs, touches a very fine white scar on her upper lip, like the brilliant thin trace of a shooting star, what's left from when I hit her. "Remember this? You don't think we didn't matter?" She shakes her head.

"So why have you come, Mia?"

Mia crosses her legs and studies her ankles. "For it to seem like old times. For us to drink and plot and laugh and ignore everyone. Do you know something? When I first had Doris, you know what I thought? I thought I had a miniature you. I thought all the way ahead to when she'd be seventeen or eighteen and I could tell her what to avoid and what to watch out for and to compare notes with her and really have her as my friend." Mia sits up straighter, and when she smiles I can see her face has gotten heavier, but it just makes her look her age. "Don't you think she even looks a little like you?"

"But she doesn't. She has your face and Rhuebal's sandy

orange hair. She's adorable, but she's certainly not—"

"I named her for you."

"She's not *me*, Mia. It's not fair for you to think—"

"Goddamn, Dorie, nobody's allowed to get close to you in any way, are they?"

"That's not true, Mia. It's only recently I've learned how close everyone *did* get."

"And you've spent all your time since getting away."

"Maybe so," I say.

We sit in silence until André, the café owner's son, comes to clean the table. We ask for coffee and André says to Mia, "Like hers, black?" Mia nods and he walks away. Mia folds her index finger under her napkin.

"I felt awful then, you know. You just took off on me. Maybe we weren't going to last, but you did a very thoughtless and cruel thing just leaving. I wouldn't do that even to Rhuebal."

"I didn't learn much till I was kicked around some myself, Mia."

I turn my head up to the sky and let a fresh wash of heat sweep down my face. I feel like I'm confessing and the lights are too bright.

Mia says, "You know, I think it's funny—how combative and hostile we are with people we sleep with and how congenial with everyone we couldn't or wouldn't possibly want to. As if hostility sets off a chain reaction or something. Like in all those old movies—you can always tell who's going to end up with who because they start off hating each other. Bogart and Hepburn, Wayne and O'Hara, Keillor and Zolkauer." Mia takes my hand. "I'm trying to say I understand, Door."

Mia lights a cigarette and looks at the sea, which is blue and green and frothed white in the wind. There's a shadow on one side of her face from where the sun cuts across her bangs. She's still holding my hand and I'm looking at her profile as if she were addressing the side of the hill and not me. I like her terribly, and I'm almost afraid for her to know that even now.

I say, "But we started off liking each other."

"Yes, but I wanted you most when I hated you most. And I'm not much good at compensation. I choose men I don't really like to more or less fall in love with."

At the end of Mia's cigarette is a long ash she just lets grow, and I finally take my hand from under hers and poke at the cigarette to get the ash to fall. Mia smiles and then I smile.

"So then, is it love if you decide to not be with someone because you just know it's going to turn out wrong?" My elbow is still forward with my hand up in the air. Mia takes my hand again. "Because, if so, then you must have loved us all—me, Geoffrey, even Larry." She lets me go and sits back almost laughing. "Jesus, I sound like a eulogy."

I want to answer her in some way but Woolie cries and goes into his long I've-messed-myself whine. Holding him in my lap and changing him, wiping the gook from his tiny behind and snugging the cloth against his harmless penis, I realize I have no idea of what to say. I'm confused as to whether we've just ended something or whether we're simply circling back.

"Do you want me to open the telegram?" Mia asks. I nod, and she slides her finger under the flap. Circling, I decide. Circling.

I talk with one pin still in my mouth. "I'm betting it's from Larry."

"That would be too rich," Mia says. "What would you tell him?"

"I don't know," I say, finishing with the first pin. "I think I'd start by telling him about the island. Maybe how the blue blue sky and water and brown fields and white rock look just like a glossy snapshot. Like a postcard. You know—you send it and tell everyone how wonderfully you're spending the time, the days spent basking myself copper—"

"The glistening oil," Mia says. "The Pernod evenings in front of your whitewashed house, the lunches of black coffee and goat cheese at a café where they know you."

"Exactly. And then I'd tell him how it really is—like Florida, only they don't speak the language."

"It's not the heat," Mia says, "it's the humidity."

We both laugh. I'm doing the final pin on Woolie, and he's trying to scratch his ear with his foot.

"But I'd want to tell him other things too. I'd ask him if he could picture me in Ray-Bans and loose white cotton pants and a fuchsia halter, still healthy, still Dorie, but a little thicker in the stomach and hips. A little older in the face, a little more aware that I'm not as precious as I thought I was. Maybe I'd even send a picture. 'You'd like me now,' I'd tell him. I think he'd want to hear that from me."

I look at Mia. "I have always wanted Larry to like me," I say. "If we haven't kept in touch it's from me knowing his adoration was what fueled him, and I didn't want adoration. Or I did, but I was stupid. That's what I'd tell him. And that's what I'm saying to you, too, Mia. I was stupid and I don't want adoration but affection."

"Exactly," Mia says, and it's as if we both know we are free of each other. Free and close. Mia moves her wrist up to the corner of her eye and says, "So do you want me to read you Larry's telegram?"

"Please," I say and Mia touches my cheek and touches it and touches it and she says, and we can both hear the love, "Dearest Dorie."

Only the telegram's not Larry's. Mia doesn't read it aloud. She hands it to me and picks up Woolie. She touches my face again and waits for me to move. I read the two words several times. I try them separately, too, as if the seven letters and a space have been badly transposed and the message is garbled, wrong, entirely different from what is printed. The telegram's from Tommy and it says MAS DEAD. A mistake, surely. Matty's died and there's been a typographical error. Or Tommy's trying to save himself some pennies.

The three of us go up the stone steps to the cottage, Mia with Woolie, me holding the telegram open between my hands as if I'm leading a procession and the chant is going to start any minute. Mia and Rhuebal huddle in their room, speaking in low voices while I put in the transatlantic phone call with Woolie balanced on my hip; he's gnawing his own knuckles while I wait for the operator to come back and then over all the crackling and distance Scott says, "Ma's dead." He has to shout. "Dorie, Ma's dead," like he was yelling it off a piece of paper someone else has handed him. "Day before yesterday in her town room."

"What about the Chevy?" I ask, meaning, meaning I don't know what.

"It's still there," he says very calmly, as if he knows its location is important to me.

"But she hasn't even seen Woolie!" I shout into the phone.

"Who's Woolie?" Scott asks.

I hang up. Nobody knows anything.

22

I GET the mail boat to Athens and a flight out. Mia offers to accompany me, but I tell her, No, finish your vacation, and she says, What vacation? This is a traveling version of Connecticut. I'll have to come see, I say, and she says, Do. We'd have a good time, you and I. We hug each other hard and then I'm gone. New York, Chicago, and I rent a National with a car seat for Woolie at O'Hare. Putting the bags in the trunk and strapping Woolie in, I catch a look at myself in the passenger side rearview. Suburban housewife, age twenty-eight. I've got on the plaid flannel-lined farmer jacket I love so much, the one with the brown corduroy collar. But the tips of my hair are dyed strawberry and I'm wearing five earrings: one opal stud, two 14K hoops and two danglies, onyx wedges and cultured pearls, like I've got everything I want only Mama's dead. Woolie in his seat is moving his hands like he's trying to hold off something in front of him, little fists waving.

Da-da? he says. As if he learned it from Geoffrey. He's twelve months and this is his favorite word. He waves a jellied fist and says, Da-da? When he's older I'll explain everything, but now I plop a bottle in his mouth and start driving.

It's late April but feels like March. My tan feels alien here. As if my skin should pale and take on that late-winter fishbelly whiteness, as if every last soul of us were tubercular. The trees are frightened. They've been tricked into budding out and are being punished for the misinformation. Last year's oak leaves still hang russet. They quiver and expect more rain. Gray and cold.

And I have bought as much of this as I've been able.

Cars are in the driveway as if waiting to be sold. When the people pour out of the house, I expect someone to give my tires a swift kick, someone else to ask me, Open the hood. Instead they line up for a portrait on the driver's side: Daddy and Tommy and Scott, Matty and Luther, Matty's other children that are here with their children: Matthew and Kathy Keillor, with their children, Terry, Patricia and David. Isabel with her husband, Dean Johnson, and their adopted child, Ching Lee. Scott said in a letter once she had three miscarriages and a stillborn. Rose with her cane and a man no one's mentioned. He's tall and thin and looks serious, as if he were a heart surgeon or fellow librarian. Fred and Mary and their children: Martha, ten now, a blond child with eyes tired from too much running around, and Rupert James and Phillip (Rupert for Rupert, Fred's older brother, dead eleven years now, and Phillip for Mary's father). And Frankie still gone, the lost son of his generation (as I'm the lost daughter for mine), who missed Rupert's funeral and his father's and now his sister's.

In all the time gone, Tommy, family historian and archivist, has kept score for me, mailed school pictures and snapshots with names and ages on the back, and like Scott with his baseball cards, I've kept them and I know who's who. As if I'd poured water into a magic rock garden and they've grown into place, aunts and uncles and cousins and cousins and nieces and nephews alike, all shapes and colors and lined up as if they truly believed it was time to take a picture. And they have that look as I say Hi! and go around to unstrap Woolie. I can't see them, bending over as I am, but I feel it on the top of my head, that hard penetrating look of who is she and what's she got?

There they are, the congealed blood of family, names and faces I knew and had tried to ignore even when I was with

them. Like Mama, they didn't matter, not for me, not for what
I needed or wanted. I knew about them, knew bits and pieces:
Rupert had died early, Fred farmed his own place and
Matty's, too, Matthew lived in Maine, owned three fishing
trawlers and probably wasn't happy, bad harvests and tough
banks, same as the land farmers, debts above his income,
Isabel with her professional life, Rose who had had a life
despite being crippled, arthritis so bad she hobbled, joints
swollen, moved as if ancient, I knew all that and tried to keep
it out, tried to keep it outside me. No connection with these
people. And they not knowing what to make of me. Colossal
awkwardness. The only thing connecting us would be if I were
married with kids, and even that I seem to have botched up,
showing up single but with child.

So fuck you all, it's just going to be the two days, right? We
can pretend intimacy and politeness and then get back to the
scattering we prefer. A few "It's been ages," and then we can
get to the real meat—Can you *believe* Dorie would actually
come with a bastard child? Can you believe it? And then I'll
fade out, as unreal to them as they have been to me.

So let us get the show going. Let us begin and make the
best of it. And I hold up Woolie and Matty gasps and I say,
This is Woolie, his father's still in Greece, and Woolie looks
up at the sky, which seems about to rain, and says Da-da?
and they are on me like a wave, Daddy first with his one-
armed hug, I'm embarrassed, still not sure how I should do it,
turn sideways so I just hug half of him or what, and then
Matty and Tommy and Scott and then everyone. And Matthew
says, "Yea, and we shall kill the fatted calf," and people are
wiping their eyes and laughing, still not sure how to take me,
but game for faking it.

"I wish it were some other kind of homecoming," Tommy
says as we walk up to the house.

"Like what?" I ask him.

"You know, like a wedding."

"You think I'd have come for a wedding?"

Tommy lets this pass. "Why'd you name him Woolie? That a nickname?"

"Look how black his hair is. He even has it on his shoulders. He's a brown-skin baby. His full name is William Fields Keillor."

"He certainly doesn't look like you."

"That's good, isn't it?"

"Yes and no," Tommy says. He lowers his voice. "Funeral's tomorrow. We put it off a day."

I hand Woolie to Isabel, who wants to hold a baby. "Ching Lee was three when her papers came through," she says. Dean has her cradled in one arm.

Inside there's food and we set to. Tray tables are set up. The big dining room table has the leaves pulled out, and the file cabinets stuffed with farm accounts have their drawers uncustomarily shut. Everyone's brought food. I sit in the living room with the children. Martha's jiggling Woolie on her lap, Woolie's eyes are wide, trying to take in everything, and Martha's asking her mother, "Is Woolie my nephew or just a cousin?" No answer. Everyone eats with a big appetite. The children sense something about to happen and they already know they won't be told in a way they can understand, so they're bored. What they don't understand but sense is that the adults are waiting for me to explain Woolie. I have blown in from another country with a year-old child who looks Greek.

Luther goes so far as to pick up Woolie, who's now on Rose's lap, Rose's friend Clifford sitting on the chair arm watching her, and says, "So who's the father of this dark baby?"

Big silence. Finally Matty says, "Luther, it's none of your business." Then she looks at me as if she knows I'm going to tell her later. Details, woman to woman. I like her, but I don't see myself telling her much. If I can't explain a decade of whim to myself, how could I to my grandmother? Or to my son? Mama would have shrieked with insane jealousy, and then she would have cradled Woolie to her chest, noting his spit-up as just another something gone wrong, and then she would have said, her eyes gleaming desire, Tell me everything. Every detail from the conceiving fuck to the final bloody cries and the slap.

But Mama had to go and goddamn die on me.

Besides to Woolie, for whom in sixteen years or so I figure to have a suitable chain of events worked up, it's to Mama I anticipated telling all. We could've sat on the front step with liquor in our coffee cups and Woolie hard crawling or toddling or falling among the junipers and the front flowers and our feet and I could've said, Mama, it's time, and I really believe she'd have listened.

So I don't pay Luther any attention after dinner with his stupid blunt questions, or anyone else. I'm far away right now, I'm three years ahead of myself, talking with Mama and there's enough distance and time gone between us so it's like really talking, and not this slip-sideways shouting.

Daddy looks at his watch, which is pinned to the bottom of his shirt pocket so he can read it easily. He says, Okay, now, and everyone looks at him like he's calling a meeting to order. Even the children get quiet, except Woolie, who's tugging at Martha's ear and saying Da-da? Da-da? his voice high and squeaky on the second *da* like rubber shoes squeaking on waxed wood.

Out at the cars Tommy takes me aside. He's different from Scott now, they're separate people. Tommy has this sad intensity in his eyes, like he's reluctant to be so earnest. It causes him grief. His voice goes low along my shoulder and into my ear. "They found needles in her room."

"What's that supposed to mean?" I'm loud, and Tommy shifts his eyes back and forth, as if trying to zap everyone else out of existence.

"That's the talk. That Bobbie Buchardt found needles when she went to get the body. And Bobbie told Nina Forsch, who told Leona Grimert, who tells everyone, so Matty called to warn us."

"What about marks? Did they find marks?" I'm still loud.

Tommy talks with his eyes. "No one's saying."

Pictures as we drive in: Mama's hair wild, eyes mottled cherry red, the fingernails thickened and yellow, tubing wrapped around her arm, its end in her clenched and yanking teeth. I see Daddy in the room when he first gets there, trying to take it in. Daddy with that smile of uncomprehending fear on his face, like he's just taken a severe blow to his chest, the stuffing gone out of him. And while they pack up Mama, he's looking with his heels for someplace to sit down.

And then the flash forward, wondering what combination of concern and sympathy and sorrow and stampeding curiosity has brought everyone out. We have become a sideshow, the flung-out family gathered in grief, if grief is what you'd call it. For Daddy and Matty, sure, but for who else? Daddy stands through the whole wake, the blood bright in his cheeks, and shakes hands with the gawkers, the ones who'll show tonight but not tomorrow, since the finger sandwiches and desserts are catered out of Appleton—Rossi's—and tomorrow after the funeral it'll be pot luck. Daddy shakes hands with them and shows almost no trace of how their curiosity and glee hurt him. He's out standing in the open with these people and they all own binoculars. Matty's not that way. It's her daughter, too, but with her it's only the grief they express. She's less a target, Matty is, uncorrupted by age, still living with her lover (they don't think about it that way anymore, but at seventy she says she still waltzes with Luther and she doesn't mean dancing), her mind gotten sharp and flinty and she'll no longer not say what she thinks only for propriety's sake, so she's dangerous enough to be left alone. Somebody asks her why did Mama keep that room in town, and they stand there nodding like waiting for Matty to confirm what they already think. And Matty barks, What business is it of yours? and they back off, muttering, Sorry, sorry.

But Daddy is truly cordial, nearly lipless in his own nods, his accepting of circumstance. He paid to have her hair done and told Bobbie Buchardt, Henry's wife, to dress her in her favorite bra and rayon blue sheen blouse.

They're coming up to me, too. The others—Tommy and Scott and Mama's brothers and sisters (except Matthew, who's been gone so long almost nobody remembers him)—they can see every day of the week almost. But I'm here now and this is a short opportunity. Even Porter Atwood. Porter catches me as I'm coming out of the ladies' and lays a hand on my shoulder.

"I don't understand it," he says. "I'm trying to get this figured out but I can't."

"What?"

"With your Ma, I mean."

"What about Mama?"

"Oh, nothing. I was just wondering, is all. I mean, are you coming back here full-time to look after your father, or will you continue to conduct business at a distance, through surrogates?" Porter's face is the blotched red of an afternoon nipper, and his eyes have that crying, rheumy look. I'm sure he expected the benefit of the doubt, but I can smell the gin on him. I've had years of experience with gin-breathed men, and Porter's trying to pull off the rural charm version of that. Instead of the scorpion slide string tie with his polyester suit, he's wearing one with a lucited pressed dark rosebud—his funeral string tie. I can see the labels in his head that go along with the ties in his closet—scorpions for deal closings and overseeing foreclosures, flowers for funerals and hospital rooms, maybe a carved heart of stone for his many quickies.

Porter keeps going. He's probably nipped a few in the men's room just now, or in the car earlier. He says it infuriates him that I buy farms and let them sit. Or worse—I rent them back to the people I've bought them from. And everything from a distance. "Like you've got clean hands," he hisses at me. "Like you're the saving princess. Only let me tell you something. You're not saving anybody. You're just prolonging the agony."

"Oh, I've wrung most of the meaning out of their lives as surely as you, Porter, I agree, plucked them clean and thrown the bones back for gnawing. But what upsets you so much, Porter, is it's me that's done it, not you. And you can't touch me, Porter. Right in the middle of all your planned subdivisions are acres and acres of land I own and you can't touch me because I don't need the money. You can't sweet-talk me, can't threaten, can't plead, can't sue, can't outbid, can't buy. And you so much as lay a finger on me again I'll kick you in the balls till you sing out your ass."

Porter produces the Seagram's from his coat pocket and shakes it in my face. "Drank this with your precious Mama before I fucked her," he says. "Fucked your grandma, too. And before I'm done—"

And my knee comes up then and he yells, "Haw!" 'cause he's seen it coming and fends me off, uses just one hand to push me sideways and I hop back on one foot and when he stands up, self-satisfied, I hop back in, my whole leg coiled this time, my thigh throbbing. He can see my panties and his eyes widen, delight, and then I uncoil. My heel crashes into his pelvic bone, I can practically feel the mush through my shoe and Porter goes down, blood out from his teeth where he's bit his tongue and he's sucking air but nothing reaches his lungs, it stays high in his chest and he's making little whinnying sounds like he's a just-birthed pony. His Seagram's hits the carpet and clunks unbroken into a table leg but the sound is enough to snap heads around and what they see is the folded-over Porter and me leaning over him like I'm giving comfort.

He's still trying to breathe, his eyes pushing tears. I give him credit for not crying out loud, for maintaining that shred of decorum and wax paper macho.

I whisper in his ear, "There's nothing more galling to a man than losing an even competition to a woman." I fetch his bottle for him and press it into his hands as if he were an infant. He nods when I ask him if he wants help. Tommy and Scott get him on his feet and cradle him to the side door.

And yet I am without satisfaction, like when you mend a ripped screen door or empty the garbage pails and wastebaskets and then wash them out with ammonia and nobody notices. For a few minutes I've been the janitor of this wake, and I don't even get the elation of wiping off my hands. People think Porter's succumbed to emotion.

I want to hold Woolie now, feel his weight in my arms and the soft shapelessness of his head on my chest. When I hold him like this it seems his head really does cover my whole chest, that he somehow expands to take up the whole of me. Kathy has been holding him while I was in the hallway.

"He's a darling," she tells me. "All that curly black hair."

I sit in the back, holding him in my lap, bouncing him lightly, talking nonsense in his ear. My hands move his pudgy arms in front of him as if he were a marionette. He resists and reaches above his head to pull at my nose, clawing with one tiny sharp fingernail the inside of my nostril. Gently I tug his clenched hand off my nose, then off my upper lip, and smother the crown of his head with kisses. I become almost drunk with the smell of his shampooed black hair, soft and soft and soft. I want to stay here like this till it's over, till they tell me it's time to leave.

"It's time you saw your ma," Daddy says to me. He's sitting on his haunches next to my chair. "You really can't hang back here the whole time," he says. Woolie reaches to grab his nose. Daddy gives his own head a shake and Woolie keeps grabbing. "I mean, it's expected," Daddy says.

"Who expects it?"

"She does," he says quietly. "You know she does."

"Is it true what they're saying?" I whisper.

"What's that?" Daddy says.

"The needles."

"Her liver, Dorie. She just drank herself to death. Is that a comfort?"

"No."

"It wasn't for me, either."

I stand and just remember to catch Woolie under his arms. I'm wondering to whom I should hand him, holding him like he was a Kris Kringle present, only I've forgotten the recipient. Finally I swing him onto my hip and stride up to the front like I was expecting this all along. Only I wasn't. I had it figured in the normal fashion: "Mama, this is Woolie. William Fields Keillor. His father is a twenty-year-old Greek who waits on tables in a little village called Aggi Galini on an island called Galica. You might think, looking at him, that I named him Woolie after he was born, but I already had that name for him from the moment his egg took hold on my wall. He was lint, Mama. A bit of wool, clinging fuzz. I know you would've wanted to see him so here he is."

Everything on the outside feels numb, but there's something inside me tight and alive. Dimly I realize I'm speaking aloud, that there's a room full of people talking among themselves with ears cocked.

Now that I've started, I want to tell her everything.

How if she's been a salmon in her life, leaping and leaping and always falling back, then there's been a shark fin on me. Move and move or settle and die. "All I've ever wanted to be was *away*, Mama." She can understand that. She kept moving herself, even when she was going nowhere at all. We call that choice. A free and independent world. Move about as you feel like it. God smiles on everything. Mama was a salmon. I see her with her eyes closed, trying to find the table to put down the needle, like the rumors are true. I see her with her eyes rolling back and her limbs full of blood, the lovely hot tickle of every pore opening, the warming and sleeping pull of everything inside shutting down and yet alive, yes, the alive and elsewhere rush.

Only the rumors aren't true, aren't real at all. Mouths stay going because without the fantastic it's not believable. She had to have been on drugs! Otherwise she's just like you and me. Not possible. Amanda Brown like every one of us? But that . . . that means—

Yes.

Maybe Daddy started the rumor for the sake of Augsbury's collective sanity. He was the first in the room, after all. She'd been gone two days and he called Dave Erndt Sr. to let him into the room. "Broke my heart," Erndt was heard saying later. "Man have to ask somebody else for a key to his wife's room like that."

Daddy, the true believer in populist causes. Letting rumors be spread about his own wife so the town as a whole feels better about itself. Like they've been here always, they've remained and will remain and so have a better claim to Mama than I do, Daddy's reasoning being the greater good, which is how he reasons everything. He voted for La Follette for governor. Wanted Humphrey to win the presidency, and even McGovern. Telling people who he voted for in the soft voice of his he usually saved for when he wanted us to understand machinery when we were children. "And that big gear turns, see, so that littler cog can turn that gear and keep the belt moving up and these ledges on the belt keep the corn coming up the chute. See the teeth? They keep the belt in line, keep it feeding proper."

I swing around to look at Daddy with his pinned white sleeve and the little silver clip on his black and forest green tie and his visible ache, his smile worn through to dull pain every time he shakes another hand and nods along with the murmured sympathies. Daddy as rumor monger? I laugh at myself. That kind of cleverness is beyond him. He's been struck across the head with a two-by-four, and he's still reeling. He's gone simple, telling anyone who'll listen about the presidents.

"I voted for Reagan once," he's saying. "The first time. I'd

kick myself except the next guy won't be any better and anyway, it's not all his doing."

People bring him flowers, which he hands to Tommy or
Scott to put by the casket, or else Bobbie Buchardt or one of
her sons intercedes and says, Thanks, and Daddy says in
agreement, Thank you, and the flowers move along like
they're something precious. Daddy seems profoundly embarrassed every time somebody shakes his hand. Like there was
a tote board set up with specific dates and the name of each
man listed and one by one they shake hands with Daddy and
their names are crossed off. Men going up to Daddy absentmindedly scratch their privates as if it were a reflex of memory.

I pull up Woolie a little tighter to me and look down.
Daddy has her dressed up as she'd have liked. Mama was the
sort of person who would wear a patterned lace underwire bra
underneath a clingy aquamarine rayon blouse with the two
gold-plated chains at her open throat. Mama's looking thinner
around her shoulders and the bra shows through the fabric, as
stiff and pronounced as ramparts, like molded grillwork, like
the front of a car. Even dead her tits are grinning a reproach
of unintelligible dimension.

"Justify yourself," her lace-swathed tits are saying.

And so I hold up Woolie again and start talking.

"Mama, this is Woolie," I repeat from before. "Mama,
you've probably heard and thought ridiculous how women are
choosing the father of their children like they're shopping for
vegetables. Selecting color or facial shape or athletic skill or
intelligence. Linebacker sperm, or a Nobel prizewinner's.
Well, Woolie wasn't like that, Mama. His father waited
tables, like I told you. He was eighteen and worked for his
father at this little café I went to every day. They all knew me,
Mama. I was the American. He served me coffee and ouzo
and wiped the table clean every fifteen or twenty minutes,
just so he could come and smile at me with his perfect teeth.

He had wet black eyes and a shy handsomeness, and he was
obviously very happy being himself and able to get so close to
this American woman who came every morning and afternoon
for food and drink. And one day he came up to my table
saying, Miss? Miss? his eyes all shy knowledge and he asked
if he couldn't take me to the cinema in the evening, they were
showing one of those James Bond films that travel so well,
and I told him, Certainly, and he nearly knocked the table
over he was so happy. And later, when it was getting on toward morning and I'd gotten up to look out the window he
asked me eagerly, Was that the kind of sleep you like? He
said it just like that, Was that the kind of sleep you like? and
I told him Yes, he made love nicely. So nicely, Mama, I
wanted to get out of bed afterward and sit wide awake by the
window, just to savor the feeling. He was a very pretty boy
and very earnest in his attentions. Standing by the window, I
could smell the ocean and see clouds crowding up one side of
the sky like a bunched skirt and the air was getting lighter
and clean. And it was the first time in ages that I thought of
you, Mama, because I wanted to rush out and tell you and
Daddy both that you could expect a grandchild, that it was
going to happen.

"And sitting up in bed, he lit a cigarette, which smelled
just like the spring burning. Remember, Mama? Remember
how we always wanted to help and you wouldn't let us. You
told us we could watch from a safe distance but that was all.
You told Daddy to watch out for us, that too many farmers put
off the burning till fall, when they were too busy anyway and
the chore got entrusted to sons and daughters who didn't know
what they were doing, who saw no meaning in it, just burning
grass, and in October with everything so dry whole fields
would go up when it was only ditches that were meant to burn
and Daddy would always say, I know, honey, why do you think
I do this in the spring? And afterward he'd have us shovel up
the gray ash for the garden. Remember? The smell of just-

burned grass sweet in your nose? And then we got old enough to help, to do a proper job of it. I loved that, Mama. And that boy with his French cigarette after his very nice lovemaking made me think of that.

"And later still, when I was fixing us a breakfast of cheese and hard bread and tea, the teakettle's shriek sounded like the screams of running children, and I wanted to tell you that for the first time I was anxious about the future. While I was swelling with Woolie I wanted to talk with you. This balloon inflating inside me, Mama, my skin going s-t-r-e-t-c-h and shiny until I thought it was going to tear, and nobody to comfort me about ruined figures or episiotomies or C-sections, like I could have talked with you about that. And even later, Mama, afterward, when the balloon was going down like a leftover from a party, my skin wimpling and getting dull and thick as leather, and I hated and loved everybody. I was scared that all I've forgotten, thinking it didn't matter, really did matter. But I had let it slide, and now here I am telling you everything and you're goddamn dead, and no one's even told me how to act."

I turn around to face them. "What do you want?" I ask them, the faces with the eyes. "What do you want to see? Silent streams of tears? The huge grief, the public wail? You want me to spit at her and scream? What?"

"Like her mother," someone says and I see them coming up to me, Daddy and my brothers, and Woolie's hands are fumbling at my neck and ears and he's going, "Mama is cry." And Scott eases him out of my hands and gives him to Matty and Woolie starts crying and I feel exactly like Woolie, confused and tired and more than a little lost and I just want to scrunch my eyes and let go wailing.

And then Daddy folds his arm around me and I feel the pressure just as strong on both sides but only the one hand on my back and I can feel his breath hot on my hair. And the gristle of beard because he's forgotten to shave a second time as he usually does and his chin hairs poke at my scalp like twenty-point sandpaper. But that's all right, really. He's my father. I beckon for Woolie and Matty hands him back. Daddy and I hold him between us like he's a seed for the earth.